Tripping Nevada

Part One of the Stone Saga

by Joey Thomas

Paperback ISBN: 979-8-9861481-4-4
Hardcover ISBN: 9798387866388
EBook ISBN: 979-8-9861481-5-1

The contents of this novel are an achievement of fiction. Any names, characters, places, and circumstances are the invention of the author's imagination. Any uniformity to anyone, living or dead, is entirely serendipitous.

www.facebook.com/Joey-Thomas-The-Writer-103809168364428

I dedicate this book to those who have grafted lessons onto my soul: Dr. Heidi Boyd for the honesty and companionship in searching ourselves out in our youth; Kimberlee for the strength and purpose along this continued search for the magic that is reality; Casey for sharing that magic you've always seen behind the veil; Clay for pointing out time and time again, that I am worth more; Scott for the education in nature and intellectual pursuits; Alan for always treating me like a little brother he liked, thanks for making me a BlackBird; Charles Ray for lessons in manly endeavors and the bonds of family; Lalane for the laughter and love. Sheila and Mark for letting us come and go and hang with love and great conversation; Grandma (Clara Mae Fletcher) Thomas, for being the sweetest soul and for effortlessly holding me to a higher standard, without shame or malice; Brandon and Amber for pretending that I'm cool; Beth for your unconditional love; Sirena Dragon, Rema Haile, Kylan'i T'e, Ka'i Sam'e, J. D. Hogue, and Kimberlee Thomas, thank you for the JOY and COMPASSION while unifying my Bark, Scales, and Skin. Kristen Simpson, Tana Roark, Hanna Elliott, and Jake Green for letting me in their sacred circle and the growth in love. I could go on to name most everyone I've ever spent time with, thank you all for the lessons I've gleaned in your presence, for your time, and kindness.

PTSD or Insomnia

The Dodge Duster was full of space, enough for the hope he clung to, breathing room for his fractured self, and enough audacity for Hank to ride along.

Nick lay curled up in the backseat of a vintage Dodge, Duster. He was too long to stretch out but, he sleeps this way most nights and his body found it comforting; as if he was hugging himself. He felt as if he was trying to convince himself he was sleeping. 'Fake it until you make it,' he thought. Afraid to move and awaken himself any further, knowing that if he opened his eyes, they would stay that way. He's been driving the last day and half and knew he needed to sleep. He'd been feeling adrift and lay here, thirty minutes, an hour, maybe even an hour and a half, but his mind was abuzz, like the Vegas strip.

Buzzing with flashes of incriminating evidence that suggested he was, indeed, a piece of shit; a worth-less, good-for-nothing, waste of space; as Hank eluded to all along. Lightning strikes of his mother's face, the day before she forgot to tell him goodbye. And, another fractured replay of her in pain, years later, which couldn't be real, because she never came back.

The young man wondered if he was stunted, because his usual sleeping position is termed fetal. It would make sense that he was immature, being abandoned at six, left to his own devices. Except, he wasn't, was he? No, it couldn't have been so quaint as all that! NO! He was left with a broken giant, who saw his own failures in the boy's face. Trapped atop the beanstalk and too big to hide; ever so small in his insignificance. He was small in his submission. Tiny in his hesitation, infinitesimal in his fear to breathe deep! Minuscule in his inability to do a damn thing right, blamed for running his mother off. Hank, often retorted such accusations under the influence, "I could still have her, if it wasn't for you! Piece of Shit!" The great news, was, that Hank was always under the influence. Yay!

His mind was at a boil. He was a poster child for PTSD, a *domestic* war survivor and beneath the hive of rage, that shot hateful words about his tender skull like a perpetual ricochet, he was further pissed that he should still be waging such war within himself. It was understandable, but goddamnit, he had escaped; he was free! Nick was only thirty hours and sixteen minutes into his exodus, and he was the only one left to wound. There was no one left to blame or stab or incinerate. He wanted to break free of the car and run screaming like a loon into the night, but his deception was not worn through yet. He was asleep Dammit!

Uncounted minutes later, his persistent deception won out and he slept. He slept in the silence that only emptiness knows, but he wasn't alone. He was watched even now, but the giant and the prismatic crew the giant created; he could never escape.

Nick knew he was nice, that he wanted the best for others, just a fair shake in the world, really. He thought himself a good person, but one with no real talent, or wisdom to effect the world. He was ineffectual, a bore, and tired of hating himself. His memory was as fractured as his personality, due to the haze; the regular blackouts. Once the personal Tet Offensive was over, he slept like a baby. Stunted? Perhaps. It was this way, most nights. It was his normal, whatever anyone else wanted to label it.

The Next Day

It wasn't me that hurt you this way
somebody made your heart unreachable
you can't let it go.
I could've really loved you
I never wanted to say so long China
Shanghai Flower

So Long China / Winger

The SCREECH of brakes was long and restorative. The Primer-Gray muscle car serpentined in a slide across the deserted highway, until it stopped abruptly. The young, brown-haired eighteen year old turned to his passenger with a grin, "Perfect! We're here," he said with a joy he seldom felt when talking to his persistent companion. The young man pushed the gearshift into R, propped his right arm upon the back of the cool, gray leather bench seat and turned his head; distracted before applying the gas pedal.

"You didn't answer my question. What are you doing?" Hank sounded serious, which he never was. At least, not in this form.

Nick Stone was very quickly pissed off, because his frustration with the man was built up…like the theoretical space elevator. "I am stopping for a breather, maybe even an overnight stay, I want to write while my idea is still clear in my mind. A perfect, starry night sleep-over in the middle of fucking nowhere! Why, you ask? Because I can. Because my body wants to unfurl and it's all about the journey, right?" Nick didn't want an answer, actually, he hoped the man he fled would be gone. He should be in his underwear, in his run-down recliner, in the broken-down-house, in Fairbanks, Illinois. Not here, in the goddamn car with him. Why wouldn't he leave the boy alone? Nick knew the answer, unfortunately, said more about his state of mind, than it did about Hank.

"Well, I neva,." sang the voice of a husky, Southern Belle. Nick almost grinned at the sight of his three hundred plus, six foot six, Steps wearing an awful brown and tan flowered dress with a bonnet to match. The dress was bad on this frame, the deep blue eye shadow was worse, all the more embellished by his fluttering eyelids.

Nick watched helplessly as his foot slipped, smashing the gas pedal, causing them both to bounce forward in the lurch of the car's need to go backward; of Nick's need to escape the man, still. He smiled at Hank, as if it should scare him that they were speeding backward along the highway and Nick removed his arm from the seat turning completely forward, as if to dare the universe to bring on its worst. As Nick realized that Hank wouldn't be hurt by the accident he was about to cause, he scanned every mirror at his disposal, trying not to look back as he egged the engine on. He knew Hank was a figment of his imagination, but he still had to save face, now that it was safe to do so.

Nick looked from driver's side mirror to rear view to passenger's side, trying to correct as little as possible, "Keep it between the mustard and mayo, Dude," he heard Tommy's voice from years before. His periphery picked up a change in the uninvited passenger. Nick dared to look and was captivated by the crash-test-dummy get up the large man wore. His drawn face was all in as he pumped his fists and said, "You got this Nick. I believe in you, Son!"

Nick closed his eye, breathed deep for clarity and patience, because vehement sarcasm was fraying his smile. The man never once offered him praise or support, but here he was, or so Nick's mind wanted him to believe, supporting his demise. He tried to let it go, to reinvigorate the feel-good feeling that this new found freedom gave him. Nick opened his eyes, as he felt himself in the right spot and pulled the steering wheel severely right, before he verified his location. It was a challenge, fun, freeing, and reckless as all-get-out. It was, invigorating, at least. Nick's eyes grew large, as his heart began to pound at the speed with which the large rock formation was growing in proximity. Just when he thought it was too late to stop, he slammed on the brakes and held the wheel firm. The car dug into the sandy soil and slid to a side angle stop four-feet from the rock.

Nick closed his eyes and celebrated his victory in surviving, "Whoooooooooooo!" Head up and eyes open, the world took on a green hue, probably from the adrenaline spike. Hank began immediately, "You are the failure I knew you would always be," the man said simply. It was this tone of utter disappointment, but not surprise, "I told your mother, you would never be worth her time on the streets. The best part of you ran down her leg, I told her...can't even kill yourself right." Nick bristled at the mention of his mother and saw the crash-test-dummy was replaced by the dirty tighty-whiteys that fit the man like a saggy, worn out glove. It was his first uniform, second only to the State Trooper regalia he wore to work five days a week. Nick decided that allowing his own tortured mind to enrage him was an unnecessary self-sabotage. Why bother, he breathed deep and let it go. He didn't have to do this. It didn't have to be this way. If only he could believe that.

The worst mental itch, that Nick wanted so badly not to scratch, was the realization that he was pushing his own buttons, jabbing his own chin, and had no clue as to why. Did he need the man to be here, a habit he couldn't break? Or was his escape from The Steps, finally, so unbelievable, that his mind needed the solid footing the evil man offered. He was something of home, after all, a sense of normalcy.

The knowledge that his step-father, Hank "The Tank" Forbus, was most assuredly still in Fairbanks, Illinois, was not the most disturbing knowledge Nick owned on this trip. The fact that, said step-father, joined Nick thirty miles out from that torture chamber of a home in an undersized pair of Aquaman Underoos, was visually alarming, as well as, *the* crux. He was right here, running away with Nick, who was running away from him. Worse than all of that, Nick knew he brought him here. His broken, torqued mind didn't know how to let him go. The bloody-red cherry on top of it all, he would join Nick in his best side-kick attire. Earlier this day, he was dressed like a cowboy, whose too tight shirt puckered between every button and whose jeans weren't buttoned, but also weren't pulled up above his waist, because they were too tight. For some reason, his toes were visible through the torn open boots. Nick figured he just couldn't wrap his head around seeing those big feet enclosed in boots, literally. Now, he donned his dirty underwear. Yaaaaay!

This wisp of a man (and it was not lost on Nick, that this was the only way the three hundred pound plus man, would ever be a wisp of anything, as he was now mere thought, a phantom of considerable wispy, weight), was trying to explain to Nick that there was no sense in trying to run from a bad situation, because no matter where you go, there you are; pointing out, as he did so often, that Nick was his own worst problem, creating ever new problems as he went; that he was doing it again, right now, was his sermon. Only now, Nick was beginning to believe the man, spectre, was onto something. *The Steps* white hair caught the light in places, his left-side-parted-do, restrained from years of the same combing style, framing his unhealthy, inflamed face. He looked out of the same puffy eyes and sweaty brow that Nick remembered from three nights ago. The poor bastard just looked uncomfortable in so many ways.

Nick didn't have a problem with weight, too much or too little. He loathed this man, however, so it was allowable to make fun, because he was mean; hard on the little things, small like Nick had always been.

Nick looked into that face and thought of the years of beatings, as his bonus torture, his mother running out on him was the great prize, cleaning up after and held hostage by a drunken Illinois State Trooper was the icing on the cake. The fact that no one would believe this upstanding decorated officer was an alcoholic and abusive father, was all the more reason to take the risk at living reckless to feel alive.

"You know, you are a real whine-bag! Jesus, you cry

and piss and moan about life...well tough shit! Grow up a damn minute and realize life sucks and the quicker you start throwing the punches, the quicker you won't be the one on the ground pissing your pants!" relayed Hank in his usual halitosis layered tone. "Your friend here did just that, took charge and made something happen. Why can't you be more like him?" Nick was silently astonished that he could smell the man's breath. Then, confused at just who in the hell he was talking about. What friend?

This was actually the most the man had ever talked to Nick, well, he guessed that wasn't exactly true, as this wasn't exactly Hank doing the talking? What was true was that this was the only version of Hank that talked so much without beating him, before, during, or after. Nick had no clue who he was talking about or what this person did that Hank was so in support of. How do you manifest a person and have him know things you don't know? Nick shook his head, unbelieving, and climbed out of the car. He had to be talking about Tommy. That was the only friend Nick ever had.

Nick's brown hair was unkempt, wind blown in the moment, but always unruly. His red flannel shirt was form-fitting and unbuttoned over a gray tee. His jeans were torn and worn, only holey where it didn't count. His carpenter boots were Tommy's, just as this sweet, growling Duster was. He always told Nick that they both owned it, but it was Tommy's dad who bought it for them, and even though Nick helped out in every way he could, it was Tommy's learned mechanical skill that held the racy Dodge together.

Nick couldn't believe the Fake-Hank was going to try and argue such a point, anyway, it was he that was the bad situation Nick was running from. Jesus Christ, couldn't a poor boy get a break? He already had to learn to live with the ass for twelve years, now he had to explain himself, over and over again? "No," he told the desert landscape about him, turning to the large boulder beside, "I don't have to explain myself. Even if I have to hear his perpetual arguments, I don't have to participate."

The right side of the car, Nick realized, was blurry. Even the windshield, just under the rear-view mirror and all the way over to the passenger side was blurry, with little spots of blur here and there in the passenger side floorboard. Nick silently quipped that it was Hank's blobby aura, but it was odd. It looked as though Hank were superimposed upon a purposefully blurred out image. He too, could smell one of the most satisfying scents he believed he'd ever smelled. It was musky and sweet, with hints of vanilla and lime and he had no idea where it was coming from; surely not this sideshow Aquaman. Also, his right leg was singing, high in the thigh. If it wasn't bruised, it soon would be, but why. He couldn't remember having hurt it.

As quick as Nick found his rage, these days, it seemed he had better things to settle upon, like this middle of nowhere, road trip. This expanse of sky and flat land and the freedom to wander, to sit, or lay and think without a chore to do.

Nick smiled and closed his eyes, letting the sun bleed through the blood of his eyelids. He basked in the memory of how his senses experienced speeding backwards. It felt like being underwater in the bathtub, when he was eight. A new and refreshing rush of speed coming from the wrong direction, like a sense awakened for the first time. The time in the bathtub was also the sweetest because Hank didn't exist under the surface; his squawk box couldn't be heard, nor the sound of his snorting or farting, or working up phlegm from his reclining throne. Even the smell of his dirty, drunk ass, that permeated the house, was lost beneath the beautiful barrier. Nick screamed a rebel yell for everyone who ever found escape. He opened his eyes, now, in the barren, scrubby landscape. He wanted to be happy. He wanted to be positive and for those around him to be optimistic about the world at large. He wasn't sure if he was happy, just yet, he wasn't sure if he ever could heal completely, but didn't question those things, just yet. The one thing he could say was true, the most honest thing he knew, was that he believed anything was possible. He hoped to be one of those, capable of such, some day.

The stone was massive. It was a love seat, of sorts, inviting him to sit down, to lay about upon its hardened surface. He decided this outcropping of rock, which was the size of a train car, sat here for thousands of years, maybe even hundreds of thousands, just waiting for him to come and enjoy it. He decided to do just that by camping here for the night. Where could you find a hotel with a view like this; besides, he wondered just how many stars would reveal themselves so far away from the city. Nick smiled at the wall of dust, still floating slowly away and he soaked in the open, huge sky that Nevada had to offer. It registered to him, in that moment, that the blurry around his unwanted rider stayed behind after the rider was gone, but he could live with a blurry spot of atmosphere that didn't talk back or make fun of him, though it was disconcerting. Perhaps, it was dust in his eyes.

The sun was one finger from the horizon, which told Nick he had roughly fifteen minutes before it got dark, at least that is what the survival experts in all the books he'd read indicated. He grabbed the Indian blanket his mother had left behind so many years ago, from the Duster's spacious trunk and prepared his bedding for the night. There was a shelf on the stony formation about four feet off the ground (the cushions of the love seat); a perfect spot for Nick to stretch out. He would find out later, there was a box formed behind this, a room of sorts all secluded by the same stony walls. He lay out his notebook next to his cigarettes and lighter on the bottom shelf. He was working on an idea and couldn't think of a better place to write. He had romantic ideas of writing in grand scenes just like this, like painters in Paris. Up to now, he'd only ever written in his dank, dark room. The world he was creating, the one he'd been building on since he was ten, was large and bright enough to save him from that darkness. He'd found a young boy and his sister in his mind, characters that felt as solid as the broken down bed he lay upon to inscribe them into creation. Brighter than the rooms he negotiated in this crushing world.

Nick grabbed the half eaten Number-One-with-Cheese, Sonic Burger from the long front row seat and took a bite as he stood in the open driver side door, admiring his surroundings. He noted that the blurs also rode the outside of the passenger side windshield, with no explanation or significance, he let it go. He patted the five-hundred-dollar bills still in his left front jean pocket with a smile. He had a few twenties in the right pocket, but the hundreds he stole from Hank three days before, just before the graduation ceremony no one attended for him, save for Tommy's dad, Sammy. The over six-hundred dollars was the least that scuzzy son-of-a-bitch could spare. Besides, it was all change. It took Nick four trips to carry the five, gallon jugs into a bank in Bartlesville, Oklahoma, to feed the machine that would exchange him bills for the coin. He netted six-hundred, forty-eight dollars and ninety cents for his trouble, though. And, it was nice to imagine how pissed the tyrant would be to know he'd been had.

The light of the day was fading now as he ate his lunch/ supper. He pondered if that made this lupper or sunch? He was excited to get to it. He had a new idea. He'd been writing during the last hour or two of road tripping, watching this story play out in his head. A deliciously dark one, at that. He wrote well past the sun's light, but the twilight of dusk allowed his young eyes to write for an hour past. As the story unfolded, he couldn't help but think about the blur around the windshield and front seat and floor board of his car. Maybe he should work that in somehow, but what the hell was it? The image kept popping into his head as he found new words to describe the scene he'd envisioned on the ride here. He loved the bloody and macabre, it was fun in his head, to read or write, just as long as that is where it stayed. He didn't have the stomach for real blood and guts.

Story well begun, Nick lay his notebook back on the stone, grabbed up a Doral Red, his skull emblazoned Zippo (the skull a white negative on the black lighter) and headed for his bed, cherishing the smoke that filled his lungs and flavored his finished meal with tantalizing, rebellious and momentary perfection. He'd only just learned to smoke. He tried some with Tommy, but always got choked and Tommy would laugh at him, not that he was a connoisseur of the butt. He only did it to be rebellious, to pull away from his parents as teens are obligated to do. Nick knew Tommy didn't mean anything by it, but he couldn't stand being laughed at. So, rather than let it be a problem between he and his only friend, he stopped trying. Five hours into this journey, though, just as he was beginning to feel safe and free, he stopped and purchased his first pack of cigarettes, his first bottle of fluid and flints. The Zippo was Tommy's. He said he got it from a girl and gave it to Nick after he quit trying, said it was a present that would come in handy one day. The gas station attendant had made the hard sell with the flints and fluid, explaining that he didn't want to get caught out in the middle of nowhere without these. She was also cute and called him, *Darlin'*.

He finished his smoke, breathed in the moment and succumbed to the sacred timbre this scene welled up within him; it was the colors and breeze and feel of it all, the beauty and invisible magic of the world's inner workings at play. He watched the twilight darken to reveal every star before he fell gently asleep in the warmth of the aged blanket, the coolest breeze upon his face. He swore he could still smell his mother in it, but it was most likely nostalgia. There seemed to be star upon star, crammed in just for his delight. Above him looking down, he was a funny sight, all eyes and smiling face in a cocoon of red, white and black cohesive thread.

Cold, Nick woke up to the full moon, his first Nevada moon and it seemed bigger than ever. Probably, because it was Tommy that found the orb sacred. Nick never paid her much mind, but it also made him question geography and where the moon was bigger, or closer. He might never sleep inside again. The saintly orb was bright and painted the landscape with shadows. He'd never seen a night so well lit. He found the stars fuck'n amazing, Jesus, there were so many, he only stopped looking because they began to blend together and the clarity lost. His bladder, suddenly grabbed the megaphone and screamed for release from the Dr. Pepper he drank earlier around his burger and cigarette, and it wanted out, now!

He arose, unraveling from the blanket, his body drawing up in a flex against the chill, as he stepped behind the rock, realizing as he did so that modesty could be a curse. He stepped into the shadow of the boulder, finding the little room within the stone and quickly tripped over something that gave under him. He kept his footing, but jumped away from the thing with a start, pretty sure it was an alligator about to chomp his leg off.

The gears of his brain finally clicked into place, to his socked feet, it felt as though he had just stepped on a body...a human leg to be exact and damn it, it was dark back here. Ugh, this felt eerily like the story he'd begun earlier, always writing himself or current scene into his tales. Trying to think of what to do, Nick popped out his Zippo and struck the wheel. The light it gave was minimal, but it did its job, revealing the lifeless young blonde he'd just stepped on, a cheerleader, if her uniform was any indication. Nick didn't jump again, but the chill in his spine was all consuming. *She looks like...*he searched the Rolodex of actresses in his head and came up empty. He'd be damned if she didn't look familiar, but that was too unsettling of a thought to entertain. He would have swore, she was from his story. A character from what he'd wrote, what, hours ago? But, that couldn't be.

Whoever she was, she was dead. She looked unblemished, save for what might be blood at the back of her head, it was hard to see. Also, did he smell wine? A sweet, yet sour...'no, wait a minute,' he thought, 'its the same scent I smelled in the car earlier.' He couldn't figure out why. He pulled his gray tee up to his nose, wondering if it was on him. He'd shucked his flannel to settle in under the warm blanket. It didn't seem to be on his shirt, but you know when you try to smell your own breath and all you smell is your hand? He couldn't help but think it was the same.

Nick instantly felt eyes on him and clicked the lighter's lid shut. He nervously scanned the moonlit landscape around the enclosure and then rubbed at his neck, at an ache there (it felt like he'd had his neck in a vice at some point). Then another thought occurred to him, but Hank was the one to speak it, "Perhaps she is still alive, conclusion jumper, Jesus." Hank was streaked in moonlight and black face paint, in a military issue tan, tank top and camo fatigue pants. He was soaked in sweat and his red rimmed eyes stood out in the darkness with a sense of feigned urgency. Nick considered this and dropped to feel for a pulse in the young girl's neck. He felt nothing and moved his hand three times just to make sure he wasn't missing it, but the cold skin said it all.

It was as he feared, she was dead and all he could think, was whoever did this might still be here. Nick froze under his urgent fear and screaming mind, that told him to hurry and get the fuck out of here. He stepped lightly back around the body and back to his Duster's safety (all the while, Hank played drill sergeant yelling for Nick to double time it and calling him a coward piece of puke). Nick would have rolled his eyes at the man running serpentine, flipping to roll to his feet, and dropping to a knee to make hand signals to no one, had his trip to pee not been interrupted by a dead girl. Nick shut the door quickly, hoping to be quiet, in the process; it was still louder than he wanted it to be. He reached around, locking every door and scanning the entire surroundings of the car. “Dammit, now what?” He was fully adrenalized, more alert than he'd ever been.

He could hear Hank screaming the garbled and non nonsensical drill sergeant song, “Right, left, head-e-lep....” as *The Steps* acted out his own little boot camp.

“Okay,” Nick thought out loud, “Okay." It was the only word that his mouth would make. Apparently that was the word that a thousand thoughts running smack into one another in a sea of fear, spelled out, and his mouth was only too accommodating in its repetition. "Okay." His mind lost so many strings of coherent thought: Is she what is left of a fraternity party gone wrong? Did she just drink too much out here alone, walking, running away? Yeah, she was drunk and laid down to sleep it off in the ruins, probably well known by the local kids and...and hit her head? He didn't see any blood on the stone. But, maybe she fell too quick to leave a trace, there? She didn't look as if she'd just laid down to sleep, though she could have fallen. There was no car around that Nick had noticed. It felt like she was left. But then it felt as though she hadn't been left, altogether, just walked away from. He could feel the killer watching him, some faceless shadow hiding in a bigger shadow.

Dammit, could he just drive away and leave this? Could he live with that? It felt as if he could or at least should be able to, but..., "dammit!" His heart fought his head, his head ready to skip town, but his heart needing to protect his head from future hauntings and lashings of guilt. He had to maintain the ability to witness his face in a reflection without hating it. That was his unspoken mantra, his only real rule that steered more decisions than he knew.

Nick popped the key in the ignition and the Duster banged to life. Nick dropped the gearshift into drive and then realized that he had to get back out of this safe room, out among the clutch of killers that were hiding just out of sight. This thought scared the shit out of him, because the safety of the Duster was real, especially when it was started, in drive, the doors were locked, and potential danger was about to disappear behind him. He had to get out, because his loose plan was to drive to the next town and let the cops know so they could handle this situation, it was WAY outside of his wheel house. But, how would he direct them here. He figured this rock was a good three hundred yards from the highway and he didn't know it was called Hangers Rock by the locals. The up side, was that there was nothing between this rock and the road, but low lying scrub brush; this gave him an idea for a visual. An image of the old road flares that had been lying on the Indian blanket in his trunk popped into his minds eye. Nick saw another image like a fish-eyed lens of the whole trunk and blood was everywhere. With a jerk of his head, it was gone and he saw the flares again as his mind focused on the task at hand. His nerves must be raw, he damn sure felt jumpy. His subconscious pondered if this bloody scene was a prophetic vision or what?

"How old are those?" Hank asked sarcastically from the backseat. Nick turned to see his troubled subconscious version of his step-father draped across the backseat, like David Hasselhoff holding the Shar Peis on his naked crotch (oh, the things our prepubescent minds don't unsee). Hank, though, had no Shar Peis to cover his peas and carrots. "Let's see, your mother was still acting like she cared about us...so...oh yeah. I brought those home one night just before I beat the shit out of her," here he laughed with a side glance at Nick, waiting for his pushed button reaction, "And, then you for telling me to stop. And, you were, what, five, when I finally beat that word out of your mouth? So these flares are, what, eleven, twelve ? Prolly, not going to work, you dumb shit." He said this very casually as if it were a term of endearment, "An' I only say that to your face, because… well, because I don't think you're big enough to do anything about it." Again, spoken as a sad fact, "Glad I got those beatings in on her before she left and gave me a reason." Nick blinked his tired eyes in disbelief and Hank's high falsetto began tauntingly, "stop hitting her...she's my mother...st-st-st-stoooop."

Nick hated to get out for flares that wouldn't work while a killer was on the loose, but then, maybe he would be killed and not have to hear this bullshit. He shook his head in frustrated disbelief and exited the car. He wanted to light his blanket, still flung across the back of the stone love seat. Despite the fear, the sting of the words found their mark. It was the chilling fear that kept him from realizing he was mimicking the hateful fucker, "Naaa naa naa na."

"Aaahhhhhhh!" yelled Hank (mimicking a really annoying, incorrect-answer-buzzer). He was, now, atop the black sedan, crouching in a too small, simple black dress, and nothing else. Nick felt the fleeting swim of his stomach at seeing this frame so undressed again; especially what the skirt exposed in the unladylike crouch.

It always took Hank about twenty minutes of being home from his day shift duty to make a three beer mug and strip down to his nasty ass skivvies. Actually, it took a trail of clothes from the door to the bathroom and all of one minute to get undressed; and what a show; shoes kicked off just inside, pumping knees and bare feet working out of his khakis, dragging them inside out to fall and remain behind the broken down dirty yellow couch. Smoke was ever present as he walked in the house afire, lighting one smoke from the last. He always had a pack in shirt pocket, or tiny chair-side, end-table. He would then, sit in his recliner and bark orders to Nick to beer him or grow the hell up or mow the yard or to go to hell, watching the History Channel non stop.

Nick found, in the present, a twinge of nausea, at his car was being stained by this asshole. “These will work. The flares will work."

Nick bent to pick up the three flares he could see and suddenly Hank was inside the trunk, a bleeding mess like the dead dog. "I have to try, have to try. The world is depending on me..." in a muffled Droopy (the animated Basset Hound) kind of voice. Nick had to reach into the mess of a man, and feel for the flares. It disgusted him to have to pretend to reach through. He held a bottle in his hand, something fluid, but it was lost in the image of the man and not a flare. Ah, that felt like a flare. Sure enough, it was, and he scrounged until he came up with another.

Nick struck one of the flares immediately and stood it up on the lower shelf of stone; and grabbed his notebook to toss back in the trunk, for safe keeping. In a quick panic of just how long that would actually burn, he jumped back into the primer gray Dodge. As he brought the engine to life, he saw a shadow about twenty feet ahead of him. It was tall and stocky, and then it was neither, as if melting. He flipped on the lights in one fail swoop, despite his distraction. He was an athlete of multi-tasking, even clutched by fear. Whatever he’d seen ahead of them disappeared with the headlamps, and he drove without hesitation. As he made a straight shot for the highway, he could see the flare lighting up the blanketed rock shelf, behind. The stone made a laughing jack-o-lantern in the darkness and for the third time in six minutes, chills ran down Nick's back. The blanket, somehow completed the image of a Mexican Sugar Skull, but at least it could be seen.

He did hesitate to stop again, but knew he must strike another flare to place at the road way, to mark the location. Second flare alight, he drove consistently faster as the darkness shifted and morphed around him.

Nick wondered just how far he'd have to drive and hoped he could get the police back in time to find the flares. "You dumb shit, I know you don't know what you're getting yourself into, who you are messing with, but damn! You know it's all hopeless and if you don't, where have you been your whole life....or should I say, *hole life*?" Hank teased now from the rear view mirror (still the blur rode around the passenger front and right side of the windshield. Nick swore he could hear screaming, loud and from far away, but it wasn't Hank. What the hell was that? Maybe the wind through an unsealed window?). Nick wondered what that next green sign a hundred yards up would reveal and why the hell Hank was wearing a gimp's leather mask with the zipper unzipped across the mouth suddenly and why there was, unfortunately, no ball gag. Nick shook his head and got back on task. The sign said:

I 50

Austin

5

Mount Augusta 53

Reno 241

He only hoped Austin was large enough to have a police department and drove on watching the speedometer, along with every other dial, not taking in any of the information but feeling as though he needed to look, again and again. He pushed ahead with fierce and foggy concentration. His mind was racing, 'Go, go, go,' racing through his head like a mantra. His 120 mph was brought to a drastic decrease by the first hair pin curve and held at bay by the next, not five-hundred-feet beyond.

Austin City Limits

So here we are
It's hour one
and it's a nightmare
There's nothing left
and yet it's good to be alive
There's no use crying
cause the universe is not fair
The wicked and the innocent
are fighting to survive
Child, stay down, stay down
You better run for cover underground
Child, stay down, stay down
You better shut your mouth
Don't make a sound!

Hour 1 / Scorpions

Nick was within a mile of the city before he could see civilization off to his left (on the loneliest road in America, which is highway 50 or Lincoln Highway) and standing sentry, was the population sign:

Austin Pop: 167.

There was next, a sign that warned of the drop in speed ahead, so Nick felt the hope he'd lost at the sight of the population sign start to well up again (as if a slow city speed limit meant a safe city and a safe city meant a concerned community large enough to help him through this circumstance). Just past the *Pony Canyon Stop and Go,* was the Lander County Sheriff's Office and Nick pulled in just eight minutes after speeding away from the poor girl's body. He parked to the southeast, to the side of the building. He didn't like the idea of pulling up in front, too well lit. Hank being a state trooper and a rotten excuse for a human, gave Nick little trust in law enforcement, but he couldn't leave that poor girl out there like that. He was torn, feeling that he was walking into a trap, but he dared not hesitate or he wouldn't do anything. He didn't think he could live with that. He caught himself at the door, trying to make a mad dash inside. He took three deep breaths before allowing himself to open the door. A clinical beep announced the open door, and a moving chair sounded from the opening to the left of the counter. A terrifying uniform stepped across behind the long counter.

"I need to speak to the Sheriff," Nick sounded like he was still fighting puberty. He was petrified.

A dark haired officer with a face for business addressed Nick's submissive plea, "Alright son, take a breath and tell me what's going on, " he said as he walked back to the long counter's opening. The counter ran from the right wall, leaving a walkway to a small office to the left and another straight ahead. The officer was in that walkway now, arms crossed as he waited for the information.

"I'm sorry....I'm Nick Stone," Nick said pulling out his wallet to expose his driver's license thinking it would be asked for at some point in this ceremony, mostly because his only dealings with the police was one speeding ticket. Handing his I.D. to Officer Dillon, according to his gold name tag, "I was just passing through and stopped for a break just five miles back (gesturing east to his left), and found a dead girl...a cheerleader...blonde....." Nick didn't know what else to say or how much to offer but was struggling to sound coherent. "Oh, I set some flares, but we'll have to hurry." The years of torture under Hank's roof summoned sweat to break out on Nick's forehead and armpits; something Officer Dillon's trained eye picked up on.

"Alright Mr. Stone, why don't we go take a look and we'll go from there." The officer eyed the driver's license and the young man before handing it back. He stepped back into his office, put on his uniform jacket and stepped around the counter, grabbing Nick by the arm with little force, but a ready hand that expected trouble. Nick felt the officer hesitate at the door, but wasn't sure why.

Nick was scared, but thought it best to just go along and be as submissive as possible to a point, a point he hoped would not be reached. Just as Nick expected, the young officer escorted him to the back seat where he knew he would be locked in. *'It's okay, you are not hiding anything, this is procedure and he doesn't know you or what you are capable of, so he has to be careful...it's okay,'* Nick told himself trying to calm his breathing quietly to mask his nervousness. Suddenly, it was as if someone was tripping Nick and he fell forward, catching himself with both hands on the edge of the open car door's frame. He'd seen a blurry spot erupt where his hands were, just before he fell. This was beginning to be a concern. Was it a tumor?

"You okay, son?"

"Yeah, I just lost my balance, my leg is hurting for some reason. My eyes have been...messing up tonight, as well. Maybe I'm not having a stroke." Nick half chuckled.

The officer had no response to this, which was probably best. He placed a hand at the back of Nick's head to keep him from hitting the car's roof. The fact that the kid wasn't handcuffed meant he didn't need his head protected, but old habits and all. Nick didn't see the officer eyeballing his throat, "You ever been choked by anyone, man?" Nick was confused by the question and couldn't help but feel defensive. Standing fully erect against the officer's hand, Nick felt something shift as he considered the question. The need to lash out against the officer spiked through his system and was immediately gone. What the hell? He looked at the officer in confusion, but fortunately, before he could say something stupid, "You look like you have, very recently."

Nick just shook his head, bewildered by the question, and exactly what was happening to him. Then, he remembered the ache he had in his neck earlier and noted that his throat did feel raw, "Oh, I did feel...I mean, it ached earlier when I woke up, but I didn't hurt it, that I can remember." The officer let it go and continued to aid Nick into the backseat. Once the door shut, Nick needed to hold it. For some odd reason, it soothed him. He tried not to let the strain show.

"Yeah, you keep singing yourself a little love song to keep the blue birds flitting about your head, but you're FUCKED!" laughed Hank in prison striped PJs and handcuffed wrists in his lap, "That is what they all say in the back of my car and half of the stupid som'bitches, I knock in the goddamn head and dump on the side of the road." Hank was sitting next to Nick in the backseat, he smelled of smoke, though he wasn't smoking a cigarette in the moment. Nick closed his eyes and tried to limit the shake of his head, to hide his insanity from Officer Dillon.

'Dammit Hank, you are all the hell I need right now,' Nick thought as loudly as he could toward his phantom, he thought it best to ignore the fat ass to his right, and found it easier than he thought, probably due to fear being a great motivator.

"You okay there Nick?" asked the deputy, pulling out onto the highway.

Nick met his eyes in the rear view, "Yes Sir, it just shook me up...I've....I've never seen a dead body before."

"Okay Son, tell me what happened as I drive us there...you'll have to directed me when you see me getting close." Nick noticed the officer immediately drove the right direction and wondered to himself if he'd said anything to lead the officer to know where he'd come from and thought he remembered gesturing at some point.

He admired the officer's ability to pick up on such small clues, at least, he hoped that was the case. "Yes Sir, I stopped to eat some leftovers I bought back in Grand Junction."

"Utah?" questioned the officer.

"Uh, yes," Nick assumed the officer wanted to know what the hell he was doing here and probably noticed he was from Illinois from his license, but thought he would let Officer Dillon ask the questions. "I fell asleep at some point, on this big rock, and when I woke to, well.... relieve myself (suddenly feeling like he just pissed all over Officer Dillon's territory), and I tripped over her body. She had a blue, white and orange cheer-leading suit on...or *has,* I should say."

"What are you doing out this way, Nick, you got family in the area?"

"No sir, that is why I headed this way," Nick was quickly trying to decide on how much of his life he wanted to give away, not wanting Hank to catch wind of his where abouts. "I am headed to Sacramento for work."

"Oh yeah? Work, for who?"

Trying not to hesitate and still keep things straight, "There is a sports apparel company that my Dad used to work for before he joined the Air Force," Nick lied. Officer Dillon may not have believed it, but he stopped asking questions to Nick's relief. He didn't know how far he could follow this thread of lies without tripping all over himself and exposing this tricky web he started. Nick scanned the landscape to change the subject, "Oh. I lit a flare hoping it would last until we got back."

"We?"

"Yes, you and me....whoever I found to tell about her, that is. I wasn't sure how long flares burn," Nick explained, sure he'd just given too much away, uncertain of just what. He felt like he was verbally walking a high wire and not good at it. From the grin on Hank's face, he thought the same. The man was now in a sex bondage get up with his hair pulled up in pig-tails and harsh make up on his face. He was sticking his tongue out at Nick, joyful that he was in trouble.

"Anywhere from 15 minutes to an hour," said Officer Dillon speeding up the car, "That's what the box in our office says. Bit of a broad window, isn't it?"

Nick was pretty sure it was hopeless, but grateful for the ease in conversation. "Nope....it's already too late....he'll never find it and then what is he gonna think, huh? Dumb-ass, should'a left well enough alone. It'll be a knock in the head for Dumb-ass!" taunted Hank, back in his prison garb and confining bracelets. Still, an aroma of smoke.

"Is that it? Wow, it just sparked out. Good thinking, Nick."

Nick was pleased with the, 'Ataboy,' as if they were on the same team suddenly. "Knock in the goddamn head." Hank offered with a tap of his handcuffs on his head, the jingle somewhat comforting for some odd reason. The patrol car pulled off the road and sure enough, Nick could make out the red, white, and black Indian blanket in the farthest reaches of the car's headlamps.

Excited, Nick reached up to point and found the cage in his way. He settle for wrapping his fingers in the crosshatched wire (the right fingers, his left hand was still holding tight at the door). "Yes Sir....that is my blanket stretched across that rock...and that is the rock that...just behind it is…the body." The officer didn't say anything, Nick could tell he was in mission mode and just let him do his thing. He'd know the truth momentarily anyway, right? The best thing was to let it unfold as it would. Nick was overwhelmed with relief that they found the place, that

Officer Dillon was now in charge and would handle things. Nick would, very soon, be on his way upward and onward. Now, he could be on his way knowing he did the right thing. Damn, he felt such a weight lifted. He merely watched as the officer pulled to a stop where, not twenty minutes ago, his Duster sat. He watched him exit the car and disappear behind the stone formation.

"Well....you might as well assume the position," said Hank now from the front seat on his knees, looking back at Nick like a little boy through the cage in his own Illinois State Trooper uniform. "The position, being, your forcibly unpuckered asshole and you assume it's going to be violated…because…it is." He was running a finger around the rim of his other hand's fist, and then hard in and out of the circle, "Cause you're fucked!" He looked back to Hank's face through the cage, but it wasn't there suddenly. He felt a small twist in his abdomen and wondered what could go wrong. He breathed deep twice and closed his eyes. He was thinking the officer should be back by now, using the radio for help or backup or the coroner.....something. He opened his eyes and still no sign of any life outside of the car, this little prison he was now stuck in. Maybe that was good though, he couldn't be blamed for anything that happened, right? If something went wrong, and he had a terrible feeling, that it already had. The darkness surrounding the sides and rear of the car stood out in stark relief to the dome light above his head, the one that was currently pointing him out as a vulnerable bit of food for any wondering predators. He realized the officer must not have shut the front door. No movement in the headlights lighting up the stone. Nick laughed nervously at the thought, that the dome light was highlighting the other Stone. He stopped a scream that echoed out of his throat, not wanting the deputy the hear it, if he still could. Why did he know Dillon couldn't? What kind of new hell was this?

Mommy

"Mommy.....Mo...."

"Shut the fuck up.....Goddamn can't a man get some sleep in this fucking house!" screamed Hank Forbus on his way to slapping the boy across the mouth and into the wall where he collapsed into sobs on the floor. The six-year-old weighed all of fifty pounds and was easily propelled by the man's meaty hands.

"Hank! You know he has..."

"Oh, don't *you* start. Yes, he has nightmares like any good Mama's boy. Fuck! If you touch him....so help me. Christ Bec, you can't reward this kind of weakness!" Rebecca Stone flinched in her reach for her son and froze, slinking back to the bed in defeat. Her look to Nick was heartbreaking, but further solidified that she was of no help against this ruler, this Tyrant of Plinth Street. "Boy, find your room and don't let me hear another damn word from you. You hear me!" Nick had a plethora of nightmares after that night, but got better and better at keeping them to himself. In the brightest of these, he struggled to land a punch, and drowned beneath the surface of his own self-doubt. The darkest, well, they involved the same husky demon that haunted his waking world; variations of him, at any rate. Getting the fuck out of Dodge was always the plan...Thank the gods for Tommy's influence and push in restoring a rusted out Dodge, Duster. After that, getting out of Dodge in their Dodge seemed like a fine start.

Rebecca Stone never married Hank, nor did she ever love him in Nick's opinion. Though, he couldn't be certain of her head-space; he sure never thought she'd leave him behind. She settled for what she thought would be a father for little Nicky, a state trooper, had his own house, and only a little handsy. David Stone was her first love and Nick figured he still was, wherever he was. Who knows, he would think sometimes, maybe she is with him now. She told him once that his Dad was a dark stranger, the most mysterious, beautiful man she'd ever met. That's about all he could ever get out of her and Nick had an image of him from just those words and wondered often how accurate his image was. He couldn't help but see a rough but happy manly man, flannel shirt wearing cigarette smoking cool dude, never upset because he was always in control of himself and anyone around him or his family, that might cause a stir. It always stung, being honest that he wasn't a part of that family. He also wondered so many times after she was gone, why he didn't ask more; more often, more questions? He wondered if she ever looked for him after she left. He liked to think they were together somewhere, perhaps walking the rainy Paris streets or lounging on a white clean beach, even if it was without him. The sweet boy wanted them to be happy.

He watched his Mom punched for trying to speak to his step-father, the man she insisted he learn to call his Dad, before the worst of it. He watched her wince and grab her fractured ribs on a sunny beautiful day, when Nick made her laugh. Saw the black tinged eyes, stained from crying and darkened from punching. He knew what she had endured in her effort to make it all work, almost died for him. He wasn't bothered by the fact that she couldn't take it anymore. He used to cry that she didn't take her six year old son with her, but he began to realize on his ninth birthday (third uncelebrated birthday), that there was no other way for her. That she actually believed without her to antagonize Hank, he would take care of the boy, afraid she wasn't able, financially or emotionally. He knew all of this too early for his years, but he also knew she left him with the darkest part of her life and there was a spark of rage, slowly kindled to life by that. How many months had she tried? Nick was already six when they got together. He didn't want to blame her, but the hell he lived through since, was because of her inability to think, to act as his parent, his savior from the world at large. She let him down, no matter her reasoning.

There was no party for Nick on his tenth birthday, either. As a matter of fact, Hank never knew when Nick's birthday was, or at least forgot if he ever knew. Hank would have said that was precious of Nick to believe that he gave three shits, and precious was for weaklings, which was made up of women and fairies and goddamn stray animals. Honestly, Nick wasn't sure it was his tenth, fairly certain he was six when his mother left.

Nick found some clarity on this particular day, because he gave himself his first real present. He waited for Hank to pass out in his broken down recliner, and he pissed in his half finished beer. It was a lovely gift for Nick, because Hank's rhythm was to awake around 3am with a cigarette craving and finish that last beer before clumsily slumping off to bed. It was a little thing, but it was a first huge step for the boy that was the fan.....you know, the fan that the shit hit again and fucking over again. It was enough for Nick to know he had to take only so much, that it could go the other way too. There were other occasions through the next eight years, it's easy to fuck with a drunken-stupor personified once you knew his patterns. There were plenty of fists in the face too, because it went that way often, but Nick took what he could and grew smarter and quicker and stronger.

He wanted free of this goddamn bubble. This tainted trash heap of oily skinned bubble, he wanted to burn it down to the hell that awaited somewhere beneath it all and if he fell through, so fucking be it, he would make waves in the fucking furnace!

Nick wasn't fully aware the blame he felt toward his Mother...He figured he didn't save her and she didn't save him....even-Stevens. He sure in the hell didn't blame her for running away from the sick fuck, he got stuck with. And, Nick had his issues....well....sure, but who doesn't when you really get to seeing how people are built and what they run on. But, he was now free and what…a bonus? "That's right...a running buddy!" adds Hank. "Whenever you think you got it figured out, I'll be there to make you question....your pride, your sanity...hell, your self worth. I got your back buddy. I'm your man!" In Nick's most gracious moments of clarity, he knew his mother was beautifully broken as well, but she didn't just leave her mother's nice china behind, she wasn't just reckless with a fragile opportunity for an education, she left her son, like a half smoked pack of cigarettes that you feel almost torn over leaving, but you can always buy more.

Being the Fan

Being the fan was a nasty, dirty hole that you found yourself in, not ever knowing how you got there, and waiting for the shit to be thrown. It was being eleven, home alone from school, doing the dishes and cooking supper so your step-father might find a better mood and not hit you tonight....and he hit you anyway, because the soup and grilled cheese you made reminded him of your mom, for whatever fucking reason. It was being fourteen and answering the door to find that Samantha, that pretty girl that sits three desks behind you in Algebra, has come to see if you might be able to help her with tonight's homework because she's watched you and knows you know how, but then being interrupted by the heavy wooden door knocking into your head hard enough to bring blood and run off your first chance to ever make her smile. It was watching her turn every few running steps as she fled in terror, catching your eyes with her fear, strong enough to keep her from ever talking to you again. It was your broken heart having to listen to your abusive step-father yell, "Hell no, I ain't got nobody and I'll be goddamn if you are. It's your fucking fault your Mama left us in the first fucking place! Now clean that blood up and get the fuck out of my face!" It is the regular, intellect numbing, beer tinged halitosis stream of hot profanity that still hangs in the air and rings in your head. Being the fan is something Nick has become intimately familiar with and recognizes that he is, yet the fan again, because he wakes up with a face full.

Nick wakes up. That seemed surprising all by itself.

Why was he asleep and where the hell was he? Damned if his right leg wasn't singing. What the hell happened there? Okay, he was still in the back of the patrol car....and, "Ummmm....." DAMN, his head was thick and groggy. His back door was open. He knew that police car's typically had back doors that had to be opened from the outside, but maybe that could be altered, or perhaps, not all units had them. Maybe, the Lander County Sheriff's Department couldn't afford that luxury, though the squad-car looked the part.

"Yeah, FUCKED....like I said," Hank offered, peeking in the open door, and then out into the darkness, after making the *I'm watching you* signal of two fingers pointing at his own eyes and then at Nick.

'Had Officer Dillon come back and opened his door? Why was he so groggy, as if he'd suffered a concussion?' Nick brain buzzed with utter confusion. There *were* no clues, though. Nothing to offer him any answers. The front of the car looked blurry, like his car's windshield and front seat had in places. He couldn't be certain, but the radio's coiled connection to the hand receiver, might be frayed. '*Jesus, was it cut? Was the officer attempting to use it and got caught by the killer? Was he killed right here? Or'*, he breathed trying not to spiral out of control, '*perhaps the killer wanted to kill the radio communication, and the officer is still out looking?'* Nick again felt the surrounding darkness close in, feeling the killer watching his every move in the dome light lit car. He also recognized the deja vu of having had the same feeling in his Duster minutes ago. Or, was it hours now? '*He's just outside the reach of light, so he can taunt me and club me over the head as I step out. Was it the killer that opened my door? Why wouldn't he have just killed me then? Did he knock me out?'* Both of these last two possibilities made it feel as though the killer let him live. Perhaps he (or she), had a code, and thought him innocent or not part of the problem?

Hank appeared just outside the open back door, in his Aquaman Underoos, pissing them. He tilted his head at Nick, as if trying to figure him out, "Are you pissing your pants right now?"

Nick dared to check, it almost felt like he was relieving himself. He decided he was too goddamn suggestive.

With no plan what-so-ever, Nick stepped outside into the dark. The fear of being clubbed over the head was a small, rusty taste in his mouth, the taste of fear and survival mode. He did feel the desperate need to run into the darkness and hide, he had to know; curiosity would kill this cat yet.

He looked to where Officer Dillon was last, the stone was bright with the reflected head lights, but his eyes received a reprieve as he looked behind the stone. Nick closed his eyes tight, fighting the fear that told him to pull his lighter and see what was out here to get him. He forced himself to stop and breathe, as his eyes adjusted to the dark. When he opened them again, he could immediately see the beam of the Officer's flashlight, on the ground where the girl should have been. He grabbed it up (the chill on his neck from the certainty that he would be shot or clubbed over the head at any time), shone the long, heavy light around the scene, and saw a splatter of blood and no girl, or Deputy. '*I didn't shoot the sheriff....or the deputy down.*' actually sang through Nick's disturbed mind. '*Now what?'* He lit up the area behind the stone, hoping the Officer might have gone back that way, but then, he realized his error in that line of thinking, '*He wouldn't have left his flashlight here on purpose.'* Which meant, he was knocked out or killed, and taken either way.

The beam of light made Nick feel vulnerable again, but he was torn between wanting to see and not wanting to be seen. He decided not being seen was probably the best option considering there were probably two dead bodies not far away. He clicked off the officer's light and stepped back into the stone room. He rested in a squat, there, quietly controlling his breathing, and listening for any sign of someone else being out here. After, perhaps thirty seconds, he ran away from the head light's shine, and once in the shadows, darted out at an angle from the patrol car, some seventy-five feet. He quickly lay down to scan the scene for any movement, or shadows that shouldn't be there. He felt the wonderful breeze wrap around him and started to feel somewhat safer, what with not having been clubbed over the head yet. It sure seemed as if he was alone, out here in the middle of a murder scene, and nowhere,

"What are we doing?" loudly whispered the night-ops-dressed fat man beside him. Nick could just make out the pink rimmed eyes within the painted black face and rolled his own, glad the lummox was at least whispering, even violently so. It was bad enough that he couldn't get away from the asshole, but he even had to take the time to think through the fact the he was glad about a figment of his imagination whispering so as not to be overheard by the murderer that may still be in the vicinity. At least, the whispering allowed Nick to listen for and better hear any close footsteps.

What Nick struggled with most was the ease at which he lost his cool with the fucked up phantom and often screamed back. He had to watch that, it is one thing to have a one sided yelling match in the car (he could always feign singing to anyone that saw), but straight jackets awaited people that performed such private arguments for the world to see and hear. Doing it while hiding from a killer, though, well, that was just bad form; or goddamn stupid. "Look, Boy, We're vicious twinkies! YEEEAAAHH!" Still whispering loudly, the enlarged night operative slid the serrated edge of his Tactical Bowie Knife across the underside of his fingers and grinned a big, goofy grin. "Here, cut yourself, now," and held up his hand to Nick, "Blood Brothers?"

'*Well fuck me'*, Nick thought as he watched him shake off the unanswered blood brother attempt and lick his bloody fingers before screaming like a UFC fighter pumping himself up for a fight. Nick closed his eyes and took two deep breaths, focusing his ears. He opened his eyes to find his companion gone and hoped that he'd focused him gone, but could just be glad that he was gone, no matter the reason. Nick thought his best course of action was to check the car for keys, since he neglected to do that.

He didn't want to go back, he felt as if he were looking in on the scene from here, rather than a part of it. He couldn't help but wonder, what would the killer be waiting for? Playing some kind of game? He could have killed Nick when he knocked him out. Speaking of which, how the hell was he knocked out? Could the patrol car have been hit by another car? It was hard to be sure in this darkness. That could explain a knock on the head, though. '*That son of a bitch rammed me*,' Nick thought. He rubbed his head and felt the pain that could have been from the impact of a car crashing into the car that caged him, but wouldn't he remember the impact? He didn't know anything about concussions, but found it easy to believe that a head injury could effect his memory of such an ordeal. It was the only thing that made any sense. If someone had opened his door to knock him out, wouldn't he remember seeing it happen? Nick's thoughts interrupted by a break in the dome light, as a shadow opened the driver's side door and appeared to be doing something with the radio. Nick swore he heard laughing, but from where, he just couldn't place. It sounded closer than the car. Nick looked around in the dark, in a futile attempt to see if there was another car in his line of sight, because if the police cruiser had been hit, where was the other car?

Then another idea struck him. He thought surely he was making more out of all of this than there was. This must be the Officer calling in to the department and he suddenly felt so foolish, out here hiding, that his body shifted toward Officer Dillon, relieved with the saving grace of this reality, but there was something about the silhouette that told him to freeze. So, he froze on the first step, hoping he didn't give away his location with his desperate reaction. Apparently he didn't, the figure was still rummaging around in the front seat. Nick didn't know what the person was doing, but was too scared to stick around and find out. He needed to get away from this situation and could only think about getting back to his Duster and the hell out of Dodge, for real this time. Here he was, he'd done the right thing and look where it got him. Where ever the girl's body was, it looked as though her death was never going to be avenged, investigated, nor justice found. All the solid evidence gone, it seemed.

He felt like he was far enough away from the car to just stand up and jog away, but it felt like he would be seen in this moonlight, so in a deep squat, he backed away a hundred yards or so...until his thigh's ached and overrode the adrenaline that pumped through his system. That's when his bruised leg began reminding him that it hurt. It made him want to limp with every step.

Seeing the light go out as the door slammed shut, he turned and ran back to the road, past the pain. His fear was that if this guy took the patrol car, he would head straight for the highway and, in turn, straight at Nick; if he didn't run him over. He didn't much care for the idea of being road kill. He also didn't care for the idea of being spotted, especially by a killer. He ran with the sound of the car and, fear of getting caught, nipping at his heels. Finally, past the pavement, he hid on the other side (hoping the scrawny, sparse scrubs would be enough).

'Oh Shit,' his mind screamed, as red tail lights danced; headlight shine and shadows began to paint the rock. Nick realized his blanket was not on the boulder where he'd draped it. He also dove (like the baseball players he really

admired for their athletic discipline and seeming lack of fear of throwing their bodies and face at the ground really hard), for the first time in his life. He allowed his body to fall motionless and held his breath trying to minimize the dust he kicked up for the driver to see. Relieved, that the car drove in a diagonal direction back to the highway, he lay on his side watching the lights push toward Austin, fearing it would at any minute turn and serpentine around trying to find him. He heard the catch of the rubber on pavement as third gear was found, the lights lurched, and diminished. Nick rolled onto his back, allowing his fear to blow away with the wind as he spat dust off of his lips. He saw the stars, so many visible here, and saw something flame across the sky, like a bottle rocket, orange and sparkling. It was absolutely beautiful and he couldn't help but find the beauty in it. He was so ready to be free of this pocket terror he'd driven into. This was all so…

"Well shit, Daredevil, hope you didn't hurt yourself trying to run from your first real opportunity to be a hero!" exclaimed Hank with a level of sarcasm that bit Nick's emotion.

"WHAT THE F......!" Nick screamed and beat the dusty floor. "Goddammit! What was I suppose to do? This isn't a goddamn comic book." Nick ranted, trying to let his practical sensibility override his desire to be that hero at any and every opportunity, as if the world around him needs saving. He got up and dusted himself and the broken pride on his sleeve off and followed the road from a safe distance. He would make it back to his trusty Duster and then figure out what to do...or simply say 'Fuck it!' and leave, which is exactly what he was leaning toward. "Fuck you, Hank."

There was just enough moonlight and waist high sage brush that Nick felt secure in his ability to hide from any passing cars, not that there were any, but remaining invisible was a commodity he wished to hang on to, at the moment. About a mile and a half in, he slowed to a jog, giving in to the sharp stabbing pain in his ribs, at two miles he stopped at a waist high rock for a breather. He realized he'd worked up a mild sweat and thought it best to avoid that, in case he got stuck outdoors for the night. The breeze was quite a bit cooler than it was when he first lay upon the boulder to snooze. His breathing returned to normal when the coyotes began singing to his left. It was as beautiful as the stars above that he wanted so much to appreciate, but it was also concerning. Just how big was the pack and would they be able to overtake him if they so desired? Might they cut him off from town?

Nick decided to stay on the move and began walking the rest of the way back to Austin, three miles, or so. Once he caught his breath he was able to jog again and repeated this cycle the entire trip back.

His head was clearer and he decided that once he was back to his Duster, he would look for the patrol car and then return to the bloody scene to see what he could find. He couldn't just drive away after getting Officer Dillon involved. He had to know what happened to him. He wanted to know about the girl, too. It made sense that whoever killed the girl, also rammed the patrol car, knocking Nick out in the process. So....."Oh shit!" Nick stopped walking as he spoke his alarm aloud, "I must have interrupted him."

This began a new gaggle of goose bumps up his spine. "He watched me...or did he see me and lay the scene around me? I didn't see any evidence of the girl until after I awoke in the dark, though, I never did go behind the rock before that. Hell, he may have woke me inadvertently," Nick tried to remember any sounds that may have awoken him on his rocky perch. "He could have killed me, which means he was probably just trying to set me up. But, why would he kill the deputy? Maybe he didn't, maybe he just hit him over the head as Officer Dillon tried to commandeer his radio. But, why would he drive the cruiser back to town and where is his car?" There were just too many variables and no answers swimming around his battered head for him to land on anything solid.

"Well, you know what they say," Hank asked Nick as he stood dramatically beside him in a black suit pulling off his shades like *H* from CSI Miami. "There's no spatter that matters like blood spatter....Batter, batter, batter." He cocked his head to the side looking back at Nick and put one ear piece of his shades in the corner of his mouth; to Nick's disbelief, he heard *The Who* kick off '*Who Are You*' as if the television show just began around him.

"I've absolutely gone bat shit crazy," Nick said stoically and began walking again, leaving *H* to his imagined Hollywood crime scene.

Back in Austin

Nick cut through behind houses and businesses staying south of the highway, not wanting to be seen, and because the Sheriff's Office was on the South side of the highway (where he'd left his car). He was torn between slamming into the Duster and hauling ass, and checking on the officer he'd directed to his doom. Nick thought he was, almost, fully aware of how dangerous his situation was. He was all about being prepared for the worst, but his positive nature left him open to evil intention all too often....at least that was his experience before he began tripping Nevada. He didn't know anything about the killer, if there even was a killer. In truth, the girl could've overdosed at a party and just been left, which was a world of difference from their being a killer on the loose (one that he interrupted, perhaps watched him infect the scene with police). Something odd happened, but the evidence didn't dictate a murder. *'Maybe, Officer Dillon moved the girl...wait! He would only do that if he killed her or wanted to cover it up, right? Otherwise, he would have left her, until the scene was covered by forensics. But, he wouldn't have left me in the car. Unless, he is watching to see if I skip town; a runner too scared to talk wouldn't be a problem for him. I don't know? There is just too much I don't know.'*

"Or....let's see....hmmmm," offered a jogging, short shorts sporting Hank, annoyingly playfully, his hands up with wrists flaccid, "Maybe Colonial Mustard used the dildo in the study, Whoa Girl! No, no, hang on....It wa.....Hup!" Nick chuckled to himself, that even his subconscious could trip over its own fat fuck'n feet and, again, left behind the comic relief while he was jogging and lisping in his best attempt at being homophobically humorous. Nick sneaked behind the Post Office and crossed South Street at a run, clinging to the shadows of the buildings. Just down from the Sheriff's Office, Nick decided he would check the windows to see if there were any signs of life in the office before jumping into his ride and backtracking for clues (and he was still, triple guessing that whole clue gathering idea - Scooby-Doo he wasn't). Nick, suddenly feeling lucky he hadn't run into any dogs behind any of these buildings, speaking of Scooby-Doo.

It would seem to fit the scene of this dusty old town, backyard guard dogs. As Nick found the edge of the Pony Canyon Stop and Go, his chills returned and his breath was knocked out by a quick punch of realization. He didn't even consider his Duster might not still be there. Now, he felt a shade of fear he hadn't yet hit tonight. He pushed both front pockets, hoping to feel his keys and there were none to be found. "GODDAMMIT! screamed his mind, echoing it through out his darkened skull. He saw a hazy blur where he thought his car should be, but many things were hazy in these street light shadows.

"Ruh-Ro Rag.....Rooks rike rur fucked!" Nick would've laughed, had he not been in the middle of a break down. Worse yet, Hank looked like a Pod People creation as his head rode the live action body of that Mystery Team mascot. Nick's mind reeled and he stood gasping for breath from the chest clinching panic attack that now had control. A list of horrible events, that happened since sundown, ran through his brain: finding a dead girl, getting an officer killed, being toyed with by the killer, finding his car gone, stuck in this nightmare. Nick fell to his right knee, and then limp against the back of the brick building, on his right shoulder. His vision went dark and he blacked out. He never lost consciousness completely, he just couldn't see or hear anything, until a blanket of sweat cooled by the breeze, made him shiver, and brought his senses back. His shoulder was scraped from the raw feel of it, and his knee felt dislocated, though he could move it. His neck, still sore from whatever the fuck happened in the patrol car, sang out just a touch louder than the right side of his head; the last part of his body to collapse into the brick.

Nick's brain tried to urge him on with a sense of mission, but his body was having none of it. He merely lay there, half fallen. *'Hell, I can't even fall right,'* he thought, before opening his eyes to see, what finally dawned on Nick, were yellow eyes. They were not nearly far enough from his own, ever growing brown ones. The fear, not enough to compel his broken body, froze his already chilled insides with an urgent need to believe he was seeing things. His tired mouth wouldn't even release the scream that filled his thudding and frozen heart.

The eyes drew closer and Nick was just able to make out a silhouette, that made his eyes want a time out. The heat and stench of rancid breath blew across his face. It was Hank, somehow transformed. He wasn't recognizable, but Nick knew it was him. This should have been a comforting realization, but the sight pulled at Nick's fright, like a wolf wrenches meat from a carcass. Nick's eyes adjusted to the darkness, as horror quickened his focus. This monster turned its head to the side, slight tilt up, closed its eyes and breathed another long, deep breath, as if smelling everything in the air for miles (like a shark smelling the drop of blood running down Nick's neck in a world full of air).

"He smells you, this other," vocalized a voice from another time; a time before man with a sensual, monstrous, bi-tonal moan that skipped right past the chills and caused Nick's stomach to churn. "and his skin is of the shadows, fitted to his mood like a burnt skin. His mood is....," pausing for another ravenous, savoring of air, "Covetous." The black, melting-plastic beast stepped closer and bent down on huge cloven feet (Nick could only hear this, but it was unmistakable) with its arms out from its sides like twisted chicken wings, until it was face to face with Nick, melted nose touching nose. Nick's eyes fought his curiosity for closure. The skin of this creature, appeared like it was soaked in pitch, or made of it. Yellow, oblong-star patterned eyes, gleamed with intensity as it breathed Nick in completely, again, releasing a putrescent sulfur stench that released Nick's stomach contents into his throat, as the creature licked at his face with a slug-like tongue. Steam and smoke surrounded Nick's nose and mouth with the breath of this demon.

Nick's head lurched back with the sudden heave, striking the brick. Nick vomited loudly and fully. He knew the force of it should have slammed his head into the creatures, but he was relieved to find his space, his own. He then saw yesterday's *Lupper* upon the grass strewn concrete, as he fell to his busted shoulder. Rolling back in exhaustion, sore head on brick, he breathed deep, closed his eyes, and fell asleep.

He awoke, after what must have been no more than five minutes, and began the long talk into action. "Just sit up, then we'll do something else." He felt sick and just wanted to sleep. Jesus, none of this had anything to do with him. Whoever's responsibility it was, it was not his. But, even if the girl wasn't his duty to avenge, he did see a deputy killed. We'll did he? He actually didn't see a goddamn thing, as a matter of fact. He wiped his mouth as he confirmed this knowledge and peeled his poor body off of the hard brick, like a price sticker on a cherished book (feeling as though he'd left some of himself behind in the process, just like he always did with the goddamn stickers). He rubbed his shoulder and only wished he could comfort his whole body this way, to ball himself up in the palms of his hand and knead himself in warmth. He was sore as hell and tired, because, he knew damn well he was going to finish this, in death, or in answers.

Okay, he needed to get up and do something, the question was what? The only answer that would come was, "Find my car."

Save for one answer more, "God I must be Psychotic."

It would seem that life with Hank left him more than just a humorous, annoying shadow (and the feeling of that last word, left a warm cramp in his gut). He'd never been scared of his own shadow, but it seemed he didn't know what all was at his back, at the moment. He looked from his kneeling position at the brick corner and saw the Duster, just where he'd parked it. The problem was, he saw it blink out of existence and then static in and out until it was just gone. He rubbed his temples with closed eyes and tried to make his mind okay. He was more uncertain than ever, of being able to do that for real, of ever really being okay, ever again. He thought of the tale of the legendary Philadelphia Experiment as he waited for the car to reappear.

Life with the Man

A bright sharp pain and the sound of someone gasping, desperately for air, woke Nick with a start. It surprised him that it was he who was fighting for air. He unfolded like a jack knife and saw his step-father standing at the side of his bed with a smile that meant he was being mean. It was the only feeling he enjoyed, it seemed.

"GET UP....RISE AND SHINE.....Piece of shit! I want you to do something before you head off to school!" he was slurring and rough as fuck. Hank slapped at the boy's face with poor aim, as he stepped back. Nick didn't know if it was day or night in the green tint the world took on after waking in such a hell-fire hurry.

Nick's hands were still up defensively, as he pulled in a ragged breath. He noticed it was still dark in the slit between his shade, and the window. Hank was nice enough to turn his light on before terrorizing him, how sweet. It was 3:16 a.m. by the red digital display of his alarm clock. He decided not to ask, and just get dressed. If he'd learned anything since his Mom left, eight months ago, it was that questions got you slapped. And yet, as he swung his feet off the bed to get dressed, a hard, huge, hand made contact with his small head, anyway.

"YOU NOT EVEN GOING TO ASK WHAT IT IS? You are a lifeless shiece of pit, like your mama in bed, fucki, Wus!" The man was slurring worse than Nick had ever heard and he realized that Hank was still wearing his police uniform and wind breaker. It was way out of routine for him. The man was typically in his skivvies as he stepped into the house, and stayed that way until he dressed for work, the next day. Where had he been?

"She was a lifeless corpse in ng worthless. Jesus....I want you to dig a hole fa the doggg ah hit while m was out. It's in the trunk of mmm patrol car...and clean at up when you're done. I'm goin ta bed. The shovas is in the shed......and put it back when yur done....Fuck Sick!" Hank finished bouncing from wall to wall down the hall to his own bedroom. Nick heard this as he felt of the raw hand print on his cheek, then rubbed at his raw throat, to scared to try and clear it, aloud. He heard the mammoth fall onto his worn down bed, as he crossed into the hall, out to whatever great present lay in the patrol car's trunk.

Nick held his face, tears stinging his eyes. His seventh birthday was last week and this is the closest thing to a present he'd gotten from dear old step-dad. He hadn't expected much from the man, who begrudgingly took over where his mom left off, but a piece of cake or a grouchy, "Happy Birthday, Boy," would have passed for government work. Instead, it was the only pet Nick would ever have.

A stray German Shepherd had shown up three days ago. Nick had stolen some food and fed Skippy at a condemned house, nearby, so Hank wouldn't know about it (just bologna sandwiches, but Skippy didn't seem to mind the particle meat Nick abhorred). Nick was so happy, he now had a true friend who could be with him after school and on weekends. He didn't yet know how to tell if it was a boy or girl, and he didn't really care. This new friend was his birthday present. The dog must have been out roaming the area and why was Hank out anyway? He never went out. He'd never seen him so drunk, either. Come to think of it, he smelled different, not like beer. Nick thought he must have gone out to drink, at a bar or in his patrol car.

The warm death hit him before he saw the black and tan body of his friend twisted up in the spacious sedan's trunk, partially lit by the street light in Hank's yard. Realization punched the seven-year-old in the gut. It was then that the evil man's words sounded in Nick's head again, "I want you to dig a hole fa the doggg a hit while I was out." Blood running from the open mouth and pooling on the dark brown metal where the trunk's crumpled black lining was absent. The warm musty aroma gripped his stomach and gave it a flex. Nick threw up as he turned from the car, not wanting to have to clean that up too. After twenty minutes and four tries, he finally worked up the nerve to put his hands on the dog. It was a quick, scared touch and then it took another three tries to grab a hold of the dead animal's fur and test its weight. He felt an uncontrollable fear that the fur would rip free. That his only friend would fall to pieces in his hands.

He didn't want to be out here when Hank came waddling out for work, so he pulled with a heave and the forty-five pound canine slipped from his tentative grip and fell into his vomit. It felt so disrespectful, so awful. Nick cried all the way through the digging, but the work eventually took all of his tears. His anger helped, too.

He was pissed that the angry, bitchy man would hurt Skippy. He knew the man meant to, that he sought the dog out, probably even went to the house to find him and drug him out to kill him. Probably saw Nick feed him the first day, spying on him. Nick knew the man had never seen him enter the abandoned house and that this last scenario probably wasn't true, but he was pissed and wanted to believe it anyway. He dug and dug, until the anger dried up and became exhaustion. He'd lost time while he was digging, it felt good to work in anger. Slicing at the man's yard with the shovel, stabbing the ground he owned. It was symbolically satisfying.

Nick saw the little golden tag just before letting him slide in the hole. "Maybe the next place will be good to you, Skippy," Nick said solemnly. The sun was coloring the sky, as he walked back to the house to retrieve the cleaning supplies, which consisted of a bottle of generic glass cleaner with a dishrag draped over the top. Nick used the rag to clean up the blood and put it back over the top of the bottle under the kitchen sink without a second thought. Seven year old feral boys and cleanliness aren't exactly known to be on a first name basis.

Nick's mom leaving him was his first real lesson, the dead dog was his second, and the bloody rag was his third, two days later. He learned that a bloody rag, from most any situation or circumstance, was evidence. Evidence of wrong doing. Evidence that a crime was committed. It was also apparently worth a broken arm and fractured rib, which Hank gladly provided Nick for his recklessness.

Nick learned that true anger could be held....held close and protected, like the first precious flame of a hard earned fire, stoked by a gentle breath and whispered into life with a hopeful prayer. Nick began stoking his own fire and it fueled him all the way to Nevada. Sometimes....wildfires rage on and on and are all encompassing. That wasn't a lesson Nick learned yet, but things have a way of catching up to us, wherever we find ourselves.

That day, Nick was walking home from Arthur Elementary school, crossing West Boise Street, cutting through yards as he always did on his way to Columbia Drive to walk the two miles back to Fairbanks, which led back to Plinth Street. He saw a boy he recognized from school stapling a paper on a telephone pole. He didn't know the boys name and decided not to engage. The boy was coming, anyway, obviously worried about something, "Have you seen my dog, Nick?"

He'd never talked to him, before, but he introduced himself as, Tommy Hauer. He would be the only human friend, Nick would ever have (he never had the heart, nor courage, to tell Tommy what happen to Skippy). Nick was startled, knowing immediately it had to be Skippy that the boy was looking for. He walked over to see the fliers Tommy was holding with alarm in his chest. He saw the image of Skippy and felt the weight of the blood on his hands at the sight. He looked at his outstretched shaky hands and wanted the dishonor off, now. He looked at the boy and fought his own stomach, fought the shame with uncontrollable tears. "I'm sorry," he said shaking his head, "I'm sorry I can't help." he grunted through the streaming tears, as he launched into the two mile run home.

He'd never run so far before and fell into the space behind Hank's house, where there was a spot of grass and no one to see. His lungs burned, raw from the crying and the distance. He struggled for breath and when his lungs finally calmed, Nick threw up his lunch. It was meatloaf day and he'd never thrown up this particular meal before...it had turned and it was so vile, it made him throw up until he dry heaved. He cried hard and loud, knowing no one cared.

He could see the disturbed and darkened dirt of Skippy's grave to his left and when the tears were gone, he crawled to the disturbed earth and begged the dog for forgiveness. Nick was so tired, but he didn't want to be out here when Hank got home. He finally walked like an old man up the steps, into the house, and straight into the shower. He got in under the cold water that always precedes the warm, with his dirty clothes on and let them rinse clean before undressing and letting them fall the shower floor. He choked a few times on the water, as he heaved and cried once more, under the spray. It was the realization that water couldn't clean a guilty heart, couldn't sanitize a broken, abused soul. It was the understanding that he might never feel clean again that reverberated such an ache throughout his body. But, it did help, or maybe, it was the exhaustion that drained away the sharper feelings.

He showered with his clothes on, this time, out of shock and defeat. He'd begun doing that, so he didn't have to wash his clothes with Hanks; another chore that was his, now. Hank was evil and that didn't wash off either, in Nick's mind, it tainted more than your skin. He thought of his mother, while in the shower and wondered what she was doing in that moment. He wanted only for her to be there when he got out, to grab him up and embrace him. They would run off together. He was old enough now, that is all she was waiting for. Any minute now, he would see her there. Right there where his eyes focused on the dark spot through the moldy, clear shower curtain. He saw her then, in a black and white polka-dotted dress on her knees in a beautiful garden in front of a big important house. She looked up at him and smiled and went back to planting her mums or whatever they were....he didn't know flowers. But that looked like a safe space, a nice place to plant flowers for your new family.

He set about his chores before the monster came home. But, it was different this time, he had aged somehow, grown in some sort of way that he could feel. He wasn't happy and that mattered for the first time. He began to feel like a prisoner that would someday change his own situation. It wasn't hope, it was red.....like a flame and it tingled deep in his gut. For the first time it wasn't a wish, it was a reality that he'd not caught up with yet.

Hank's patrol car rumbled into the driveway. Nick heard the same white rocks of the driveway pop under its weight. His heart jumped into a new rhythm, but this beat was slower and steadier than usual. And, it wasn't that he felt any safer, he just didn't care quite as much, that he might be in danger. He'd grown farther than his knowledge of words that day. Nick never made eye contact with Hank and only looked towards him to pick up warnings. He found himself watching Hank as he opened the door, that day. He didn't know if the dull hatred made itself known upon his face, but he felt it hum just beneath his skin. He tried to stop himself, not to tip his hand that something changed, but he was a slave to the hum. Hank popped the old ragged front door open and caught Nick's eye. The cranky, childish man froze three steps in his front door, his gaze trying to read Nick's. The boy was washing dishes, shoulder level to the counter's edge, and starring coldly back. Nick didn't have any words or actions in his mind, just a reptilian gaze. He watched Hank's face ripple with anger that swiftly changed to sadness, perhaps, and then just as quick, confusion. He knew Hank must be tired from the later night of drinking and full day of work. Perhaps, that saved him. Hank dropped his eye without a word and went to his room, not to resurface for the night.

Nick merely watched, cold and dead and unfeeling. He would have been more proud of himself, but the moment went unnoticed inside. His unfeeling passed as well, but it would be back to help him deal and Hank learned the look, eventually steering clear when he was sober enough not to feel insurmountable, (which wasn't often).

Mustang Deborah

The air smelled clean, with the most pleasant breeze. It was one of those days that makes every aspect of your life appear weighted on the positive side; like anything was possible. She felt strong, capable of anything. Her grades were good again, the strain that lay between her and her parents six months ago was gone, and she had finally gotten the hang of this cheerleading thing. That, and she realized that what she liked about it had nothing to do with being popular, or in the clique. She enjoyed the challenge, the athleticism of it all; and she was proud of being a Mustang, that was their mascot; something so empowering about that. She enjoyed being strong enough to do a one legged squat in Jason's lifting hand. Not all of the group was as shallow as everyone acted, either.

Tommy Matheson, who she now realized was a rotten boy, had broken up with her six months ago and she was a bit depressed. It seemed as if the ground had dropped out from beneath her feet. Her time with him gave her an attitude of rebellion and then, with their relationship over, her demeanor was even worse. Everything she enjoyed doing and being, up to that day, seemed colorless and senseless. Her sensibilities, with him, had already started to become dark and cynical, but now that he'd dropped her like a hot rock, anger and cynicism were the overriding feelings. Summer vacation held no excitement for her, for the first time ever. Leaving the state with her family to enjoy that vacation time, seemed an imposition to her. Having to feign happiness felt exhausting to her. The occasional girl-friend sleep over, was not even on her radar. She felt done and had a feeling that it would never get to good again. Her whole life up to that point had been a rut she couldn't wait to get out of and she was just mad enough at the world to believe that she would always dislike her parents. She was so sick of them always striving to be up in her business.

It was the last few weeks of school and the slip in grades that brought it home to her parents; just how rebellious she was feeling, how lost she was becoming. They expected a bit of mourning over the boy, but grades were too important to let go. As parents often do, they didn't know exactly what they could do. Every time they tried a new tactic, a new way to say it, she always ended up angrier than when they'd started.

Pam and Janice tried to make plans with Deborah, but she was not having it. Pam said she wasn't going to let Deborah's summer "Pity Party" be the only party she attended all school break, but that just made Deborah storm off in anger. Deborah even made an exaggerated point of telling Dad that she wasn't even going to read or work this summer, she was done with all of it and would stay in bed all day and on the computer all night. She wanted to be everything they didn't want her to be.

Fortunately, she was wrong, about losing the good forever, about losing all her interests, and about staying mad at Pam and Janice. It took her four hours of road tripping to California with Mom and Dad, before mom got her first smile and minutes later an actual belly laugh; from that point on the vacation was good and turned out to be the best yet.

The vacation was, in Deborah's favor, immediately after summer break's start, as it set the tone for breaking Deborah out of her funk early into her summer. By the time vacation was over, she was okay, *right as rain* as her mother liked to say and ready for a new start, with a new attitude.

Now, she was three months into her freshman year, two months into cheerleading practice and one month into what might just be the relationship of her life. She was very excited about all of this, it all felt decidedly different than before, she felt grown up now...well, more grown, anyway. She was trying to be careful and not get ahead of herself anymore, which is considerably hard to do when you are a teen. She was yet to share her happy news about her relationship, however, as it was with Sara Beatty. She had no reason to believe her parents would refuse to let it go on, or that they might even be shocked, but when she tried to tell her mother, she couldn't help but believe she would be disowned. She had a feeling *that* wasn't a cat that would go back into the bag once let out. So, she swallowed her words and told her mom she was considering trying out for drama. Her mother hadn't had a chance to say anything, derogatory or uplifting, but Deborah lost her nerve and decided to wait.

Today was one of those days that made it all feel okay. She knew as soon as she awoke that morning, that it would all work out like it was supposed to. She also decided that it would be whatever it would, that she would make the best out of whatever situation came, because she was starting to realize that she couldn't control anyone but herself and that was chore enough. All she could do was control how she reacted to the reaction of others. And, she was determined that she was going to be mature, lady-like and grown up; not a drip, but playfully perspicacious and responsible, to boot. Now, as she fell from the height of Jason's toss above the rest of the crew, her smile radiated like the sun preparing to set behind the mountains that ran the western horizon before her (and she had a view that most missed out on in the rise and fall of the toss). The pyramid was next and then her favorite cheer, the one about their rivals, the Bandits. She was happy and hopeful and loving this first day in the rest of her life. Deborah didn't see a strange vehicle between her and those glorious mountains, that would soon be blocking the sun from her view. She didn't see the man sitting in that strange vehicle, watching her with what might be construed as lust in his stunned, hidden eyes. She didn't see him back the next day to watch and take mental notes on her schedule and possible entourage.

Thomas Cates: Back at the Start

The middle aged man sat in the fuzzy light of the used up Sun, that allowed a threatening shroud to encroach across the flat and dusty land. He crouched upon a boulder, like a bird of prey awaiting the occasional rodent. He was a muscular man in his early forties, disciplined and confident. And, why not? He was a good person. He was freely offering his help to the young women across the country, those innocent young girls that the awful, dirty men of the world would gladly misuse, abuse, and break.

He had a vision into things, inside people and their ways. He saw past the acts of the everyday monsters. No one else seemed to see it. He knew, though, where justice could be found and he knew how to bring it to the light of day....and the darkness of this oncoming night would be his arena. His mission was to save, it was a light to tear that darkness asunder.

His arms flexed, muscles evident, in the short sleeves of the gray tee he wore. His hair was chaotic and loose and afire when the sun was inclined to shine on him. His stubble was coarse and darker than his brownish-blond mane. His tee and jeans were expensive designer labels and it showed, he looked cut out of a magazine with the dramatic fading Nevada day above and behind him. That is how he tried to see things, from her perspective.

The rock that held him was a headstone to the rectangle of stone monument that he favored. A short shelf, backed by another shelf some five-feet above that. Behind it was a hallowed out room of sorts, a sacred space if ever there was one; a ceremonial alter in front, private grave in the back. He christened this natural formation as Cates' Place. *It ran through his mind twenty years ago and it stuck. He'd called it* The Gates of Tara, *first, but it felt too hokey. It felt cheesy and too teenage angsty, where as* Cates' Place *sounded like a diner from a novel. It felt real and texturous to him, but Tara deserved recognition because she was the reason they were here. Twelve years ago was not his first attempt at justice, but it was* when *he got it right and set his pattern. It was a ceremony now and he was mastering the promise he made his Sister, twenty long years ago.*

"I know you are probably thinking that I'm some creepy serial killer, but that couldn't be farther from the truth," he half laughed (as if that was the silliest idea). The young, blonde cheerleader's sun-kissed skin was complimented by the orange of her Arizona Mustangs uniform; a vibrant color he could plainly see four minutes ago, now paled in the dusky light, along with the white and the blue. To him, perched nine-feet above her, like a vulture, the shadows in the little, rock room were consuming the girl. He liked to look in their eyes during this part, but it just took too long to get everything together this time. The girl (the afore mentioned blonde, tan cheerleader), didn't play along, at all. Nabbing her was easy enough, with a bandana smelling of homemade chloroform, but she awoke early

and fought the good fight. It was so damn frustrating that they never ever understood, he was really trying to help them. Jesus Fucking Christ, he wasn't just some psychotic killer! He had principals and there was reason to his rhyme. And though, he could see where they could get the wrong idea, damn, give a man a minute to explain, or even better, let a man's work speak for itself.

Thomas Cates was here to help and as he set his mind to unifying the appropriate words to explain that higher purpose, he also realized that they would never understand while they were bogged down within this attractive, yet distracting physical body. He supposed he couldn't blame them for fighting him, no matter how pure his intentions, how gentle he would be in the act, they were losing what they were taught was all important to them, life. It was his intention to help them avoid all of this drudgery, the stained, blackened souls that came with living too long. Besides, as Tara taught him, death was only the beginning. And life, well, life was just so much misery and weakness slammed together over and over again.

It was his hypothesis that the chemical energy, the galvanism we are enslaved by that fills our bodies with life, was too distracting; that our every moment was all dramatic feelings and sensitive reactions that prevent us from really see things clearly. Of course, they didn't want to die, but only because they didn't know what came after. He envied them the chance to die, he was tempted to join them, most everyday, but he had a mission and that came first. He also knew that he would always feel the need to explain, to collect and place these pearls of understanding for the fearful eyes that watched him work. Lost and silent in these thoughts, he scanned the dull pink light of the sinking Sun. He caught far off headlights and watched those as he spoke. He made a quiet note that the Sun's light was roughly thirty minutes from dying away, though there were deep shadows all about.

"Sweetie, My Sister, Tara, was twelve years old when our mother died. I was sixteen and Mom pulled me close to her cancer ridden, bald and beautiful head and told me to watch over Her, to protect My Sister. She whispered it with such feeling. She was crying," as now was he. He paused when his breath caught, "It wasn't a request, it was a wish...it was a prayer. I'd never been prayed to before, but that must be what it feels like, because the full weight of Tara's life and happiness was forever after upon my heart and shoulders. I had no idea how very heavy that weight of Her tiny little frame could become."

The headlights were obviously coming this way. It is Nevada, which is to say flat with one road to everywhere. This didn't effect his pulse in the least, Thomas Cates never worried over a situation that hasn't happen yet. Preparation was being ready, all the time. With reflexes that merely responded when called upon to do so, without having to have a Goddamn conversation about it. He took note of his surroundings and adapted his work accordingly, at every moment. "See, My Sister and I thought this was difficult, and it was heart wrenching, but we didn't know difficult yet. It took dad a whole year to completely give in to his own weak mind and drag Her down with him. Tara was just starting to smile again," Cates' chest hitched again as his face wadded up like a fist in the diminishing light. He turned it away from the girl even though she couldn't see his face, or anything else. Emotion found his words, "She had the prettiest smile, full of innocence and joy. She was pure like the light of the sun, too," he remarked as the headlights grew brighter and the pink light, duller.

"Dad was always a drinker, but without Mom's light in his life, his darkness took over. He was short with us and then just bitter and pissy," now the fringes of his words sounded of bitten rage. "I didn't know for two months....Two Goddamn months! Can you fucking believe that?" Cates moaned as tears streamed free, "I asked Her what was wrong one day...She looked so pale and sick....heart sick. Finally, She told me...see, Sweetie, dad was molesting Her. I wanted to kill him." Thomas grunted and growled with remembered hate that burned just as hot as it ever did, with the properties of a rekindled fire. Thomas wiped his right thumb at clearing his face of hurt, "I reigned in my emotions like a good boy and I went to the police station the next day. I was doing the right thing, or so I thought. I'd seen Detective Howard at our school previously that year. He talked about saying no to drugs and all that jazz. He was a good guy though, and I knew I had to do this right, for Tara. I couldn't kill the asshole, what if I went to jail?

What would happen to Tara?"

Cates judged the headlights at just a mile away now, "Sorry Sweetie, I don't like being distracted. I train to be stronger than that, I apologize for my lack of focus, you deserve better from me. The gist is that the stupid son of a bitch went to jail, dad that is, just as he should have. Now, Tara was safe and I was the man that made it so, her forever protector. So, naturally when Social Services snatched My Sister away from me and put Her in a foster home....," he growled again, "I was the man that did that too. If I'm allowed the credit than I have to shoulder the blame too, right?" Thomas, in one efficient movement slid his feet from under his body to land on the ground below, and his body seemed to float in the lack of effort. He dropped all nine-feet into the room of megalithic rock, his feet, to the outside of her legs and then crouched again to touch the skin that showed above her torn top. He rubbed at the torn fabric and caressed a patch of tan skin.

He closed his eyes at the feel, "I hope you don't mind that I found you on FacePage. I needed to know who you are. You are no Debbie, or Deb, by the way. You are Deborah, a queen to be loved and worshiped. I have saved you for just that reason." He was shocked at how far he'd let his hand grope. He felt too much and pulled his hand back like it burnt. "I'm here to save you from that. Anyway..."

"I tried to see Her everyday after school, but I had to work and the whole Goddamn system was against us. I never saw Her again. Within the year She was

dead." He lowered his head and shook it in incomprehension, "DEAD!" he screamed. "This is why you are here, Sweetie, I'm here to save you from life. Please understand, Tara was molested by our father and when I saved Her with the help of the system, She fell victim to the very family that was to be Her saving grace, by the same GODDAMN SYSTEM! The husband, wife and daughter...Every Goddamn one of them hurt Her....I wasn't even aware of all of the abuse that befell Her in that new hellhole, until I broke into social services and stole Her files. By then, she was dead and it was too late, I was too late. I know what you're thinking, 'that is not my life, I wouldn't ever be subjected to such cruelty,' but believe me when I say, it befalls us all unless we take the appropriate steps to stop them. This is the best step, I've studied it and studied it, from every angle and you have to trust me, this is better. Tara tells me so, from the other side, in our dreams together. You get to shift from childhood to enlightenment, to evolve straight into the sage spirit that would have come after all the hatred and pain. You don't have to suffer all of that anymore. It is done. No one will ever be able to sully your beautiful body, to darken your bright mind with their weak, sexual needs." His hand on her shoulder now, rubbing just inside the neck of the uniform, feeling the cold, supple skin.

Cates went silent, as if picking at a thread he lost, "That is where this picture came from." Cates had removed it from the back pocket of his jeans and held it in front of the girl's lifeless face. "But Tara found Her own justice when I let Her down. She poisoned the lot of em' and then with one last look at the city lights, She jumped from the thirteenth floor of their apartment building. And I know She jumped, as if off of a high dive. I dream about it all the time. She was finally free and She did this with as much excitement as She'd ever felt in Her life...with relief. I always see Her stepping out onto that roof, seeing the stars, with a kids smile, as if for the first time. Just like we used to do when we were little," a bitter smile touched his lips as he heard the gray car roar past like he willed it to. He gave an inner nod to his power over the world, when he put his mind to it. "I know it's dark, but this is her. Pretty, huh?" And then, just to spite his arrogance, the automobile slid and screeched with loud lurch, a good five hundred yards past them. The mere sound of the clamped tires was a slap in the face of the very belief that his mind held sway over matter, but then, he was so over taken by this cool liquid feeling of deja vu, as if he was in the car, also. It was a challenge and though he was thrown by his immediate enjoyment, he enjoyed the idea of a challenge.

A wall of dust continued on like the ghost of the car leaving the body. Cates could hear screaming, adolescent Whooping. His mind quickly filled in a story of a fighting couple, young probably from the looks of the sporty gas hog. He's gotten them lost and she is pissed. He is too damn stubborn to admit they are lost and won't ask for help, though asking for help in

Nevada is typically difficult as most of it is absolutely in the middle of nowhere, everywhere. There was, finally, the small clicking sound of a gear engaging and to Thomas' intrigue, the gray machine roared in what sounded like reverse. He couldn't see it from his place in the ceremonial room, but he could hear the whine of reverse getting higher with increased effort.

He peeked around the side of the monument for a quick look. The damn thing twisted and turned and damned if it didn't straighten up right for them. Now there was no story that his mind could pull from this collection of disorder, other than the man inside had had enough and pulled recklessly off the road to have done with her. He wondered if that meant kicking her from the car or killing her by wrapping their ride around the stone? Perhaps Cates would win the presence of another soul to save in the former scenario. And who knew what might be made of the latter? There was one more option that stung his happy thoughts. It could be someone trying to stop him.

"What the fuck?" Thomas asked Deborah with a look as if they could share in this curiosity; they were, after all, in this together. Now Thomas' pulse raced with misunderstanding and chaos. His muscles tensed in disbelief. He suddenly knew he was found out. He was seen. Who was this after him, out of nowhere? He was suddenly sure that was the case and almost pissed that he was fool enough not to realize it until now. His feet carried him backwards as he eyed the racing car, he wanted as much stone between him and this enemy as

possible. His mind was screaming, "This fucker is going to slam right into Cates' Place! Is he crazy?" Cates was very concerned for the girl laying just within the formation. This was going to fuck up the whole works. This whole attempt had gone wrong, for fuck sake! Thomas lost sight of the car as it closed in on the rock, as he gave up and ran the other way, clearing two hundred yards before he stopped to realize he should have heard a crash by now, if not felt it. The commotion echoed into and around the stone, losing its cohesiveness and offering no real indication of what was going on.

Cates couldn't help but enjoy the feeling of deja' vu as it washed over him, again, as if he knew exactly what was going on inside the car. He was even certain he could see, broken scenes, pieces of the boy and the girl, so much like his girl. He found it hard to breathe as these two scenes converged in his mind, he also wasn't used to the scheme of things working against him so. Cates turned to look back at the kicked up dust cloud drifting back over where the car must be. He was not at all certain of anything at the moment. He knelt to breathe and steady himself while he watched his plans unravel before him. He might actually have to kill someone tonight.

Thomas Cates argued with his own mind in the moments that followed as he never had, never before having witnessed anything more askew from his expectations than what was currently unfolding. Five minutes went by without a sight or sound, to the point that Cates began to question whether he'd actually seen the car at all. Was he actually hallucinating? He felt as though there were someone else in his mind, inside his head-space fighting for control. He played with the thought of walking back to test this, perhaps he was alone and just, losing it. Perhaps, the difficulty of this particular mission had him expecting stumbling blocks, where there were none. He thought the couple in the car must be arguing, but there was no sound. Disquieting actually. Finally, just before the darkness over took them completely, a young man (with light brown hair donning ripped jeans and a red flannel shirt open over what looked to be a gray tee), sauntered around His place...His spot...as if he owned the Goddamn place. Unbelievably, the young man was throwing out a blanket of the same red as his flannel shirt, upon the lower shelf of stone. He was making his bed on Cates' Goddamn Rocks! Who the hell did he think he was?

Cates pulse relaxed into a rhythm as his muscles realized this jack-hole was not aware of his presence, or that he stood between Thomas and his ceremony. Thomas wasn't sure how to feel about this change, this unplanned event, but it clearly spoke to the fact that the world wasn't plotting against him, just further proof that it didn't spin around him as its all important creamy center.

He had been sloppy in the beginning, and that pissed him off. He tried to assure himself that it was about saving these innocent creatures from the meanness of life and he had done that in the end, no matter how messy. Life was hard on the small things and it was up to him to change that. Tara deserved so much better than she'd gotten and so he would make amends at every turn as long as he had breath left to breathe. Thomas now bent behind a bit of scrub, saw the young man step back into view, now barely visible due to angle and diminishing light, but he apparently, had a meal to eat. "Don't let us get in your way, boy." Within ten minutes, he decided he had a book to write, and the piss ant wrote for an hour and some change. Persistent annoyance!

By then, he was only visible as the shadow that occasionally moved in the darkness he was apart of. That darkness was suddenly threatened by the light of a flame. The red eye of a lit cigarette expressed itself with a rhythmic pulse from inhale to exhale. "Make your self at home, you *son of a bitch!" Thomas said this aloud, daring a confrontation. "Gooooddamn." he uttered in monotone, and again in one movement, dropped to an Indian style sitting position, to wait for the right idea or opportunity to expose itself. He was itching to just walk up and continue his ceremony behind the stone wall that separated the young man from them, but he was subdued by his curiosity. Just who was this young man and was his presence here more than random colliding atoms? Cates was patient enough, but wasting time was not something he could abide. Now, he was merely torn on what might come of waiting. There was a taboo desire to tempt the fate of getting caught, but it would mean either killing the young man or subduing him for recruitment.*

Thomas couldn't believe the boy was going to write out here in the dark, he used what must be a lighter to glance over the pages from time to time, but he wrote feverishly, with no light. It made Thomas very curious about the subject matter and whether the boy was challenging himself or if he always wrote in the dark. Though, now it was impossible to tell if he was indeed still writing or merely enjoying his smoke.

The cigarette rose in one last arc and flew in somersaults, as the wind took hold and helped the spent butt momentarily escape gravity, exaggerating its trajectory. Cates felt this was a sleep preparation and wondered just how bold he should be with this new comer. Should he merely finish his ceremony while the young man slept, or should he take a chance on disposing of the unripened male? Something about the young man reminded him of himself and this prompted an alluring possibility that he might be a sacred heart, a twin in the mission. The thought of a companion in the darkness touched him deep. Perhaps it was possible. He would have to be tested, of course, but that was doable. This was a treacherous mission, very necessary and righteous, but not one everybody could handle. You had to be willing to get up close and personal with your own mortality. That is what tearing a body apart does to you, forces the understanding of just how easily life can be dispatched, unlit. Cates only ever dismantled three humans and they too were interferers, he wouldn't perform such atrocities on the pure.

Thomas knew this part of the world well, and the quality of sleep it provided, under these stars, within the arms of this wind, meant sleep of a better brand. No stuffy room anywhere held sleep this sound and just. He waited thirty minutes just to be safe and then made his move. Cates walked very casually to Cates' Place. The wind was loud enough, and he downwind of his prey, to save any worry of overheard footsteps. Cates was confident in his ability to overpower most anyone, if not from strength, from sheer anger. There on the lower step of Cates' Place was an agile looking teen, lit well enough by the light of this sliver of moon. There was patchy young stubble, but a strong jaw...of good character. Maybe he was a good kid, but he was either in the goddamn way or perhaps, a new and unexpected comrade in arms. Then Cates had a twinge of something, perhaps it was character too, but he decided if this kid would sleep and allow him to finish what he started, he might live to drive away from Cates' Place. Though he wouldn't go untested. He might be the answer to the obstacles that Cates had to jump through, throughout this mission.

Something shifted while he waited though. It felt as if the winds of fate were beginning to stand against him. He also considered it might be age catching up with him, but he allowed that idea to slip away like the boy's spent butt on the wind. He couldn't be any more conditioned than he was now. He was certain the factor wasn't him, and he didn't believe in coincidence. The notebook lay beside the young man, the top few pages blowing in the breeze and providing its own white noise. This intrigued Thomas, now reading what the young man had written. He always loved a good story and was an avid reader. He didn't know what to make of the words, the story seemed to be about this very moment, but he felt bolstered, like a poetry that is felt more than understood. He placed a hand upon the boy's heart, and felt it drum beneath his firm chest. He thought, devilishly, to tweak the boy's nipple, but just laughed at the thought; reminding himself that this was no joke.

Cates stepped into the rectangle of stone and knelt to delicately stroke the girl's face, "It's okay Debbie, I'll finish this, but you are already saved from this horrible darkness of life that finds and destroys all innocence. The ceremony is in the saving you from this life, and you are safe, Sweet Girl. I couldn't save Tara. I failed Her, so She saved Herself. I learned through Her, my purpose. I know not all of you will have the strength it takes to do that. I also know, that this anniversary is used by Universe to manifest those who need help, in my path. I don't choose. I'm drawn." The soil beneath the young woman was solid and untouched, or so it looked. Every May 20th for the last twenty years this sacred ground had been dug up and received Cates' offering. The ceremony had been refined a little each time, but never strayed from, only added to or enhanced. The soil was enriched and sacred, but saw very little, if any, sun due to the formations around it. Cates put a hand on the girl's right ankle. It was a practical action, he was going to grab her left ankle, as well, and pull her back far enough to re-dig the hole, but his hand lingered as it never had before. A color exploded within his lower gut and bloomed forth, maroon and pastels and neons, an unknown sensation in Cates' nervous system. He accessed every surface of his hand and rubbed up past her knee, appreciating the life that built this, still, strong body. Cates felt his perspective alter as if the lighting shifted somehow and began to feel sexually alive. He could smell the room in which he'd first masturbated. See the lighting through the heavy curtains. He felt fierce desire to caress and share his sensual love. This desire touched him deep in places unknown to him until now. There was no darkness in his love, but he knew the carnal act of forcing that love, was as dark as life could get. Killing was horrendous, rape was real evil. He realized that Deborah couldn't consent in her current state and knew he should stop. 'But,' he couldn't help but question, 'is it rape if she no longer is connected to this body?' His physical body wanted to have, now, and so his mind turned to conversation into a valid stance.

He forgot where he was and that there was a possible eyewitness within twenty feet. He was overridden by the stimulation memory, like muscle memory, but more covetous. His hand was now every sense he owned and he bathed in this touch of her skin. This was all new to him, feeling where the heat of this young woman would have been strongest. Touching her womanhood, overcome with automatic yearning and suddenly Tara was watching.

Cates jerked his hand back to his chest horrified, he fell into the rock behind him hitting his head and shoulder. He had to get a hold of himself, this wasn't part of the ceremony; not part of his saving mission. He was instantly furious. Was it this young outsider, in his place, bringing darkness to this place? It made sense the more Cates thought about it. He'd never been late in the previous twenty years, this had never taken place in the dark. This perpetrator had sullied Cates' righteous mission and this could not be tolerated. With hate behind his eyes, Cates exited the chamber after a heart-felt apology to the young woman. He stood stooped over, just ten inches away from the evil new factor in this equation. The boy was dreaming and his REM eye movement intrigued Cates and stayed the murderous intent for the moment. Perhaps it was something in the face, but the anger Cates felt fell away with a breath. He would forgive the boy, as if it were having to forgive himself. That didn't excuse his mission betrayed.

Kneeling over the young man's face, just inches away, Cates own face turning like a predator studying its prey. What did this mean? What purpose was this person to play in Cates' own fate? Cates never questioned if the young man's life was in his hands, of course, he could free this spirit at any moment he chose, but the curiosity of who and why this young man was here, here of all places, *grew like a fire (with an internally audible whoosh). He was here for a reason and Cates couldn't argue that it felt as if he was to become a part of this. There was something, a scarring, a past in fire that showed in his brow, in his skin perhaps. Cates felt more and more drawn to him the more he watched him dream. He felt he knew him, but why? How?*

The boy's eyes opened in reaction to the wind on his face, his face a mask of confusion as he searched the darkness for an answer to where the hell he was. As he sat up and remembered his journey thus far, his bladder made an exclamatory suggestion that he empty it before it took matters into its own hands. He rose and quickly circled the stone, stumbling inside Cates' Place.

Cates was quick, he'd recognized the end of REM Sleep and its path into consciousness and ducked just a few feet away to watch. He'd gotten close enough to read some of the written words on the top page, risking the audible billow of pages in the breeze long enough to do so. It was a story about a road trip, his road trip it seemed, perhaps this was a budding writer trying to experience the next great American novel. But, it sure sounded to Cates as if, the young man knew him, was writing about him. It was an effort, between the hand-writing and it being illuminated only with the moonlight, but Cates recognized his description along with the description of this place. Cates' indulgence of story was interrupted by the waking teen. Cates could tell as he stood feet away watching, the boy was in active Pee Pee Dance. "Of course," Cates thought to himself, "Of course, he's a modest one." He shook his head sarcastically with his eyes on the moon, as if she were obviously in agreement.

When the young man step into the formation and quickly out, Cates knew he'd found Deborah and simply shook his head, unsure of how exactly this would play out. He wanted to see what he would do with his new found knowledge; prepared to kill or recruit, one or the other. Recruiting would be a new unknown experience for Cates with an improbable outcome, but he liked the looks of the kid. Something very Rebel Without a Cause *about him. He felt secure in the idea of testing him, because if he failed and were ready to ruin Cates' mission, he would have to be disposed and disposal was right in the center of Cates' wheelhouse. Cates knew he would be justified in the killing if that were the case, nothing to fret about.*

He gave the young man room to deal with what he'd discovered, space to take it in and absorbed it. He watched him run to his car, climb inside and slam the door. The engine rolled over with a lovely hum. Cates tried to think ahead on the young one's every action. So he would know how far to let him go. He knew he would have to give him enough rope and time to find his way to the truth of what needed to be done. But, he felt certain the his new brother in arms would find the way to Cates before it was over. Cates had already decided what his course of action would be if the rebel decided to drag an officer back here. He assumed that was what was running feverishly through the boy's mind. That is just the way it was these days, everyone looking for someone else to take care of things or be a hero themselves. If the boy drove away never to return, then Cates would find him and work him later with more respect for the fact that he was willing to leave well enough alone. For now, either way, he would have time for the girl. He watched perplexed as the boy jumped out of the car and he had to duck away again as the flare dumped light over the scene suddenly.

He smiled as the boy pulled the blanket up over the rock wall in the light of the flare, certain now that he was a clever one. He was marking his place and would indeed be back, with or without help. Again, Cates wasn't concerned with which counter point to have to yield to. He was prepared for either outcome.

Graduation Eve

The uniform was getting tighter every day now, it seemed. Hank was ashamed of his physique, but he was just so tired. It was hard when the boy's mom left, but he was still young enough to bury it deep and fake his indifference. Well, perhaps the boy knew better? He had seen the anger, got a real good look, up close and personal.

Twelve years ago, now, it struck him how long he'd been miserable. He was tired of being angry, exhausted from the facade; half dead from pretending that each step didn't hurt all the more. But, what was the half life on self-doubt and sorrow? How much longer could this go on? His drive was wounded by her absence, and sucked out by every day thought of her, every slap, punch, and hateful tone unleashed on the boy. It wasn't just the hurt of her leaving, or the fact that she obviously believed she was better off without him, it was the bitter, aloneness.

He liked that she was quiet and submissive, but he missed her presence. He felt confident in dismissing her when she was there, but her absence left his house and routine sterile and colorless. He knew he was mostly to blame, but what was a man to do with that? You didn't talk about it. Feelings were to be swallowed and beer and cigarettes sure made them go down easier. Sure, not everything was her fault, but sometimes, he just couldn't find the way to apologize or give in. That was not her fault, but what did she expect him to do?

The boy was ever quiet, surely judging the man that stayed behind to protect him; a lot like his Mom. He did what Hank expected and that was a plus, submitting to his chores without an attitude. He hadn't had to hit the boy in, geez, he didn't know how long now. "Well, well, look who's here! Doing the dishes, no less. What a change of pace for you. Oh wait, no, that is all you ever do isn't? Clean up my mess like a little bitch! Huh?" He smiled a little inside, this innocent jeering wasn't a bad mood, it was Hank's way of fathering. It was just enough locker-room gig and sarcasm to be playful, but also to put across his compliment of just how helpful the boy was on a regular basis. Life was funner the more engaged you were and he wanted the boy to feel at home, engaged with his step-dad. The boy still acted like it bothered him, but he would come around to it. He would understand how it was meant and take it, even one day be able to dish a little out, in fun and all.

The boy looked at him from his position at the sink when the spring-loaded screen door slammed behind Hank with its usual sharp pop. He looked quickly away again as Hank began to speak. Hank was sure the boy didn't look him in the eye, mostly so he too, could keep his feelings to himself. It's what men did, share nothing and assume that everyone else felt the same way that they did, about everything. It wasn't fail proof but a million years of evolution couldn't be questioned. His father lived by this credo, just as his father slapped into him; so forth and so on.

Hank slung his uniform gun belt over his bedroom door, just ten steps from the front door (ten Australopithecus-Hank steps anyway), before tossing his head-cover to the bedside table where it sat always, unless upon his head.

Hank belched as he stepped toward the bathroom, as usual. The man's uniformed shirt already lay upon the floor behind the worn recliner, two steps closer to the kitchen lay the khaki belted pants. He was wondering if it was just his age that seemed to make this heartburn worse everyday, or if it might just be the extra alcohol (just upped his thirty pack a week to what, forty-five; fifty?), the very alcohol that made his nights bearable. Hank climbed out of his dirty, white undershirt to reveal his super hero suit, his favorite uniform, his trusty tighty-whiteys. He had several pair but they all seemed to have a rip under the elastic band in the exact same place. It was a scant wardrobe of comfort in a hot, dark world. Hank was saving electricity by doing without lights and air. He was as green as they come, he would have argued. He cared about the world, just doing his part where he could.

The boy always had too many lights on, Hank enjoyed them off to escape fully into the television. And so, his worn path from kitchen light switch to living room lamp was taken again. Hank felt a twinge of pride, knowing that the boy was watching a great example of conservation, saving energy and the fossil fuels it takes to produce that unnecessary energy. An image to aspire to, in other words, and it was up to Hank, after all, the boy was his to shape. Sure, he was discarded to Hank's auspices, but what did Hank do with the abandoned lad? He stepped up and did the job even the mutt's mother couldn't do. Hank didn't know the boy's father and Mary never shared any details of the man. For all Hank knew, he was a hobo on the street, or an alien Star-Man. He was a dead-beat, whatever else he was. Hank did his job, too, taking care of their boy as if he were his own. Sure Hank was hard, but it was a hard world and the quicker you learned that, the better you were at it. You either take the licks forever, or you started licking back.

Hank realized in that moment, that he wasn't really sure the boy could still speak, he'd been quiet for so long. This provoked need in the man to find out, to push for the boy's own good. In all honesty, the boy was his to hone into what makes a fine, law abiding adult. He hoped he too, would be a fine police officer someday, if not a state trooper like his real Ole Man. Because, what was a real father, if not the man raising the boy? He grabbed his first nights mug of beer (three to be exact), of the ten or twelve he would drink tonight, still at the kitchen counter, he stared a hole through the back of the boy's knees. The urge to unlock one of those, most tender joints with a kick was strong and he wouldn't normally have fought it, but he had a problem, and whether the boy could speak or not wasn't it. He didn't want to do this but who if not him, "Boy." Hank analyzed the reaction, as the boy, now seventeen, froze in the action of washing a plastic cup, but didn't turn around.

"Boy! Look at me." Hank always tried to be stern. He knew from his own hard father, that if you give a child an inch, they run away with the ruler and don't look back. There was a hesitation, but the boy did look back to him, in the eye for all of half a second before his eyes dropped.

"Officer Lanny saw you yesterday coming home from school. He said you were speeding off from the abandoned Dairy Squeeze parking lot after smoking it up with some three-sixties. Is this true?"

The boy held his position and lack of eye contact. He appeared to study the floor, but he wasn't seeing the old-creaky wood floor boards, dark with wax that was older than his mother. He didn't see the dirty kitchen counter and filthy wall that opened up to the dirty living room. The rooms were decently organized, but only because of how little was actually in the home; one broken-down blue, tattered LaZboy, one old-blue-patterned couch that looked as though it had welcomed many asses since the nineteen teens, a wobbly-cheap nightstand (where Hank's mug sat beside the couch) and a boxy thirty-two inch TV console that weighed as much as its owner. This particular piece of furniture held a radio as well (one you couldn't help but expect to hear *The Lone Ranger* or *Dick Tracy* radio shows playing), alas, it no longer worked. The boy was somewhere else, where ever he went when life got scary. Hank hated that stare off into nothingness. It made him want to slap him back, to feel this scolding, to scab over and be hardened into living.

"Wake up, Goddamnit! Dexter Lanny is my fellow officer, my friend and he catches you showing off? You a bad-ass? Huh? It is my job to keep this county safe, the keep its citizens within the law at all times and you go and not only break the speed limit within MY county, but then add hazardous driving to top it all off? I was embarrassed to say you were mine. You, of all people should know better and I'll be damned if you're gonna get away with it. And don't take that as a free pass to leave this county. You know you're not to leave this county without my say so!

Right?"

The boy just stood there, no reaction to speak of, except to the trained eye. Hank saw his face redden and flush over. He also noticed the slight quickening of his pulse, which created a subtle tremor to the boy's frame. This pleased Hank because he knew the boy had respect for him, even if it was through fear. The boy actually looked like he was shrinking. Hank wanted to pull him out of that. He softened his tone in the attempt.

"Now that you've finished the car with What's-his-nuts' dad, the one that you're so goddamn proud of, the one that you sling around town in, breaking the law in. I'm gonna hold those keys for ya, just for a few months, maybe. Depends on your attitude between now and then." Yeah, that sounds like a real Ole Man. A diplomatic, concerned parent who could bc trusted; one a boy could be proud of, except…

This struck a chord in the boy. Hank was almost taken aback by how assertively the boy looked him in the eye, how serious the boy took this threat. At the same time, he wasn't really surprised by how much the car meant to him. It was something he and his best friend started, a project he finished with the boys father and in turn a gift from the same man. It was this disconnect from him that Hank loathed about the car. He might have enjoyed working on a car with the boy too. He didn't know much about mechanican and he wasn't much for projects, or even spending time with the boy, but the boy didn't even ask. That's what hurt. Hank felt an assertive push from these sore feelings and held out his hand for the sword in this particular stone, "Now."

The boy actually hesitated, enough so that Hank wondered if he should allow his anger to well up or play this one cool. His anger was not typically something he questioned or attempted to control, but there was something about the boy suddenly, he looked taller, broader, stronger somehow. Hank couldn't quite put his finger on it, but it was there all the same. Was it really just something in the boy's thinking that could evoke such a change, or just the lighting that seemed to shine on him from out of nowhere?

Hank didn't believe in all that power of the brain bullshit. Hell, if that unicorn poppy-cock was real, he'd have been a line backer for the Fighting Illini twenty years ago. Perhaps, he was just really seeing the changes in the boy since his mother left, the physical growth (or that other thing with his mother, but Hank wouldn't think about that). Perhaps this too, was Hank feeling his age, seeing the scales tip in the boy's favor. This brought forth strong feelings in Hank, feelings that angered and saddened him both. Hank's hesitation fueled his anger to action. The boy stood stock still deliberating silently over what came next. Hank open handedly slapped the boy's face with all of his fading strength and yelled the house full, "I'll be Goddamned if you're gonna stand up to me! You think you're big enough to call the shots now, huh? I'll be damned!" Hank's anger brought forth words he was just too fearful to allow to be heard by the budding young competition for dominance. Words like *just try it* and *give it all you got* and *I'll give you the first shot...hit me anywhere you want, as hard as you can*; because he was afraid. the boy might just try it...and win. Perhaps, that is what this was, the young male rival attempting to take the crown.

The boy was rocked off of his balance, but not downed. He could see the boy working through his next move as he recovered his balance. It was the straining arms and spasming fists that worried Hank. To Hank's relief, he watched as the boy's eyes, the eyes of his mother, dropped, finally, and he submitted yet again. Hank was worried that he looked weak to the boy, that he had waited too long before slapping him, but the boy placed his keys in the wide palm, reddened from the slap of flesh.

The boy, head down, looked at the keys as if they were his only salvation, his last chance at survival. There was something in his stone-faced submission that worried Hank; anger, rage? Nah, he wouldn't leave the only man who cared? He watched as the boy's eyes squinted almost completely shut and fluttered, as if he felt a pain. Hank knew he'd won when the boy turned back to the sink without word. Hank did his best to hide his shortness of breath as he ambled to his captain's chair and tossed the keys onto his discarded pants already on the floor. He did his best to catch his breath in silence, but couldn't pull it off, so he turned the TV louder.

For the first time with Nick, Hank felt unsure of his actions, but he had to teach the boy. Didn't he? Like the slaps in the back of the head and harsh jokes, calling him a fairy, or a loser, or even taunting the boy about his loser of a mother. It was good for Hank growing up, so it was good for the boy. 'End of story', Hank thought but didn't quite feel settled on the issue. He wondered if he were feeling scared of the boy, or for the boy? He quickly drank the rest of his beer to drown out the feelings. Feelings were for *less thans*. Hank was above feelings. Hank was a man of action, like his father before him. Sometimes it hurt growing up, you got over it.

Graduation Eve, Again

The uniform entered the house before Hank did. Nick was always astounded with his Step's ability to remain so spiff, so spit shined and professional looking as a state trooper and then transform into a slobbering, alcohol soaked idiot with the shifting of his cruiser's transmission into park. "Well, well, look who's here! Doing the dishes, no less. What a change of pace for you. Oh wait, no, that is all you ever do isn't? Clean up my mess like a little bitch! Huh?" Nick turned reflexively, but had learned with experience, that the less you saw, the less you were seen. He could visualize the parade of ceremony by sound alone, the slam of the screen door, Hank losing his shirt, undershirt, pants and socks together, discarded droppings like breadcrumbs to follow to bed later; then the uniform gun belt's unique swish as it was slung over his bedroom door. Then, the pop of his uniformed hat as it landed on the bedside table where it lived. The consistent and well timed belch between the bedroom and bathroom, where he would complete the butterfly like transition into a lazy, crotchety, step-son beating alcoholic, which entailed his second most worn uniform, tighty-whiteys and nothing else.

What an image to aspire to, Nick could see the man falling apart; becoming more of something that felt — less. A gray-haired barrel-bellied, ogre-knarled, hulk of a aged man. He actually said nothing to the man and had not done so in, hmmm, he didn't know how many years; eight? He'd learn silence as safety, keep you eyes down, opinions unspoken, and burning fury unseen; closing-in gave the monster more space; swallowing desires kept the bruises away. Hank's presence took up the three closest rooms, disturbingly so, his grunted silences were golden and eagerly manifested. He listened to the nightly path, ushering in the darkness, that Nick tried so desperately to transform with the few, dim lights the house was weaponized with.

The man didn't want his hateful, button-pushing questions answered. They were tools to diminish, and when they were more, they were weapons to draw out a fire; only to keep the spark consistently drenched in defeat. Hank wanted Nick to fight just enough to have an excuse, not that he needed one to slap the young man, or to launch a well placed boot around the back of the knees (always causing the boy to buckle as his manipulated joints gave way). Nick knew the man was only on the prowl for more reason to react with violence. It occurred to Nick, that just maybe, The Step's reality looked a bit different sunken into his dead, shell-like husk of a meat-suit. His larger than life stomping feet drummed ceremoniously through the house. This was good, the march started meant a monster sated. But, the stomping feet had to clear the fridge and make the throne before the boy could be safe; and the beast was getting closer. 'I'm invisible,' Nick tried to manifest, 'You can't see me,' 'I'm not here'. Nick's mistake was not understanding that nocebos were as valid as placebos. Adding the negative inflection to what was unwanted, gave the fear focus and made him glow like prey to a wolf.

The man grabbed his first nights mug of beer after banishing the light, and stared a hole through the back of the boy's knees. Nick could feel the urge in the man, even with his back turned and a feign attention to washing dishes, Nick could only lock his knees and wait. He should be hearing the march continue, the falling with abandon into his broken down LaZboy, but that wasn't happening. Nick could feel the man just standing behind him, the hateful aura spreading to pull him in, "Boy?" He could already smell the rotten tobacco festered breath. He didn't like the man this close to him, for many reasons, but that was a damn good one.

Nick shuddered to freezing at the word, the tone, the attention, but didn't turn around.

"Boy. Look at me."

'Oh Shit,' Nick was struggling tonight, had been all day, with the desire to fight back. He couldn't talk it down. He needed to shut it off, but it fought to live. It felt like a growing entity that would break free from his back and unfold over his head, all Praying Mantis like. Tomorrow night was graduation and he was leaving. He knew if he didn't at least argue with the man before he left that he would feel as though the man won to some degree. More than that, though, he felt the need to rub it in the man's face, to taunt him with the raging anger that bit at his insides. He wanted to rub in the perpetual hanging cigarette into that hateful mug. He knew freedom would feel grand, fresh and exotic. He also knew that at some point he would catch his face in the mirror, any and every mirror outside of this piece of shit, broken-down old prison, certain he wouldn't like what he saw. Cowardly puke of an abandoned pup (what occurred to Nick in the moment was hope, he would love an abandoned pup, why not love himself). Nick looked back, inspired, for all of half a second, before his eyes dropped out of habit. He felt a certainty that this was somehow a pivotal moment.

"Officer Lanny saw you yesterday coming home from school. He said you were speeding off from the abandoned Dairy Squeeze parking lot after smoking it up with some three-sixties. Is this true?"

Nick cringed at the tone. He didn't know where this was going, why it might bother the man in the least? He studied the floor as his mind raced with anger and fear, worry and rebellion. He reddened at the thought of having been seen.

"Wake up, Goddamnit," Nick further diminished under the flurry of hate, feeling for the first time a power to fold in to a finite point that would push him back out with some new atomic power to blow up in the man's face. "You a bad-ass? Huh?" These words hit home, had the man read his mind? "...within the law at all times and you go and not only break the speed limit within MY county, but then add hazardous driving to top it all off? I was embarrassed to say you were mine."

'*Mine*? Did he say *mine*? I...I don't know what I am, but I am not *his*! What the fuck?'

"And don't take that as a free pass to leave this county. You know you're not to leave this county without my say so! Right?"

Nick was flabbergasted that this walking poster child for piss poor parenting was actually going to take the moral high ground. He'd never heard the man talk about morals or values. Maybe that was what he was barking at the TV sometimes, Nick never paid much attention to what he was blustering about. The boy was too busy not engaging to glean any twisted lessons the beast might want to share.

Nick's anger flushed within him, flashing like a flare dropped from a plane to distract the missile threatening its safety. Nick's pulse pounded in a vein that seemed to run from his knees to his right armpit, tightening his body with a need to move. Nick's leanings waxed and waned between kicking downward at the side of one of the fat man's knees or sticking to what he knew. It wasn't just fear that held him, it was remembered fear, years of the inability to physically do a damn thing about it; years of muscle memory that ticked in his abused brain like an old pocket watch in front of a microphone. It reminded him at every tick, that he had to wait, that eventually an opportunity would present itself, but that this wasn't it.

It was never *the* opportunity, never the *right* fucking time. He wondered for the first time, would it ever feel like *the right* time, until he made it so? That waiting was his only grace and there were far tastier graces for bold creatures brave, or foolish enough, to grab for it. He supposed the trick was to know which was brave and which was foolish, but he also wondered, in this moment, if it wasn't merely a matter of perspective, dependent upon the outcome. Or even if the outcome mattered, as long as you believed in your cause. Then, words of war blew out of the loud ass mouth.

"Now that you've finished the car with What's-his-nuts' dad, the one you're so goddamn proud of, the one that you sling around town in, breaking the law in. I'm gonna hold those keys for ya, just for a few months, maybe. Depends on your attitude between now and then."

Nick felt struck. How fucking dare him, to even mention Tommy or his dad, Sam. It felt blasphemous to Nick. Nick met his eyes with a need to drive something, anything dull or sharp, through either eye, but hard and far and into the brain. This project, the car was so much more than the sum of its parts. It was Tommy's smile, his contagious laugh, and the experiences they'd shared. The friendship, the time, the care with which they polished and placed every part, while intertwining their story. The chance to watch a father and son behave as they should. Healing perspective. The old growl of the Duster's engine and the freedom it granted. Hank couldn't wait to fuck shit up, to muddy up the only stain free parts of life that Nick clung to so desperately and innocently. The man actually held out his chubby hand and pressed the point, "Now."

Nick couldn't believe this mother fucker. '*YOU CAN'T HAVE MY FREEDOM,'* rang through Nick's head over and over; a new directive. Nick knew something was different, something clicked audibly deep down within his bowls, where his soul connected to his spine, he thought. He knew now what he had to do and what exactly he could live with. He submitted to the moment because he understood now that he could make his moments, take them and make of them what he wished and this was not his chosen moment, but choose he would. He placed the keys in Hank's hand with what felt like a lash across his back, he winced inside to his core. Nick vowed to himself, 'You didn't win you sonuvabitch, you don't get to win.'

Solitary Suicide

The blade in Cate's hand was sharp. It was his special, his blade for their ceremony. He always thought of it that way. He wouldn't be here if not for Tara, chosen to carry out the work he was so focused on perfecting. Forever grieving that he wasn't about to save her. He had learned from each sweet girl saved, what scared them, soothed them, saved them from fear or ache. He wanted to warm them, caress lovingly, so they might leave this world with the joy of what was to come.

Cates' laziest moments consisted of sitting on his ergonomic seat, a knee pad and padded seat. When he wasn't lifting weights, boxing, training with his throwing knives, running, biking, swimming or studying physics, music or chemistry, he sat in this, this favorite chair, and sharpened his cutters. If he was still and not hanging upside down on his inversion table, he sat here. His tastes were simple, but elegant, such as this studio of glass and metal. His tastes were clinical and clean, hard and sharp.

This one, the blade he now sharpened with brio, had only ever pierced his *skin, besides, he never cut the precious girls. It was his special because it marked his progress onto his left arm. His number of missions tallied there, and when the missions were through, it would end him too. Not that he would die of a thousand cuts, but two decisive wounds that would give him the release he dreamed of. He wanted to end it everyday with this exotically patterned hardware. It was a gray*

Damascus steel-bladed straight razor that he loved. Its weight in his hand was stable and grounding. The handle fit his hand as if custom crafted for it. The color scheme spoke of hardened things to Cates and it soothed his rattled mind. The Damascus pattern spoke of controlled chaos. He read aloud the brand name etched in the middle of the blade, "Geist". It was the German word for mind. The play on words caught his attention years ago, second only to the patterned blade and handle.

The truth was Thomas Cates always felt like the alien limb that one can't wait to rid themselves of. There wasn't a part of him that was alien, he was wholly not made for this world. He was always intrigued that it was a bundle of bad nerves, allowing poor input and output that could cause such a phenomenon as Alien Limb Syndrome. That is what he knew he consisted of, an entire system of mephitic nerves. He imagined he was filled from toe to tip with pretzeled and corkscrewed filaments, pinched and twisted by the gravity blown at him from every angle.

The razor seemed to dim these loathsome feelings, the way it floated in his hands, the feel of it slicing into his arm. He liked the thought of keeping his mind sharp, his Geist *scharf. He also liked the thought that his mind would be the end of him. The pretty patterned blade pushed in at the eight hours of stubble on his throat. It wasn't uncomfortable and he knew full well what any more pressure would bring. He wanted it, wanted it bad, but was more overcome with the guilt of not finishing.*

Who would he be leaving the mission to? There was no one in line to take up his fallen arms and fight his great fight. It was up to him and he would finish for Tara, if only for Tara.

Cates didn't see anything wrong with suicide. It was obviously everyone's right to do with his or her life as they chose and choosing to leave this dark, horrible, hateful world was not a cowards move. However, leaving a job, a duty as necessary as Cates Mission, was unforgivable and wrong. He saved countless lives from the awful futures that awaited them. He watched the innocent lambs, their feet wading through a darkness they just weren't trained to see. He saw it on them all, just as he saw it on the blonde as he passed by the Arizona Mustang's football field where he first saw her cheering. It was an awfully sexual routine, which is all it ever was these days. Little girls flaunting their blossoming bodies in short skirts, thrusting their hips and tanned legs. Jumping and falling to expose their panties beneath. What kind of wholesome parent thought through this particular sport? Jesus Christ, it was every bit as wholesome as the baby girls in full makeup for the fucking pageants. He never understood the need of adults to make their children look older than they were; to parade them around like little versions of themselves; on display; on exhibit. She was too innocent for that kind of indecency. That was something else he seemed to see that went unnoticed by the world at large. This pissed him off, this crudeness and indifference of genuine innocence. His mother would have found this deplorable. It just tainted these pretty little girls and gave the jocks and coaches and fathers in the stand a menu for their future mistresses. Dumb ass typical male chauvinist PIGS! The whole fucking lot of 'em.

The pain grew sharp as the flesh easily broke opened around the edge of the blade and let the blood loose. He was so tired, so goddamn ready to feel nothing. To drift away in the electric soul that was trapped here without his mom and sister. He thought of the flight his bluish-green electrical soul might take when he found his mission complete. He wondered if he would know. Would he ever feel certain that he was done? He didn't know, and this seemed an overwhelming weight at times, but a certainty he suddenly felt was that it wasn't this dark day. Cates did this at 8:45 p.m. on every anniversary of Tara's death (and when he just couldn't seem to cope). She leapt from that mislabeled thirteenth floor on a Sunday at 8:45 p.m. That was when the Lincoln Town car that caught her body convulsed in explosion, blowing glass for yards in four directions. He learned this from the stolen social services report in the manila folder, embellished with the large red CLOSED stamp. That is what his Sister was to the world, closed, so minimal, unnoticed. This thought made him cry with rage. Well, Fuck Them!

Cates pulled the rectangular blade from his throat, caught the maroon drip from the minute laceration there and sucked his finger clean. He noted the tinny taste from the healthy blood. He got up and placed the razor in its wooden, leather lined box for another day. Three weeks from now Cates would spot the girl out on the bright green field under that perfect blue sky. Her tan legs kicking in rhythm with a line of girls on each side. She would be in the middle, the center of this world and so much brighter than anyone in sight, to show him just how special she was, how very innocent; that she was next. The kicks would lead to the hip hop booty shaking nonsense, but the girl would be so bright and positive that she made even this lewd movement seem pure. She would be unblemished, so beautiful.

Her routine performed beyond the black hogs head that blurred just at her feet. It was a symbol that held motivation for Cates. It was how Tara made certain he made the right choice. After all, who was he to judge who was innocent, or evil or even misguided? He was still human and could be fooled and mistaken. But Tara was beyond that now and this was her intervention. She always let him know. They were a team with military precision, she set the laser marker and he unleashed the strike.

After Tara's death, in Cates' first attempt to make his own leap, he ran through the city to Tara's jumping place. He would jump too. This was weeks after her death and coping was becoming less and less what he wanted to do. He would find her where she left this world and they would fly to whatever came next. She would show him all she'd learned of this next world and they would run and fall and laugh together.

He was out of breath and frantic and stopped for no one (not even the young man he knocked to the ground as he rounded third street). Cates ran through the lobby seemingly unnoticed and completed the twelve flights of stairs at the same frantic speed (he didn't want anything to stop him). He found the door to the roof and just before he found flight at the edge, he tripped over the hogs head. The fall was hard, jamming both wrists as he slammed into the gravel laden concrete roof. The pain made him question the fall he was about to undergo. But, more immediately, he wanted to know what the hell the hideous thing he'd just trip over was. He tried to imagine the scenario in which someone brought it up here. He even imagined an eagle flying by and dropping the heavy thing, too exhausted to carry it to its nest.

It was severed from the animal and dried bloody bits and pieces hung from the ragged cut neck that terminated the head. Cates couldn't believe his eyes, and without hesitation picked it up by the scruff between the ears and held the large head up to his eyes. The smell was miasmic, but Cates was captivated by the glassy dead eyes and the unreal sense of seeing this dead decapitated head here of all places. What was it doing here if not to tell him something. He couldn't help but expect to hear it grunt in his hands. He imagined its eyes turning to look at him, visualized its snouted mouth animate with a gruff, raspy voice. His concocted hog's voice said, "Tara told me to tell ya, 'Fuck 'em!'

and 'Hey, what's up little brother?'"

It made him think of the pigs of the world, like Tara's foster dad. Hell, like their own dad. "Goddamn PIGS," he roared and felt the first cultivated seeds of mission. His injured wrists sang (gravel embedded in his palms), but he overrode this pain and held the head aloft as he screamed this again and again. It all became clear, his new mantra began on that roof, "Ridding The World". Ridding it of the opportunity to blemish such pure individuals as his sister had been. He would add purpose, tip the scales away from what felt like a tragic win for the darkness. Tara's death would be the catalyst for a revolution and he the tidal current of change. He was the Goddamn Storm!

He knew he couldn't kill enough of the evil bastards to make the world safe enough for the pure, but if he could take some of the wins away from them, pull the pure from between their imprisoning fingers, perhaps that could make the difference.

Back at the Ranch

Nick found his strength and composure. It was late enough, he didn't think there would be too many people to worry about seeing him, but there was a killer driving about in a stolen patrol car and possibly another officer in the Sheriff's Office, if not one coming in soon for shift change. That was enough to keep him on his toes, but he had the added worry of his own stolen car. His road trip was officially over if it wasn't found. What would he do? Walk home to Hank? No, he decided very quickly, that he would die before returning to his old life. That didn't mean he would never return to Illinois, but he would never be the worn path he become under Hank's care.

The late hour eased Nick, but he always felt eyes on him, even in the old abandoned house where he fed and played with Skippy. He never felt alone and when he knew he was alone in a small room, he always felt as if there were a camera hidden somewhere. He never questioned it, though he knew it was sometimes just paranoia. Perhaps it had something to do with being Hank's step-son.

Maybe, it had more to do with every action counting, like every moment would be weighed by Anubis, in the end. Hoping since he was twelve, that nose-picking and masturbation wasn't as bad as everyone acted. Surely, it was another societal construct, merely to highlight manners? But, who could say? It was that time of early morning that always spoke of sleep to Nick, even if he'd just awoken for the day, this shade of light was always sleep inducing.

The moon had long since set and Nick's first major

breakdown was behind him. He was behind the Sheriff's Office now and the answer was yes, he was absolutely bat shit crazy. That shit behind the liquor store just now was all the proof he needed, but what does one do with that? Turn themselves in? He thought he could tell between right and wrong, real and hallucination; if so, he was no danger. He was still dizzy throughout the run to the back of the building, running drunk, but he wasn't about to hang around where the darkness had been so comfortable reaching out to him. He knelt and breathed and watched and breathed and tried not to think about it. He actually wasn't thinking clearly enough to focus on any one thing, but his body was still too highly aware of so much. Perhaps it was a bit of physical shock.

The lighting of this predawn scene reminded him of the last night he and Tommy worked on the Duster together. It was a secret project for Nick. After Tommy's death, Sam told Nick that his son asked if he and Nick could rebuild the old car together, said Nick could have the Duster, because he would need it to be free. He wanted to do that for Nick, give him a chance for a life that wasn't going to be handed to him. Tommy's dad had helped them procure parts and with the more complicated repairs that were still beyond Tommy's skill, but they both learned so much. It was all over Nick's head, in the beginning, but he was a quick study and eager worker. Nick recounted the week after he'd first encountered Tommy, when had asked Nick about Skippy. Nick was still so guilty about the poor dog, but left unspoken, Tommy cheered him up, introduced himself and asked Nick over. Nick got laughed at for asking, slapped for begging, and punched for his first attempt to stand up to the Mad Steps.

It was Nick's shame over the dog that caused Nick to watch Tommy from afar. He admired the way he acted, the way he carried himself. He was the kind of guy Nick wanted to be, cool and calm and somehow himself. He didn't boast, or lie, or pick like all the other boys seemed to, even later when he became the town's quarterback. That is how it is in small football towns, you are the town's hero, not just the schools. Tommy was humble, though, quick to own his mistakes and joke about his own faults and compliment others on what they thought were their own flaws. That is why Nick found it so hard to settle into the belief that Tommy's interest in their friendship was genuine; he was so cool and well liked, he could have spent his time with anyone. He chose Nick.

Nick and Tommy were close by the time he became the small town hero and though he made new jock friends, he still made more time for Nick. He was that kind of guy, with friends in every clique. His interests broad enough to allow him to be relatable to everyone. He even invited Nick to hang out with his football friends, but Nick always rejected the idea. Even if Hank would've allowed it, Nick knew they wouldn't see whatever Tommy did. He didn't want that embarrassment, but he also didn't want to ever put Tommy in the position to have to choose who he liked more. He was afraid he would lose that fight. Nick enjoyed his time with Tommy alone, he knew he wouldn't be himself around the other guys. They were too confident and he didn't want Tommy to see just how poorly he handle himself around those who might pick a fight with him.

Tommy was confident, but humble and laughed at Nick's jokes as if they were actually funny. Nick knew he was putting him on, trying to make him feel like he was somewhat worthy. Nick never understood why anyone would do that? Once he became convinced that Tommy wasn't feigning his kindness, that he wasn't setting him up for a humiliating prank, he knew he must love him to try so hard to make him feel normal. Nick loved Tommy for that. He wouldn't be the fool that believed it completely, but he would have Tommy's back forever. There was a point, Nick decided that if it was ever revealed that Tommy had been playing him all along, he would forfeit his life for Tommy's, without hesitation. Even if the town turned out to watch and laugh. Tommy had given him real kindness and hope, the first Nick had ever had. Nick knew he could die content, convinced that it was all real, at least for a bit.

Nick propped his back against the tiny Sheriff's Office, and sat in a crouch. The breeze was just enough to cool him and let him drift.

"Here Nick, I think we both know this is how this should go," Tommy's dad, Sam, was holding out the four keys to the Dodge Duster (two for the ignition and two for the trunk). "It was always Tommy's intention for this to be yours. He wanted to gift you with a way out." The primer gray 64 Dodge Duster, that the three of them had completely restored, was all his; a present from his friend, his friend — now gone. Primer gray was the color Nick always wanted and Tommy made sure it met his desire. Tommy made it happen. "I want you to know that you taking this car means as much to me as it did to Tommy. You know he really loved you, Nick. You know that right?" Nick caught his eyes as if to ask if that were true, but as his own tears made him lower his head and shifted uncomfortably. Sam didn't have a problem with Nick's tears, letting his own run freely. Nick admired that. "Yeah, he wanted you to know that you could be and do anything you wanted to, no matter your past. Ha, he had his eye on old Mustang that he wanted you to help him with. He knew you needed the get away more than he ever would. He also wanted you to not forget what you were capable of if life ever got between you two. It has a way of doing that to high school friends. He knew that and didn't ever want you to question your friendship with him." He smiled as tears dripped from his face. He grabbed Nick's neck softly and pulled him into a hug and Nick completely broke, loudly sobbing into the man. Sam made it a safe place to fall apart and let Nick cry himself out.

He couldn't believe that his only friend was gone. It was the Fairbanks' Panthers versus the Lincoln Railsplitters, Homecoming game and the last play of the fourth quarter that left Tommy lying motionless on the field. He even succeeded in landing the score that brought the Panthers the victory, but he never moved again. His neck was broken by the two large boys that brought him down from opposite sides. One caught him just after the other and rather than smashing him, they twisted his head one way and his torso the other.

Nick was there and he could see it play over and over again like a car crash. So fast, like a gunshot must be, Nick often thought. Tommy's body was horizontal in his leap into the end zone and the first tackle was a grab around the hips. As Tommy's hips were pushed to the side and up, his head was forced down, until, the other boy caught his helmet with his shoulder in an upward motion. His neck was snapped before his body hit the ground. The momentum was deafening as shrieks rang up all over the stadium. Nick knew it must have hurt, but he would be okay, this was just a football game. The moments dragged on though, the field of players on their knees and Tommy never moved. He was finally put on a stretcher and carried off. The game was over, and all Nick knew was that it was worse than he thought it could be.

Nick was worried, alone in the stands until Tommy's mom, Linda, grabbed him up to come along with them to the hospital. He told her it would be alright, it was just a football game. He voiced his thoughts that he hoped it wouldn't hurt his chances of playing next year, his senior year.

Nick couldn't read her face in the moment, but every time he thought back to it, he could see the knowing in her eyes. The knowing that her son would be lucky to walk again. The knowing that *she* hoped he would live. The fact that her son never woke up again, that he didn't survive the ambulance transport to the Decatur Memorial Hospital, made his memory of that look all the more crushing.

He spent that night over at Tommy's house with Sam

and Linda, not really knowing what to say or do, along with them. He risked the beating that might come, because he didn't ask Hank. Hank never said a word about Tommy's death, but he didn't say a word about Nick staying over that night, either.

They drank coffee and cried and talked. Mostly, they sat in shocked silence. "Listen," Sam said, his eyes swollen from too many tears, "I know your life isn't so easy at home, but you are always welcome here. And...I don't mean just for the night. Okay son? Tommy loved you and that means we love you." That was when Sam turned in for the night and left the house to Nick. He couldn't sleep, but he thought it was disrespectful to do anything else. He ended up waiting for Tommy's parents to settle in and quietly stepped outside to climb up on their roof, just like he and Tommy used to do. The smell of the asphalt shingles, the cool bite of the November night and the smell of the old Mountain Dew soda can they used as an ashtray (Tommy would always wedge the can behind the unused chimney-flashing, along with a pack of Doral cigarettes in a Ziploc bag) brought a whisper of Tommy back. Nick cried and smoked two of the four cigarettes from the pack they shared there. He attempted to wrap his head around the fact that he would never again share a cigarette with his friend, never hear his voice outside of his memories. He never figured out how to make peace with that.

This was the only night Nick never asked Hank permission to go anywhere or do anything. Hank had only ever let Nick stay with Sam and Linda Tomlinson, because Sam had asked Hank. Sam was was once mayor and now a state representative. Hank didn't know how to refuse the man. And though, Nick caught a black eye after returning home from that first stay-over — Hank said for putting him on the spot with Tommy's dad — Hank never stopped Nick from going over and staying over.

Tripping By Force

Deborah was done with school for the week and glad of it. Cheerleading practice was done, friends told goodbye and she was walking home. Pam had offered her a ride and so did Terry, but she was only two miles from home and she was looking forward to the walk. Mom had just started working late last month, normally she would be picking her up. But, no matter. The day was begging to be absorbed, soaked in, 'Walk in me,' it persuaded with a sunny, warm voice. Deborah had an essay to write and the small front yard to mow. That was her deal with Dad. She didn't mind, but she wasn't in a hurry to get to it today. She figured a nice, casual walk was just the thing to prepare her for the brain straining essay and if luck was on her side, it would be too dark by then to mow today. She watched the clump of cars make their exodus out of the parking lot, all her cheer-mates roaring past with waves and jeers all around. The music blasting from each vehicle was all distinct, varied, and pitchy due to the rushed coming and going of the vehicles.

It took Deborah ten minutes to walk off of the huge school campus. It was a beautiful campus though and a safe, wide road to walk home on, with just one turn onto Banquet Lane. That was the main reason that Mom and Dad didn't fight her when she wanted to walk, though they preferred her catching a ride with friends when possible.

Just two minutes off campus, a red fox ran out of the tree line just twenty-feet ahead on her left, spotted Deborah and rushed back in to the small forest. She was right to believe it was the same orange as her blue, orange and white uniform. She wondered if it was the colors that caught the creatures eye or her movement. Deborah smiled at the day she was experiencing. It was all so beautiful when you paid attention, when you saw the serendipitous way everything coincided, collided and so perfectly fit together into what appeared to be normal happenstance. She didn't question what it was or who was responsible, she only let her curiosity wonder adrift. She felt strong and the world felt indifferent to her, which made her feel as if she could come and go and play as she chose. She thought adults all seemed to lose that sense of play and hoped she could figure out how not to do the same.

She was lost in the clouds playful transfigurations, the breeze that caressed her cheeks and teased her hair. Also watching the wood line for other unexpected appearances, when a blue Prius sped by from behind. It made her jump because it too was unexpected and unannounced by the hybrid engine. "Dammit!" she said under her breath with a laugh at herself for jumping. She turned around to see if there was anything else coming that might make her jump. She didn't like being scared, it embarrassed her and she loathed being embarrassed. She didn't see the car headed her way at speed, because it was on the other side of a curve that lay well beyond the school, now well behind her, but the road she could see was barren. Still, she walked further to the side of the road to assure her own safety.

With the wind blowing about at her cheer uniform's hemline, the tree line to her left and a sparse collection of leaves to the right of the road that she now crumpled under her feet, mostly overrode the oncoming car. It wouldn't have changed anything, as she wasn't expecting trouble; which is exactly what she got. Trouble in the form of a man that was just that, troubled. He was quick and decisive is all any bystanders could have honestly said about the man who slowed to a stop, angled with little noise some twenty-feet behind the girl. Some might have suggested it looked as though he had planned it, as if he expected to find her there alone, at this exact time, on this exact day. There wasn't even a scream or argument from the young woman who was so happily enjoying her day before she was scooped up into the man's arms. It even looked as if she was part of the dance as she turned at the last minute and he with her.

He left his car, even as it rolled forward to a stop, left the door open and ran toward her as if he'd practiced it a thousand times. The man so quickly at her back, turned counter-clockwise with her like Fred Astaire. He used his left forearm to trip the cheerleader behind her knees and lifted her as she fell, using his right forearm to support her back, while using the red traditional bandana to cover her nose and mouth, forcing her to inhale, before she could really begin to fight. The slight struggle he had holding her was masked as he lifted her from the ground and settled her in his arms. It was over by the time they were back to his car. He opened the passenger-side back door with his left hand, exposed just beyond her tan knees. He dropped her in with care head first, quickly pushed the door to and just as efficiently circled the car and climbed in. He was in behind the steering wheel and speeding away with no fuss.

Deborah dreamed of a meadow, a single red fox

played there and bid her to come play. She wanted to so badly and couldn't stop herself from walking ever closer, but she felt a need to be scared, of *what* she was unsure. Her body seemed to be screaming for her to run, but her mind wanted to play with the new friend. Red flags waved at her from far away and were ultimately lost to her new playmate. What could a fox teach her, how did they think and play? What was she so scared of? Why was this perfectly beautiful day so suddenly full of unspoken fear? She decided she was being silly and that if she made the time for the small creature, like a fairy-tale, the fox would transform and gift her with its magic.

"You're pretty." the brilliant red animal spoke.

Deborah gasped at the unexpected, high-pitched voice and the wonderful compliment, "Thank you so much. I think you are beautiful."

"Oh, well, thank you, but you would be wrong."

"Why do you say. Perhaps you, like me, are too hard on yourself. It's not boastful to think yourself beautiful as long as you don't try to rub it in everyone's face, like Janey does."

"Oh, you misunderstand me. I don't underestimate my worth. It's just that I am not very nice. So much so, that my beauty is overshadowed by the hungers within me." Deborah didn't know how to respond, which was just as well because the mouth of the small creature opened slowly and distorted as it did so. The short red muzzle elongated unsymmetrically, as if with the magic of a fish-eyed lens. The canines of the small beast distorted toward Deborah and in a tenth of a second, the mouth grew and closed to surround

Deborah's sight. The fear chilled her neck and stifled her scream.

The darkness and foul breath, a stench that swallowed her up and she thought in horror it must be the animals' back teeth that hit her so hard in the top of the head. With this thought and the knock on the head, she came to consciousness. Chills still alight along her neck and arms. There was a roaring sound, loud enough to cover any startled noise she might have made.

The nightmare was statically darkening away as her eyes adjusted to limited daylight, though the stench seemed to linger. She realized she could actually taste the chemical smell, that it produced a mucus reaction in her throat. The gray texture that brightened in her vision, she realized, was the back of a front-row, leather seat. She followed the stitching, remembering with horror, that she should be walking. She remembered turning at the sound of something, feeling her knees give way, falling back and being caught and then that smell as the world rotated around her like a ball she was rolling in. Her throat seemed to close up as she fought the scream that rushed up the center of her body.

After Burn

Nick began to wonder if the killer followed him here, took his car, and left it at the scene when he stole the patrol car. That would be a great way to set him up, if it were found with Officer Dillon and the poor girl. That made Nick question if the killer had a ride he/she left parked nearby? He looked around to see if anything stood out, but it could be any of the three he saw from the back of the Sheriff's building. A husky, rude laugh caught Nick's attention, "Take any of 'em you like, Officer Dillon won't mind." The imagined man's tone chilled Nick. Why would an idle threat from a troubled mind's figment cause Nick concern? Was there something he should know, that he didn't? Was he crazy enough to black out and do things he couldn't remember? The closest he'd come to blacking out in his life, was just a moment ago and he could hear the world around him even as he lost his sight for maybe a minute. Had he done anything while he thought he slept? Didn't make sense. Priorities. "Now's not the time," he said aloud.

"If not now, when?" Hank stood in the light of the side window of the Sheriff's Office in his stretched thin, tighty-whiteys, looking at a clipboard, with glasses and the demeanor of a psychiatrist. Nick shook his head quietly. He felt surrounded by his own crazy.

Nick walked through his imagined Steps, feeling nothing, and saw no one in the little office of the Sheriff's Department. That didn't mean the offices were empty. He walked around where he thought he saw his Trusty-Duster. It was weird, a blurry-void filled the space and when he tried to touch it, there was a pain in his fingers; almost a shock.

"Dammit Man! Whatever will we do?" Hank spat overly heroically as he jumped to land like superman in his bright blue, generic Halloween super-suit. "I know," he answered before Nick could interrupt, "We shall cry like the vulnerable milksop that we are," he finished with a pinkie to his cheek, making a dimple there. Nick noticed the asshole was steaming from the cold and thought that odd, if not impressive for an hallucination.

"If you're not going to help, shut the fuck up," Nick added stoically, as he walked to the front door. He couldn't shake his guilt over Officer Dillon, concern over the poor girl, and an increasing cat-killing-curiosity. These were apparently stronger than his worry over getting in trouble...dammit to hell! His need to hide and sneak, suddenly gone, though he felt immediately exposed under the florescent light of the front awning. He couldn't have told you exactly who he was hiding from, in the first place, but all too often felt the need to be unseen by anyone. Then it occurred to him that maybe the Sheriff's Department had towed his car to a location off site where they held such things.

Surely, the sheriff would be here with the sun, or soon thereafter. He quickly walked to look around the end of the tall counter that walled the world away from whoever was on duty. From there, he could see into the office straight ahead. By the desk, he could tell it was the Sheriff's office. He turned to his left where there was a break table with chairs, a corner stand for the coffee pot, a tall-tan filing cabinet, with a printer on the table.

Not thinking, he turned to kneel toward the small space behind the long counter. He was hoping to find the deputy tossed in the floor, knocked out and left for the sheriff to find, but no luck. No reason to believe the missing officer would be here, but he didn't like the idea of having to go back to where he went missing, and where he'd seen his first dead body (Save for one. He could see Tommy's dead face without effort, it was always just there, behind every thought). Headlights poured over the wall above the counter, disrupting his reverie.

Nick, as one does, freaked the fuck out. He didn't want to be found behind the counter of the Sheriff's Office. He felt a chill run his entire back as he fought to decide on stepping out or hiding. He heard a car door slam shut. Too late, 'Okay, how to play this? Hide or come clean?'

'Fuck!' The door popped open, and Nick's heart hammered. He heard steps, and the jingle of keys, thinking every invisible thought he could muster, on the floor, hugging the back of the counter, like he was on a ledge. '*Glass, a clean pane of glass, so clean you don't even know its there. Wind, a body of wind is what I am.*'

"Dillon? — Dammit, Dillon, you're suppose to lock up when you leave. How many ass-chewings does the Sheriff have to give you?" The feminine voice asked the empty office with disdain.

He watched invisibly, as a uniformed, red-ponytail bounced across the span of open space and into the office closest to him. In Nick's mind, she would either settle in or drop something and bounce right back out here; he had to move. His body was one tingly surface as he braced for action, his mind struggled for which action that should be. His body thought itself capable of leaping to clear the tall counter, but he didn't know how quietly he could perform such acrobatics, so he leaned toward sliding his torso across in a parachutist's *backward turtle*. Just as he was about to do so, the officer stepped out and into the break room that opened up in clear shot of his position, though she was quickly too deep in the room to see. He leaped the counter without hesitation, clearing the counter much more stealthily than he believed himself capable. He was grateful, because swore he heard the female officer step back to the doorway. He remained crouched up against the front of the counter, and looked at the window in time to see her reflection follow the sound of her footsteps back into the break room.

He was amazed she hadn't seen his reflection, but Hank was there to explain it all, very loudly, "It's Cause We's Invisible!" The large man was only two foot tall, in overalls, a straw-hat, and gapped buck teeth holding a single straw of their own. Standing in front of Nick's reflection. 'Jesus be a saint,' he thought to himself.

He could smell her coffee, which bought him a small amount of time and the slightest noise for cover. Damn, it smelled good too. His relief felt attuned to the coffee, it saved him.

He quickly stepped to the door and opened it just enough so she would hear it. He composed his breathing as much as possible and stepped back up to the counter. He was trying to feel what his face should look like in this moment; going for nonchalant. Feeling his face without seeing it was a challenge he'd not attempted before. It was an effort, but a great distraction, allowing him to calm from the adrenaline inducing hiding foolishness. He folded his arms up on the high counter, still breathing heavier than he wished, when the green eyed officer stepped across behind the counter where he hid fifteen seconds ago. The gorgeous red hair surrounding the exotic green eyes was attractive. A fair haired Irish maiden.

"Can I help you sir?" He was fighting his usual body postures and natural way, too nervousness to think straight, or he would have used a version of the truth to make his story all the more believable. And, just as he was getting to enjoy Hank not showing up to distract him, he was suddenly glad to see the large man appear behind the officer. He knew he needed a grand distraction from his self-critical BS. What Nick could see of Hank, was naked save for the masquerade mask he wore. The skin around his eyes were blacked out behind the mask. He winked at Nick and kissed at her shoulders, as if he were a lover that wouldn't let her work.

Nick inwardly snickered at the happy distraction and read the shiny gold name plate on her shirt. Officer Shannon (sounded Irish), eyed him, waiting for an answer. "Sir?" Hank's mask was quite elegant really. It was crowned with leather jester's cap-n-bells. Below the very ornate light pink coxcomb, the pale white eyes and nose was cracked like weathered plaster and decorated with a gold trim. He looked again at Nick and made a goofy buck-toothed grin. It made Nick smile again and think about classmates trying to make each other laugh on picture day in the 3rd grade.

"Oh, I'm sorry, I was wondering if Officer Dillon was in?" Nick didn't know how he should proceed to most efficiently find out what she might know about his car or whatever the hell was going on, so he dropped back and punted; something Tommy used to say all of the time.

"He is out at the moment. He should be back shortly. Can I help you with..."

Nick smiled at the green eyed officer, cutting her off in an attempt to end this conversation as quickly as possible. Hank would have told him he played dumb well, but he was too busy making obscene gestures behind the officer's back. Nick would have laughed again, but this was not the kind of humor he found funny, that locker room bullshit. "Oh, well..." he said, turning so he couldn't see Hank pretending to grind her leg. He was trying to plot a verbal course that was vague enough not to unravel if Officer Dillon was indeed still alive and questioned. "Officer Dillon was..." Thank the gods, Nick's lie was cut short by the sound of the door, cause all he could think was, 'Shut up, just shut up.'

The door was bulldozed open by someone yelling. Nick turned to the door as the officer addressed the man at the door in the same tone she had him, "Sir?"

"Please help me!" It was an older man in baggy work clothes. He looked like an old mechanic, with black grease on his face and his loose uniformed pants were wrinkled up and spilling over the top of huge work boots. It looked as if he was already a whole day into work. He had a pristine pink scar that started at the left of his throat and rode across to the man's milky, dead right eye (like the "*Vulture's Eye*" in Poe's Tell-Tale Heart). The mechanic's wet hair clung to his brow and the side of his smudged face. The dirty skin was tanned and weathered cracked, but you could see the edges of a fake beard, clearly too dark. He smelled of mechanical work to Nick as he rushed closer to the counter making his claims. Nick felt something was off about him. "Officer Dillon was...There is a...I don't know...I..."

"Sir?" Officer Shannon offered in an attempt to calm the man into making sense, "What about Officer Dillon."

"Okay..." the man said and stopped to breathe. It struck Nick like a performance, but why? "Officer Dillon just crashed into my brother's shop. He's hurt bad." The man was hooking a thumb to his right, "Over at Danny's Auto." The man stole a quick look up and winked at Nick with a side ways smile.

"SIR?"

It made sense that Officer Shannon might get amped up at the news that her fellow officer was in trouble, but her response, too, felt off. He looked at her and she was looking at him, as if she were waiting on Nick to answer. Surely, she was just sharing her exasperation ('Can you believe this guy?'), but Nick felt like he missed something.

"Yes Ma'am. My brother's trying to help him but he ain't no medic." He finished this off with what sounded like an old-timers laugh straight out of a western. Maybe the guy was just nervous, but it sounded weirdly acted out. Nick studied him, deciding if he was wearing a disguise, he was acting this out, but…?

"Sir, don't move," Officer Shannon ran into the break room that smelled so deliciously of coffee. The man grinned and eyed Nick, a look that grew increasingly menacing as Officer Shannon broke radio silence.

"Sheriff Jenkins, Deputy Wales, I hope you guys are on your way, we have a situation. Officer Dillon may be in need of assistance, but first..."

Nick began to see, the man looked purposely dirtied; the grease a touch too uniform. Nick turned back to the counter to ponder what this might mean. Was it Officer Dillon that Nick saw climb back into the damaged police cruiser some forty minutes ago (or was it longer now)? Hell, he felt so stupid for assuming so much. He realized he didn't know what the hell was going on. Except, that Officer Dillon surely assumed he ran from the scene.

Then Nick looked around the place for a clock, as the radio came alive. He caught movement as the old-timer stepped out and looked back through the door at him. 'He winked at me,' Nick thought to himself. It was still dark without the sun's face, but it sure appeared that way. Then the man pressed his face against the glass of the door and made a taunting face, topped with a long fingered bird. Nick chuckled at the little fucker, wondering if he was crazy, too. Nick felt pranked, he realized pranked sounded so much better than set up, wondering now, if the latter wasn't closer to the truth.

"Gotcha Shannon, ready Patty and Jay just in case we need a quick ambulance. I'll be fifteen," declared Sheriff Jenkins before another, deeper voice, "This is Wales, I'll get there A. S. A. P., Sal."

Nick felt the need to leave, before he was trapped, not sure what was really going on. What was that guy about? Why did it feel like he was in a play, or watching a movie? Nick didn't know what to think, or do. Would leaving make him look guilty or would Officer Shannon lose him in the mayhem at hand? Nick decided he would take his chances and get the hell out of here, he was already an escapee of Officer Dillon's, how much worse could it get? He was very afraid, he knew the answer to that question was, much. As the closing door sounded behind him, he was immediately reminded of just how cool it was outside and breathed in the refreshing outside, he heard a choking, gurgling sound. He couldn't tell if it came from inside or out but he would have swore it was Officer Shannon.

No, it was a screaming laughter, but it sounded as if it were coming from inside. He wasn't sure if he'd ever heard such before, but he turned back to the glass to see if the female officer was the one making this noise. He saw only his reflection, but it was a mangled reflection (a tangled mess of genetic mismatch, as if he were Dorian Gray with a telling reflection rather than a disfigured painting. He felt unarticulated taint upon his soul; not guilt, but rather a good heart exposed to dark forces. He was certain his troubled mind was letting in the darkness and releasing his light; his positive nature dripping away. It was like Hank was turning off one lamp at a time, as he circled back to his La-Z-Boy nest. He realized it wasn't a movie or play, but a soap opera that he was trapped in and sick was the only way he knew how to feel about it.

He squinted his right eye with an accompanying grimace

as a long needle seemed to stab through it. He put a hand to his head and saw a vision of a dancing flame before the pain subsided. What was going on? He needed to get away, suddenly.

"Did that hurt? I was just trying to finish the stitching in your Voodoo doll, damn things missing an eye." Hank wore some sort of puppet face over his junk (a long blue fuzzy nose and red rimmed eyes), sweating fiercely. There was a light in his eyes, as if a flame were reflected in them. Nick realized he might still be able to see where the old-timer was off to, if he could keep from getting lost in those baby browns of Hank "The Tank" Forbus. Feeling the dawning of a panic, that the old, fake mechanic, might just be the killer.

Nick ran across the street to get away from the Sheriff's Office, and to watch. A block-and-a-half right, on a side street and somewhat behind this run of buildings, there were tail lights and what appeared to be smoke pouring from the hood of a car. This stood out stark in silhouette of the pink and purple sky that announced sunrise, but he couldn't have certain that it was a squad car, in the still diminished light. He didn't think, merely responded by running towards what must be the scene. It made sense, the mechanic being out of breath from running over. But, the rest of his performance, the disguise? He ran straight for the car, and then decided he didn't want to get caught up with the sheriff and other deputies. So, he steered away from the open garage door at the front, where the car was crashed, to duck behind the building. He needed to know what was going on, and, he hoped his car was inside. He would soon find no windows, but a back door.

The Mission

Thomas Cates saw the girl falling to land gracefully atop her fellow cheerleaders' formation, as the sweetest icing on the cake. She was so innocent and all gentle grace. Her muscles were tanned and taut in the exercise of flipping and jumping. She took flight before falling to be caught as the formation dissolved into single cheerers. She landed with purpose and immediately broke into a laugh at how amazingly perfect their performance was. They'd been practicing this for weeks and finally all of the pieces came together.

Cates felt her pleasure at the skill they'd discovered. He knew he'd made the right decision. He couldn't let them have her. She deserved so much more than the disgusting men of this world would allow her to have. Given enough time, they would ruin that heart-breaking smile, not to mention the nasty, mean girls that only wanted to take and hurt. She was deserving of salvation, just as Tara was. He had to steel his every nerve to stop himself from ruining this with the lack of patience he was feeling in the moment. He was suddenly scared that he was about to fuck this up. His breathing grew heavy and his body chilled with a sour sweat before he realized he'd lost control of his fear, he felt lust for the sweet girl. That wasn't allowed. He couldn't allow himself to be like all of the rest. What did it matter that she was his type, the muscular, tan body. It couldn't matter that her smile radiated the whole day, or that she moved so animal like, agile and steady. It didn't matter that his need was to love, to touch with gentle pleasure, to bring only happiness. She was beyond such things, and it showed in her glow.

He and only he could see her heart, her soul for the beauty that lay hidden. He could set that soul free, expose it to the winds as he gave her the world beyond without the pain she was destined to endure here. The horrific black-furred head lay upon the ground at her feet, marking her place in the world. It followed her like the imposed lines on an NFL football broadcast. If nothing else, his lust further proved her need to go. If even he couldn't control himself, those lesser in discipline than he stood no chance of letting her be.

He slowed his breathing, his eyes closed to the lovely girl. He placed his foot on the break and pulled his vehicle into drive. He checked the road thinking a traffic accident in front of the girl's school was not something that would allow him to follow through with saving her from the horde of men that were coming for her, not without trouble. He drove home with a smile on his face that was the anticipation of adding Deborah to his bicep's tally with his special. He might have been able to convince himself she was the first because of how sweet this felt, but his marred arm told him she would be his nineteenth. "Mmmm, that is special.

The mood of the studio was soothing, all his and private. It was all glass and metal framing above ten feet, so that even a half mooned night offered its light on things. The studio was in an industrial district, surrounded by docked warehouses and long forgotten businesses now abandoned. There was only one building whose height might allow a look into the Cates' Estate, but it was well over five hundred yards away and Cates never stood still in the floorspace that could be spied into from the assassins perch. Even at that, he'd strategically placed a textured glass wrap on that edge of his windows to further break up his brief appearances, just in case. He wasn't about chances and though the odds of him ending up with a hit on him or the cops ever revealing him as more than a shadow, were very slight, he endeavored to further lessen the odds. He now rested on his bed though he wasn't sleeping, he was strict with his time there as he only allowed himself six hours of sleep a night. Always he slept from ten a.m. to four p.m. If he needed a break at any point during the day, it was taken on his inversion table or the knee chair, as he called it. This routine was altered only when out on mission.

Due to his regular schedule, his obedience, and resulting pure health, he was wide awake while Nick was sleeping out on that rock in that breezy night. It was a testament to his discipline, his mastery of self, that he was a shadow in the night of this sleeping boy. Cates was the twisted sugar plum fairy, dancing about the ignorant heads of all childish humans while they slept, wasting what time they were given with illuminated boxes of every size, watching a virtual world rather than living in their own real one. Cates was awake and on the move, always. He was a human shark, always in fear of only one thing, motionlessness. His mind ran for the mission, not consciously aware of the wave of blood at its back threatening to drown it at any sign of stillness. The wave was filled with young women and Tara was always in the lead, just behind the red tide. If she ever caught him, he might begin to comprehend the reality that his mission, that her markers were of his making. That his twisted mind saw things a little askew from the ignorant humans he held in disdain. That he was twisted beyond repair and a killer of supreme arrogance.

Hank's Help?

Nick made it to the side of the garage, feeling as though his gut was full of cats destined to die by curiosity. He heard voices coming from the back of the shop, the slight aroma of lubes teasing his nostrils. His mind raced with questions as he contemplated whether or not to put himself closer to the voices with the hopes to over hear. His curiosity made this decision, he couldn't stand not hearing the conversation clearly when he might learn: who was talking, who all was in the garage, did they have anything to do with the dead girl, was it one of them who stole his Duster, where was Officer Dillon, and more importantly, was there anything Nick could do in the moment to render this messy situation to a happier ending than he felt was coming?

Nick had his back to the wall of the place, eyeing the Sheriff's Office, feeling exposed in the dawning light. Fortunately, his scream was stifled.

"Ha! You jumped like a bitch! Oh, but keep it down for Christ sake, don't you know that the bad guys are this way, A. J.?"

Nick closed his eyes, disappointed in the game that was now his mind. He could feel Hank's Morse-Code of alternating big eyes, as if to let Nick know they were using code names. He thought it was a low blow that Hank was going to pull out Nick's childhood game of playing *Simon and Simon*. Of course, he played it alone, as Hank prest any possibility of friends. Then, he thought, what the hell...if you can't beat 'em. Perhaps, he could play along and Hank would either disappear because he wasn't getting the rise he wanted, or play nice, for once. And then Nick remembered that this *man* was a figment of his imagination and wondered again if he would ever be strong enough to just blink him gone for good.

Nick felt silly, and yet he played along, "Rick, you bastard, how 'bout you shut the hell up. We need to hear what they..."

"Enry the eighth, the eighth I am, Enry the eight I am, I am!" Hank sang in a full throated chorus. Nick froze and ducked down, forgetting that he was the only one who could hear the horrible monotoned singing. Again, Nick looked disappointed, though this time it was self directed. He was angry that his screaming mind had the need to work against him. But, it proved that Hank was looking for a rise, rather than for Nick to play along; psychological fuck. Nick didn't know what to do with that, so he left it.

He crept closer to the back and strained to hear, knowing that his mind's static was the only obstacle, but it was no good. There was just too much noise to allow his mind focus. "Alright Goddammit!" Nick screamed into his head, drowning out everything, if only for a few seconds. He realized as he breathed deep, trying to maintain his composure, that he could smell smoke again, something singed and acrid. Were they burning something inside? Welding, he thought, but it smelled different. Then the voices clear and closer to him than they should be. Maybe these thin metal walls, but he was just six good strides to the back. They must be outside.

"He was right there, in the sheriff's office."

"I know you didn't want to kill him, but he could've

unraveled this whole thing."

"I know. I'll do what I have to do. I'm not going back to jail."

Nick knew one of the speakers must be the fake mechanic. Was the other really his brother, who owned this shop? Again, he heard what sounded like muffled laughter. He was sure they would see him, as close as they sounded, but then he heard what sounded like the back door closing. He crept to the back corner and looked around, just as he heard a coming siren. He looked back to make sure he hadn't been spotted by any arriving patrol cars, as he put the building between he and the oncoming patrol cars. The timing was too close for his taste, but they must have heard the sirens too. What to do now, besides not be seen and learn the facts?

"Don't worry, Brother. I'll distract 'em." Hank had on his Rick Simon blue jeans, boots, green infantry jacket and wide brimmed Panama hat with his hands up and together around a pretend gun, as he jogged back down the side of the building to the front. Nick was at a loss for words, and sanity, he feared. Sneaking into a building that the sheriff was headed into, to question killers, neither of which he wanted to be seen by, didn't feel like the way to go.

Waking up to Trouble

It was a solid front seat which was completely foreign to Deborah. She'd never seen one like that before, did that mean it was a police cruiser or a cab of some sort? She had no memory a face, or even the car from outside, as quick as she was taken. But, she didn't know this yet, so she searched her mind, as her eyes picked apart the scene. She was afraid to move, but thought if she could move her head back to the seat cushion behind her and up that she might be able to see the driver; careful not to catch his eye in the rear-view.

It was then that she realized what the tap on her head had been, the door scraped her head hard, stretching for the back of the seat. It was loud enough to make her afraid of him hearing, but the speeding engine roared from her place in the back. Or maybe, it is the sound of the road not so far below. She froze anyway, eyes closed, so she could play unconscious if anyone from the front seat looked back here. It occurred to her then, that there could be as many as three upfront.

She scanned the floorboard, the passenger side where her feet almost touched the door. She couldn't see anyone's head in the front passenger seat, but, perhaps someone was laying down or short? There still might be someone up there, someone that could raise up and peek at her. She didn't want to be seen awake before she figured a way out.

After fifteen seconds, she felt safe again and quietly scooted her ass toward the other door on this long back seat. Again, surprised by the simple bench seat, it wasn't broken up like every car seat she'd ever seen. She wondered if it was custom, which then made her consider if it could be a vintage car, "all cherried out" as the boys at school said. That would explain the sound of the engine, the old school roar.

Deborah scooted with ease and stealth, but it didn't help her line of sight in the least. She could just make out the hair of the driver, but to raise up any further and she risked being seen. It was a man, or so it looked, with light brown, messy hair. There were no head rests riding the top of the front seat. She couldn't help but wonder if this was some kind of serial kidnapper's custom ride made for easier nabbing. Serial, the word, rang through her head, echoed trying to make her say it, as if prodding her to say the word for the first time; se-ri-al...serial...serial killer.

She tried to stop her racing mind, to stop the oncoming panic she felt in her chest, fighting for release. She closed her eyes and focused her breathing. She opened them again with a mind on troubleshooting this predicament. Her bent knees showed below the orange, white and blue cheer uniform to mid thigh, but her mind was seeing possibilities. She wasn't tied up or restrained in any way. This guy must have overestimated his dose or underestimated her ability to overcome it, whatever the hell it was she was tasting. This made her feel stronger, more capable. What if she raised up and choked the driver until he passed out or died? She couldn't imagine choking him with one hand and steering with the other. No, she would need both to choke him with any lasting results of unconsciousness, but then, it was Arizona (assuming she was still in her home state; how long had she been unconscious?), and that meant flat earth for the most part. If he lost unconsciousness or tried to throw her off of him by swerving the car, the odds were that she could finish the job before having to snag the wheel. It was worth a shot, what else was she going to do, wait for another chance?

With this thought and a silent, welling scream that she wouldn't unleash until she had full control of his throat, she thrust her shoulders up and her ass under her with a speed that the drivers big eyes honored in the rear-view mirror. She had his throat in both hands, pulling the tender area into the seat with her weight. She felt his Adam's Apple compress back into his spine, saw the side of his face turn quickly red, to a fearful purple and the veins around his eyes stood tall in the small mirror he watched her in. He couldn't see the road as severely as she torqued his neck, just barely able to look down at her reflection. It completely stole her attention. He didn't seem worried about her grip on him, or controlling the car. He was watching her with what might have been the deepest love. She almost released her grip, it was as if she realized she was strangling her brother, having woken from a dream. Who was this man looking at her with such adoration?

"Stop that shit!" she silently scolded herself, reasserting her grip, "You don't know this asshole and he just kidnapped you." She squeezed harder, "Of course, you don't know why he kidnapped you. Is it possible he saved you somehow, from something or someone else?" She squeezed harder not knowing the answer and wanting to live more than she needed an answer. He merely watched, she felt sure he was just going to let her do her worst, as if he deserved it. Another thought increased her pressure, 'Surely he will pass out before he dies.'

She saw scarce rocks and boulders on both sides of the road, but they'd just passed the worst and largest of them, so maybe she had a chance. Except, something else changed in that moment. The eyes. She was certain they'd changed color, but that couldn't be. She was trying to believe that it was just a trick of the fading light, but she felt as if something shifted in the moment. The sentiment in the eyes, even the hair changed, she was certain; and the peaceful smile, the love, became a something else. Sympathy, maybe? She would have sworn that she felt his throat grow thicker in her weakening, trembling hands. She was suddenly certain this wasn't the same man she had just been choking. Startled, she felt her fear regain her strangling grip .

She settled into a stronger squeeze to put an end to this thing, when the driver slammed on the breaks and swerved hard to the left. She hadn't realized, so taken by his eyes and compassionate look, that he'd been speeding up the whole time she had his throat. At one hundred and fifteen miles an hour, a sudden stop and swerve tended to toss a body into motion, even an athletic one. She was up and over the bench back with what felt like no effort. She was halfway to the windshield before she knew what had happened. Her body rolled as if she were falling in cheer practice, though, falling forward and out of control; turning her back side to absorb the impact of the sudden stop against the windshield. He smiled (in honor of her fight, her willingness to stand up and take on adversity), even as he swerved with both hands and coughed, in gagging rasps, to catch the breath she stole from him.

Deborah's head and back slammed into the large windshield, buckling the hard glass into a red, splattered spiderweb. There was a quick flow coming from the back of her head, as she fell, caught by back of the front seat, with an impact that shook the car. She landed on her stomach, on the front seat's edge, beside the driver. Save for the heavy head that gave Thomas Cates the loveliest dead-leg. He looked at what could be Cate's Place, The Gates of Tara and thought how perfect. "We're here!" He rubbed his throat, spotting the blood across the windshield and dashboard, small but there all the same.

The driver refocused on the tanned body in the blue, orange, and white cheer uniform; now red, as well, in places; small places, speckled with the blood that now flowed freely from the back of her head. He realized that he'd have a bruise, but he wasn't complaining. A lovely souvenir. It was the best dead-leg he'd ever had.

The driver's mind had been multi-tasking, more fractured-functioning, since she'd gotten her hands on his throat. It fed him a euphoric experience, out of body, he was already into the ceremony he was told he so cherished. He, a written character, akin to a programmed automaton that feels perfectly at home in the personality it is handed. As if he'd been soaked for years in the experiences that fleshed out the world behind him in a long forgotten photo only said to exist...told to him by the other. This was the first of his waking, and yet…many kills into a worthwhile mission.

Decisions, Decisions

The voices were gone as Nick stood at the back of the garage, having run out of nerve, options, and time. He knew the police cruiser's would be sliding up in the front any second now. He thought a quick look *in* before it was too late might provide him with the answer to his leading question, "Where is my car?" Plus, if he was seen, he'd just have to play it off, or outrun the old fuckers. He felt certain, his bruised, overworked legs could put them to shame. He hoped. Looked like he was about to find out.

The back door, metal and commercial grade, surrounded by the same corrugated metal siding as the sides of the building, came open easily. The dark shop he was expecting was not beyond the door. Nick's eyes grew wide at the bright lights now shinning out upon him. It was an animated scene of marching images. He was absolutely certain it was a video he'd seen, *The Wall*, he thought. He wasn't certain until *the Judge* looking character skulked by looking menacing. It was in that moment that Nick realized the Judge was an ass, literally. He'd thought, through his twelve-year-old eyes with Tommy years ago, that it was suppose to appear phallic. He then wondered what else he'd misunderstood in his life up to now (with this thought, Hank seemed to be a germane subject; because he had no idea why, the thought fluttered away without inspection).

The parade of animated characters filled the space before him. Memories of Tommy flooded back to him, because it was Tommy that had turned him onto this old musical, creative-insanity that became such a cult classic for generations to come. Nick, dazed by the impossible, shut the door just as easily as he'd opened it, as if nothing out of the ordinary were happening all around him just now. As if to diminish just how much insanity lay within his head. He rested his weight on the wall, covered in sweat, he realized as the cool breeze began to chill the fever he wore. He looked up at the brightening sky but could only see residual effects of the movie he'd just glimpsed. The bright spots of color from the last scene, ink blotted the lost western horizon in negatives upon his eyes. The white house just two hundred yards before him took the color, like a projection upon it's pale surface. He knew then that he was crazy; absolutely, bona-fide, money-back-guaranteed, fucking bat-shit crazy. He didn't have a clue what to do now but be stunned and unsure if another fainting spell wasn't overtaking him. He even wondered if he wouldn't be better off, just falling to the ground to sleep away, whatever...all this was. To lay still and not have to make another decision, another move that in the end would be based on the delirium that fashioned the inside of his head, felt like a relief. Ever the glutton for punishment, Nick felt his bruised leg protest to the need to run.

An Easy Day

Saleisha felt the rough caress of something on her forehead. Her mind lighted on a number of possible reasons for the feeling above her eyes, a few disturbing. Fortunately, it was just her four week old kitty, Montague. He was a ginger (white with red rings), and the size of a can of soda. He weighed about as much as eight feathers, but could decisively pierce the skin with sharp little teeth, and remove skin with her tiny sandpaper tongue. Saleisha laughed and petted at the feline in the darkness. She immediately pondered if they were called canines in felines, speaking of teeth. Then she remembered, still petting her friend, that the sheriff had to travel for a presentation at the school this afternoon. Deputy Jacobs was still out for a few more weeks with her maternity leave. That meant that after about ten this morning, she would have the office all to herself, because Officer Wales always stayed out on patrol for speeders and common calls.

This free time made her giddy, because she had been trying to find time to Face Time with her sister all week and this would be the perfect opportunity, as conflicting work schedules and time differences were hindering their connection. Her sister had moved to London six months ago and they hadn't had much time to talk since. They mostly shared text, but it was not the same; they missed each others faces. This was going to be a great day, and an easy one if all went according to plan. She had no reason to believe it wouldn't, 'Except, of course, for the fact that Murphy's Law should'a been named Shannon's Law,' (something her Pa always said; and it was true in her twenty-four-years of experience).

She pushed the cat back, knocking the featherweight down onto the bed, which provoked a wrestling match from the tiny automaton, just as the alarm announced that it was 4:45 in the a.m.; get up time. A weight lifting session in her spare bedroom (it was arm day), a quick shower, breakfast with strong coffee over a twenty-minute episode of her favorite anime, *Sisyphus Remanded,* and a ten minute drive to work made up her prework routine. She smiled at the pink and purpling sky in the parking lot of the Austin, Nevada Sheriff's Office. She always parked in the first spot to the left of the door, because it was designated for Officer Shannon. She was proud of that. But, for the first time in her tenure there, someone was parked in her spot. She fought the frown, trying not to lose her cool.

She absent-mindedly gazed at the headlights on the brick facade and shut off her Prius' engine (she was the only law official without a designated cruiser, which meant that she typically ran dispatch from the office, she was the greenhorn, after all. Since Officer Jacobs had been on maternity leave, Saleisha had been on patrol six times and out on four different calls with Dillon. She enjoyed the change of pace, but hoped for quiet today. This unwanted customer was not the start she was looking for. Who the hell needed to be told to move today, because she was about to tell 'em? The squad car was gone, was this Dillon's new ride? It looked vintage and primer gray. Not something that struck her as his style.

She scanned the well lit foyer through the windows and

pushed the door open; it should be locked if he was gone. She was taught to always check the door before turning the key by her deputy father, just in case, and she found the door unlocked (which didn't alarm her much since Dillon did this every so often, but she still didn't like it). "Dillon? — Dammit, Dillon, you're suppose to lock up when you leave. How many ass-chewings does the Sheriff have to give you?"

Saleisha's red pony tail danced as she walked into the small office that doubled as hers when the sheriff was out (small departments such as theirs had to make consolations). Saleisha would have told you that her peripheral vision was exceptional, but she didn't see the young man behind the counter when she passed it. She checked the desk for messages there, paper notes often left by her fellow officers, but found none. No blinking queues of phone messages, so, coffee-time. For her and Sheriff Jenkins, before his afternoon errands. She stepped past the small copier, tall filing cabinet, the departments common computer, where the coffee pot stood sentry, to the tiniest bathroom. Where she used the tiniest sink to fill the pot.

She swore she heard movement, but allowed her ears and peripheral vision to do their thing. It took her a few seconds to remember the car in her spot. This oddity made her take the noise more seriously. She carried the full pot of water to the doorway and scanned the open room, before making a quick scan of the office. Still empty.

Oh well, coffee can't be denied without extreme emergency. She returned the pot to its maker, cracked the plastic lid of the big, round, blue tin and the smell of the rich, dark grounds painted the air all around her with its glorious and alluring smell. Officer Shannon breathed it in deep as she scooped the loose bits into the tan filter. She flipped the switch on and heard what might have been the door as she did so.

"Can I help you sir?" She looked into the soft brown eyes of a young man, seemingly nervous or slightly out of breath, she wasn't yet sure which, possibly both. He was handsome, but looked a mess. She was almost unsettled by his direct stare, but it also indicated honesty and innocence. This boy looked like a mixed bag to the green officer.

"Oh, I was wondering if Officer Dillon was in?"

"He is out at the moment. He should be back shortly. Can I help you with..." He cut her off before she could remark on the specks of blood that wore his shirt.

The young man smiled, and actually interrupted her. "Oh, well..." He seemed to get lost in thought for just a few seconds before he continued, "Officer Dillon was..."

Officer Shannon was taken by the fact that he would cut her off, but more so, by whatever interrupted him next. He jumped and quickly looked back at the door, as if someone was interrupting him. She watched waiting, but he seemed to be following the phantom as it stepped up to the counter beside him, apparently directly in front of her. "Sir?" He didn't even look at her, but began mumbling between closed lips, as if he were reading something and not very good at reading to himself. She couldn't make any sense of it, at first, but then swore she heard the name 'Dillon' and 'Danny's Auto' in the tangled mess he was muttering. She was reminded of seeing her kitten do this, stare off at nothing and follow it around the house.

After a minute, she felt she needed to begin directing this situation, "Sir? What about Officer Dillon?" The young man. The troubled young man began moving his hands as if he were speaking or trying to rehearse a conversation for later, he half hooked a thumb in the air. "SIR?"

The young man looked back at the officer as if he was unsure of what was going on, as if he were wondering if she could believe what this proverbial Harvey seemed to be saying. There was some deep, dark smell about the boy that troubled her. He was still listening to whatever was behind him, and she was quite sure that he thought she was listening too. She wasn't sure what to make of it, other than, maybe he needed psychiatric help. Saleisha had dealt with a plethora of local odd balls, but she felt this one offered a level of bat-shit well out of her wheel house. "Sir, don't move," Officer Shannon felt the need to get the boys on the way before Little-Mister-Crazy here proved her right.

"Sheriff Jenkins, Deputy Wales, we have a situation. Officer Dillon may be in need of assistance, but first come by the station, I have a more pressing issue that may give a lead to Officer Dillon's situation." The Sheriff and Wales both responded immediately, fortunately for her this was the perfect time of morning shift change to catch them both so quickly. She heard the door just after Wales' response and wanted to make sure her troubled visitor wasn't leaving. She ran back to the doorway and exclaimed along the way, "Sir, I need you to...Dammit!" Sal shook her head and wanted to throw something, but her hands were empty and women just don't pick up things so they can throw them...as quickly, nor as often, as men do.

A Difficult Night

Not much affected Terry Dillon in an emotional way. He was not psychotic or even troublingly closed off, if you didn't ask his on-and-off girlfriend, Darby. She would have told you that he never tells her anything. He could have never shared enough to satisfy her, because she was certain he was cheating. She knew what deputies got up to on the graveyard patrol.

He didn't like to talk unless it was beneficial, or fun. He liked action and quiet. If he had something to say, he'd say it. Darby talked about every meal, every stop along her day, it was too damn much. She'd just broken up with him again. Not surprisingly, he wouldn't have been broken up about it at all, if he hadn't just spent three hundred dollars on her birthday the night before. He was done with her games, so manic, so easily made frantic. He'd hoped this expensive birthday would help to bring that to an end, to assure her that he was committed to her, but just not ready for marriage.

Dinner was lovely and five coursed, within the swanky ambiance of Chey Cheree. There was no ring presented, but that was the point, to prove to her that there would be if she would just stop rushing things to the point that they broke up. If she needed a money back guarantee, which is what he considered an engagement ring, than she could play her games elsewhere. If she loved him and wanted to be with him, there should have been no problems. She wasn't mad about anything, that is what he couldn't understand (other than the fact that he wasn't ready to get married -

what he wanted to make clear was that she was who he planned to marry when he was ready).

She was never upset with him, they never argued, all they ever did was have fun, snuggle, watch movies and streaming channels together when they weren't hiking or camping. He just couldn't understand why she needed more proof than how he treated her, when they spent most every day and night together. He didn't get any sleep thanks to her bitching and his desire to work out the unworkable. Now he was exhausted and it was thirty-minutes from the beginning of his shift, "Hells bells!"

He was sitting on his couch, where Darby typically laid with her head in his lap at this time, telling him things like, 'Just call in,' 'I wish you didn't have to go in,' and 'I love you so much, I'm so glad you're mine.' It was here that she would look up to him most nights and talk about what they would do the next day after he awoke. He couldn't help himself but to look into his lap for her amazing face, her wonderful presence. He just didn't know why it had to be so hard to stay together when it was so good between them. It felt like the only problem was something *only she* could feel and see and experienced, once every three months or so.

It was 10:25 p.m. and work was silently at his doorstep, and this heartache had to be laid down, for now. He would cram this swelling, wounded moment into its appropriate compartment and carry on with what must be done. He could mourn in another quiet moment, this quiet moment was over and so he stood, retrieved his keys, uniform jacket and gun belt on his fluid motion toward the door.

He would find, then tag Officer Manny and Officer Swane and then he would be *It*. He was the only officer on the graveyard shift, but it was typically quiet with little to do, so he had no objections, in fact, he preferred the alone time. He knew he would be that much more thankful for it in his current wounded state. What he didn't know was that the typically quiet shift would be anything but, on this particular night. He would soon be found by a young man and a world of trouble at his heels.

Lost to the Chase

His weight was suddenly too much for his knees, but just as Nick was about to find his ass, he caught a reserve of need to keep his feet. It was a fever to run, a self-destructive spasm of tearing at the life saving tubes and apparatus running in and out of one's self. In full squat, Nick pushed himself up with concerted effort, scraping his back across the head of a bolt in the metal wall. The new pain in his back and lingering one in his leg, staved off the impending loss of consciousness. His new need to flee even himself, was a dancing vibration beneath the sweat. The chaos of a wailing car sliding to a stop at the far end of the garage reminded him of the current exigency. The heavy realization of just how deep his vein of insanity ran gave him the last push to run, as the world broke down.

The door beside him burst open and flew toward the white house in front of him. Two bodies ran out after the flying door, as if their destinations were the same. The bodies were on fire, in fact, the flames that roiled ever upward covered them so completely, they could have been made of it. They ran, it occurred to Nick, as if they were merely computer graphics in a movie, just oddly out of step with a natural gait. Nick didn't know he was looking for a sign and was never a follower, but he couldn't stop his body from running after them. It actually felt amazing to race without thought, to move in instinct rather than logic. He wasn't trying to catch up with them, he didn't believe they were real, but he did feel a need to get away. He didn't know what lay behind, what run toward him, but it might just be more understanding of the chaos that was his mind. He was as eager to flee that as any tar dripping monster. So, he ran and ran, into the back neighborhoods of Austin, lost inside his body, as if it just might find his mind out there somewhere. As if it might catch it, slap it and shake it to waking.

It just so happened that Carie Havored was raising her favorite, green golf-ball-perforated coffee cup to her lips. Her gray oversized sweatshirt with its enlarged neck line hung about her shoulders and down over her red jersey, cut-off shorts. She slurped the hot, heavily creamed beverage, because she'd seen something in a television show years ago about how aficionados of wine and coffee slurped to awaken the flavor fully and allow for more oxygenation. She'd done this ever since when she drank alone, her raising too set to allow her to be rude in company. Carie slurped absentmindedly as she watched this strange scene unfold before her. She had a habit of standing in her windows in these early hours, looking for something new, anything different that wasn't there yesterday. A UFO might have scared her, but it would be something she hadn't seen before and that was welcomed. Boredom was her enemy and it's friend, depression. Today, offered a gift of oddity.

She saw a young man outside the back door of Ray's Auto Garage, looking at the closed door as if it were something to see, and then he laid his back against the wall to the door's right (from her perspective) as if he had just glimpse into hell. He appeared to be in shock, slowly sliding down into a squat. He looked directly at her. She was immediately entranced. She felt this young man was up to no good, but hoped not, because he had a look about him that touched her heart, that made her believe he was the underdog in whatever was happening. This was far better than the morning news, a new show through a different window, she didn't realize just how giddy she was in the moment.

The boy was now rising out of the squat and looked as if he were seeing her now. This was the first sip interrupted. The rising cup froze and began to lower as the strength in her arm weakened under the assumed scrutiny. Should she hide away, should she run? She was sure he shouldn't be able to see her, but she felt caught, naked and vulnerable. Then he jerked his head toward the door he'd just closed as if he could hear a crash of rhinos running toward it. Then his body jumped, clung to the wall behind him, and leaned away from the closed door beside. His insane eyes followed whatever ran out toward her. He seemed to look directly into her eyes, again before he found his feet and began running at her. He ran with a purpose and she knew he would run right through her door and get her. She jumped back and slammed the coffee cup down on a side table, spilling half of it in the urgent need to have her hands free.

She questioned this that night in her bed, wondering why she wouldn't just use the hard ceramic cup as a weapon, but her reptilian brain was in charge and running at full speed in the moment. She couldn't see him anymore through the window, but stared agog at the door waiting for him to bust through. It wasn't until she saw his blur buzz by the far northern library window in her periphery, that she realized he wasn't going to break in and get her, at least not by the front door. Immediately she turned to look toward the back door, knowing this would be his entry point. Her body refused to move toward it, with another reptilian thought, that there was a door just behind her now that she could escape through. Carie stepped toward the kitchen doorway that opened up into the hallway which allowed an unobstructed view of the back door. Two minutes of heart thudding silence writhed costively by before she ran to the back door to lock it, if it was by some weird occasion unlocked. The door was locked, as usual, and she quickly stepped to the guest bedroom to the right of the hallway and tried to pull the curtain back in a manner that might remain hidden to the young man whose intentions were still unknown.

The curious heart of her was wondering if it wouldn't be a dream come true to open this door and wave him in as an accomplice to evade whatever he thought was after him. Confusingly, she wanted this as much as she wanted to save herself from his madness. She wanted to play along and please herself on his madness.

She couldn't see him as she peeked out timidly, growing bolder in his absence, suddenly bothered that he was gone. She immediately unlocked the back door, almost depressed that she'd hidden herself away from what would have extended this, her new favorite show. She felt as if she'd learned some hard truth about herself. She wasn't quite sure what that was just yet, but she was pretty sure she didn't like it. She was extremely melancholy now. It was a hard, slow truth; whatever she wanted out of life, it wasn't this bland, suffocating existence that sought the stranger's madness just for a breath of fresh air. And now, there was no going back to the comfort of it.

Head in the Game

Three hours into his shift, Dillon, still wide awake, was feeling drug out all the same. He knew he needed sleep, but that would have to wait. He felt wired and exhausted and the wire was in the lead. His mind was consumed with anger and loss, and the aggravation that comes with attempting to shift your focus over and over again, to stop the vehement arguments in your head. Why did she have to test him? He just wanted to love her, why did it all have to be on her terms?

He was in the side office, with the printer, coffee maker, sink, bathroom and three filing cabinets. It was a small and crammed full, with little room to walk around the small square of table, and less to take a seat, but he enjoyed this room. The lack of space meant he didn't have to share it with anyone else.

Only the technological devices this minuscule department could afford, including the seven-year-old, large computer tower and newer twenty-inch flat screen monitor. Dillon was most proud of the small flat screen, which allowed him just enough elbow room for his laptop. It was because the young officer was in this room, on his laptop, that he didn't see the headlights of the vintage Dodge, Duster slide into the gravel parking lot behind him. If he had, he would have thought Saleisha had forgotten something; that was where she parked.

Officer Dillon was startled by the sound of the door and that annoying, cheap sensor. He was surfing on his laptop, lost in the hand gestures of Kuji-Kiri, when he was interrupted. The young man was wearing a dark gray tee with dark red half-sleeves, worn jeans and gray combat boots. Officer Dillon noted silently, his mind was suited for such work. He noticed the young man appeared frantic.

"I need to speak to the Sheriff." The light-brown, hectic haired youth squeaked. Six-years in the Army and four with the force had provided ample opportunities for Terry Dillon to experience situations. It also gave him the insight that such trouble could be more efficiently handled by a quick, level head. The face and troubled voice said something was wrong.

"Alright son, take a breath and tell me what's going on, " Officer Dillon said soothingly as he stepped closer to the counter and toward the offices, reflexively, in case he needed to get around the counter quickly. The boy was amped up and Officer Dillon needed to be ready for anything.

"I'm sorry....I'm Nick Stone," the young man said pulling out his wallet and driver's license. Officer Dillon wouldn't have asked for it, but he wasn't going to refuse the opportunity to verify this frantic identity. Officer Dillon focused on the two-by-four inch card with his periphery engaged to keep the subject in check. "I was just passing through and stopped for a break just five miles back (gesturing east, to his left), and found a dead girl...a cheerleader...blonde....." The boy was stammering and seemed younger by the second as he searched for words to describe what sounded like a homicide. Officer Dillon watched the boy begin to sweat, he had to contemplate for the first time if he'd ever witnessed anyone begin to sweat from the first bead; he wasn't sure he had.

"Alright Mr. Stone, why don't we go take a look and we'll go from there." Officer Dillon left the young man at the counter and stepped back into the file room, which he thought of as his office, sliding on his uniform jacket as he stepped back out. He grabbed the subject by the arm with little force, but a ready hand that expected trouble. Dillon almost stopped at the door, knowing he should lock it, but decided to let it go in favor of getting the boy in the cage first and then he would come back; though he decided not to once he found himself climbing in the driver's seat. He left the office unlocked all the time, he'd just have to deal with Shannon's ass chewing. She was always on him about his recklessness in that endeavor. Shannon was a good officer, but she could be a hard ass.

The frenzy of twitchy muscle fibers at fire in the young man's arm told Officer Dillon the boy was scared, but he submitted to the officer's lead. He allowed himself to be walked to the patrol car and locked into the small cage, that was the back seat, without notable hesitation (though he did trip into the car door, that was odd; it just looked odd. Dillon had never seen anyone fall quite that way before). He seemed a touch breathy, but he was reporting finding a dead body, which *should* freak a person out.

"You okay, son?"

"Yeah, I just lost my balance, my leg is hurting for some reason. My eyes have been...messing up tonight, as well. Maybe I'm not having a stroke." Nick half chuckled.

Dillon had no response to this. He placed a hand at the back of the boy's head to keep him from hitting it on the top of the car. That was when he noticed the red marks on the boy's throat, "You ever been choked by anyone, man?" The boy looked confused, but just looked at him quietly. "You look like you have, very recently." Officer Dillon rubbed at the marks absentmindedly. He wanted to ask the young man about the few spots of blood on his shirt, but after his next answer decided against it. He figured either the demure boy was abused or hiding some sex fetish.

"Oh, I did feel...I mean, it ached earlier when I woke up, but I didn't hurt it, that I can remember." The officer let it go and continued to aid Mr. Stone into the backseat. Once seated, Officer Dillon saw the boy jerk his head to the seat beside him, listen and then close his eyes, raising his face with a deep breath and nod negatively, very slightly, as if this just got out of hand. The officer wasn't sure what exactly to make of this, but was glad the young man was now locked in his cruiser. "You okay there Nick?" Dillon asked as he closed the driver's side door and reached for his seatbelt.

The boy looked at him as if caught, but only momentarily, "Yes Sir, it just shook me up...I've....I've never seen a dead body before." This came off as sincere, but the officer wasn't going to let his guard down.

"Okay Son, tell me what happened as I drive us there...you'll have to directed me when you see me getting close." He remembered the young man pointing back east, so that is the direction he drove, knowing most of the town's visitors and through traffic came from this direction. He could tell the boy was now watching him with some unasked question rounding the inside of his head.

“Yes Sir, I stopped to eat some leftovers I bought back in Grand Junction.”

“Utah?”

“Uh, yes,” Officer Dillon wondered what brought the young man this way, trying to weigh his words against the manner in which he delivered them. “I stepped behind this big rock to, well.... relieve myself," the boy hesitated here (Dillon was trying in real time to sense if he was creating or remembering), and then continued, "and I tripped over her body. She had a blue, white and orange cheerleading suit on...or has, I should say.”

“What are you doing out this way, Nick, you got family in the area?”

“No sir, that is why I headed this way,” Officer Dillon understood the boy was running from who he was or who his family wanted to be, at least. “I am headed to Sacramento for work.”

“Oh yeah? Work, for who?”

“There is a sports apparel company that my Dad used to work for before he joined the Air Force,” Officer Dillon could feel the change in the young man's demeanor. He couldn't articulate why, but he knew the boy was lying and it seemed for the first time. He watched the young man gaze out his window, then, more excitedly, “Oh. I lit a flare hoping it would last until we got back.”

“We?” Officer Dillon assumed he was talking about any officer he found on duty, but he wanted to keep him shook, off center, to trip him up if he could be tripped into telling a truth he wasn't planning on sharing.

“Yes, you and me....whoever I found to tell about her,

that is. I wasn't sure how long flares burn," this last question made the rest ring true. It seemed he wasn't worried about having his statements picked apart as much as he was worried about being able to find the spot again.

"Anywhere from 15 minutes to an hour," said Officer Dillon speeding up the car, "That's what the box in our office says. Bit of a broad window, isn't it?" He needed to know where this body might be. Again, in his periphery, he saw the boy shaking his head as if he no longer believed it were possible; or that he was part of a prank that he didn't feel right about.

Officer Dillon caught sight of a red flicker, a spark half-a-mile ahead, to the left of where the road should be, "Is that it? Wow, it just sparked out. Good thinking, Nick." The fact that the boy indeed lit and left a flare, pulled at Officer Dillon's trust. And what harm was there, as long as the boy was locked in the back seat? The officer pulled the patrol car off the road and could make out a red, white and black Indian blanket in the farthest reaches of the car's headlamps, it was stretched over Party Rock (at least that is what his generation of local youth called it).

"Yes Sir....that is my blanket stretched across that rock...and that is the rock that...just behind it is…the body." The boy seemed overcome suddenly with relief. Officer Dillon was ready to verify one way or the other. The officer quickly exited the car and ran around the rock, letting his small tactical flashlight's beam lead the way.

"I'll be damn..." Officer Dillon was truly shocked, the young girl lay before him, just where the young man said she would be. He didn't know just how strongly he disbelieved that there would be anything to find, but here she was. He then reminded himself that this didn't mean the young man hadn't killed her. Just that he had been mostly truthful thus far. He checked her neck for a pulse, but the cold flesh told him the story before the missing pulse replaced the question mark with a period. He was so glad the young man was contained in the cage. He jumped and turned at a footstep behind him, he whirled with his flashlight. He thought, 'I'll be goddamn!' but he had no time to say it aloud.

A View From the Inside

"Perfect! We're here!" It was perfect, in ways that made no sense. The light of the day, the location, the air and its scent. He couldn't have asked for a better moment. The Maxx was ecstatic to be right here, right now. He felt twenty-two and new, though he was sixteen and without a back-story to weigh him down. Oh, he'd done things, but his baggage was nothing more than silent bits of film, all close-up, moving images. Snippets, where drama, pain, and utter joy could easily be felt in mere seconds of frame; where confetti fell and unfell in frames of tight faces, clipped together so perfectly that it felt like art. The Maxx didn't need the past, the past was a huge creature holding you down against your will, with its unyielding weight; meaty fists at work on your pain. The Maxx rode behind his keeper's eyes, merely watching, awaiting his need. He wasn't worried about the arguments, or hurt feelings. He was here to protect, to ensure survival. He'd just finished his moment with the girl, saving Nick from her, at least. He didn't know how she came to be in the car, but it was his love for the poor girl, his compassion that surprised her. He knew there was something new in them, something foul. Whatever it was it would show its ugly head in the end, and just like her, he would take care of it. He knew Nick wasn't that broken, so why was she here, trying to choke the life out of him?

While The Maxx squeezed every moment of its splendor, as only a sheltered or even caged youth can, Nick relished the high. Nick absently set about preparing his scene, with writing on his mind. The Maxx and Jay Jay helped him by partaking of the leftover burger and fries, leaving the cigarette for Nick to enjoy all on his own; they didn't care for such things. They knew the enjoyment he took from a cigarette after a meal. They knew this from his time with Tommy after school lunch, or atop his parents house after a late snack. The last three days, they learned a great many things about Nick and their role in his life. But, here, atop an ancient rock in the open wilds of Nevada, this was a new found freedom. The Maxx smiled at the moment Nick and Jay Jay could settle into, but he was weary of what shadows lurk behind their eyes. He didn't know how he missed it? Worse yet, he didn't know if he could save them from it.

Thomas Cates had spotted the rock while The Maxx fought to catch his breath, busy being enamored by the blonde trying to choke the life out of him. Cates found the thrill in stirring up an F5 Twister and stepping back to let the hero wrangle it. He was an even quicker study, in this first day of life, and this was going to be fun. But, he was given a back story, a way to be, and a holy mission. It wasn't even his choice, but he would have sliced anyone that tried to argue that point.

Before Deborah was launched from her position as choker, in the back seat, her hands wrapped and pressed around Nick's throat. It was his love-struck eyes that first caught hers. Thomas, now had this same young, candied sweet, tucked into Cate's Place, ceremony in full swing, just as he'd imagined as Nick drove them past. Nick's other, the god-forsaken-hero, let him take the wheel while he blurred the graphic scene next to them. Cates actually watched as Nick sped by in the primer gray Duster with all of them in tow; a clown car of cram-packed-lunacy and Nick's oblivion to it all; but then, the boy seemed to see what he wanted to. Rose colored glasses an' all that bullshit!

Cates could see ahead of them all, while they were distracted with their own roses, their own weight; just as Nick couldn't handle the full weight of his past and therefore divided it into equal parts for a lighter load. This was only Thomas' second ceremony, though he remembered a lifetime of perfecting it. He knew that this was his first real mission. There were vague details of something the boy set him too, before he was truly born, something he was tasked with in the womb. Three nights ago, and it was Nick's anger forcing his fetus to act, the boy's angry will driving nails into the world's wrists. Manipulating Thomas' power into a terrifying outcome that even Thomas was having trouble stomaching (mostly because it fell well outside of his mission).

It was this twisted interference and the fact that all of these young selves were flitting about upon this sacred ground. Like shallow hippies in a horrible Baby-boomers commercial, that had his own, ceremonious mind distracted and aggravated.

Jay Jay, was the six-year-old girl who worried about Hank, afraid of Hank but also, now scared of what they'd done to the man just three nights ago; terrified of what it said about her band of cohesive misfits. The Maxx shielded her eyes from it. Nick sang absently, while she guided him at fitting broken puzzle pieces together, playing her part, but she felt too much of what was going on. She felt a birth and a death taking place within and around them. This new one, she didn't even know his name yet, but he was the darkest, broken part of her Nick, and poor Nick was her's to set to play, to find the joy for. She even had sympathy for Hank, though there was no doubt her Grandad would'a spanked that man. This thought troubled her; Grandad? This absent thought felt like a false memory. Maybe it was Nick's, from a book or something?

The point was, they all protected her, just as they all protected Nick. She couldn't just be done with them. They were her salvation, no matter what else they might become. They were her's and it would always be so, but if the world needed protection from them all? She wasn't sure how to fit her head around that thought.

She was the pure core they chose to save, to protect from the hardening world. She wondered, for the first time, if she really wanted to be a part of such a group? What life might be like without them? She was born with enough hope, that she saw this as a possibility, but something deeper told her she was a fraction of the whole; that without Nick, at least, she didn't exist. She knew The Maxx, he came along years back, but felt like he'd always been with them. He was the big brother that Nick couldn't be for her. This new one, he felt like the killing kind, and 'MISSION' was his focus, whatever that was. She wished Nick had never needed him, that he just let the man leave. He creeped her out. She didn't want any part of his scary, dark life. Before three nights ago, the darkest worry she had was making Hank mad. She was the one that always pulled

Nick back into behaving for Hank, saving them from his fists, his belt, his mad mouth, whenever she could. She wasn't yet sure how to battle this new avatar. This was all happening so quick, but the air here, around the stone, felt ancient; revitalizing. Perhaps, here, they could set themselves right, find order in the chaos?

While Thomas grew weary of the others, Nick pissed him off! Did he really think he was a God? Who was he to tell Thomas Cates, what and who he was? He had a mission, a holy mission to bring innocent women of the world to his sister's alter. So she might process them into a better world, not sullied by the men of this one! The boy might have to go. He watched the boy and his minions after being interrupted; awaiting a moment to begin again.

Nick, freshly fed and nicotine fixed, wondered if all writers pondered the same questions. He sat Yoga-style on the large stone, notebook flipped open on his folded lap, pen to his mouth. He wondered where his ideas came from (such as, a young blonde cheerleader kidnapped by a serial killer who believed he was saving the world, or a waltzing flame, or even a graveyard vintage-gentleman-zombie). Were these ideas fed to him, thoughts picked up by his telekinetic antenna? Were they the breadcrumbs left by the many muses flitting about his head; a trail that might lead to some life-long epic that changed the world?

It was as if they just fell into his head, complete. Sure, he had to figure out just how best to describe the details, like spices in a dish, but they were already there, waiting to be seen, to be tasted and breathed. There was another idea that begged to be written, this waltzing flame of Christmas on the Fourth of July, but he didn't know what to do with it just yet, it felt too big, too much. He didn't know why such an image would feel like a present, why such tantalizing macabre imagery would hold such feelings of relief for him.

Besides, he was drawn to this serial killer's mission first, it would be a great story. A young girl and her terrifying need to destroy, was just too close to home for him, though he didn't understand just why? He just knew it felt, raw, like a wounded mouth nibbled without regard for the Novocaine's fade.

The divided mind that paced and hid and sat about the bolder, frantically at calm, found a peace, in this piece of sacred earth. Unfortunately, Deborah was past experiencing, at least in the way that Nick and his understudies understood it. Her body drained of its spark, the impact with the windshield, that left him speckled in blood, assured that loss.

Thomas often wondered, as he did now, waiting for quiet from the others to proceed with dignity, just where that spark went and how it phased out of this world. He never saw it leave a body he aborted. He would often sit in his favorite knee chair and ponder if the mysterious circuitry of the brain contained a portal, a hole, for which the soul could escape undetected, leaving the rest of us ignorant to that sparks existence. Perhaps, the entire circuitry created an electro-magnetic force, opening a doorway? Maybe that is where dreams came from, and unworldly sightings, like ghosts? And often, the bleeding slice that would further calculate his missions half-life, helping to keep his tally, would leave this belief emblazoned upon his mind with a certainty so indescribable. Then, lost in the graceful pattern of the Damascus straight razor, Thomas would weep at how very beautiful it all was, the connections between every intention, every action, every ending; so glaringly clear in those searing moments.

Cates knew how Deborah, seemingly the most important of all of the sweet girls his back story made him aware of, died. After all, it was he that spotted her, scooped her up, and placed her so lovingly in the car. It was he that pushed *the hero*, that he so despised, into slamming on the brakes and breaking the poor girl. But, Cates also knew how she was taken by his blade, with one burning, merciful slice. She was broken by his blade with love and compassion, perhaps that is why he let these underlings have their freedom? They too, were broken by love. Love, twisted, turned, and bent love, was the chaos that kept the world at cycle. Like his father's love broke over sweet Tara. It was an ugly thing, but that is what Cates was here for. To save as many as his blade could find.

He had one concern, as he took over beyond the garage, that scratched rabidly at the back of his brain; was Nick trying to get him caught? He wasn't even sure why he could even think such a thing, of such a simple boy? But, there was something going on that, a multitude of memory clips, just frames really, suggested betrayal to Thomas. He wouldn't cause any harm Nick's way, just yet, but he would have to be careful. He wasn't going to let the young man put him in harms way and perhaps, in the end, he would have to save them both; hell, the whole broken band. He felt he was, at least for the time being, subservient to their wills (at least at times), but he wouldn't allow them to deny him his freedom. This could not be.

Looking for Dillon

Officer Shannon stepped outside the door and looked for the man in all directions. She ran to the left side and shot a quick look around the corner of the building, nothing; but that goddamn car parked in her spot; that meant something, something to do with this, she felt it. She ran to the right corner, nothing, no...wait. There he was, creeping to the back of Danny's Auto Shop with his hands up. He seemed to be holding his right hand with his left. Ah, a pretend gun from the look of it, one that probably sounded like, *PATUE PATUE*. "Oh, that fucker is crazy."

Not drugs. Possibly a lack thereof. She knew she could run over, catch him unaware at the back of the building and slam his ass to the ground, but procedure and the fear of another ass chewing led her to a second option, waiting for backup. Besides, just how crazy was he? Crazy typically means strong, and capable of just about anything.

She wasn't sure if the sheriff was being over-protective, or merely concerned about his officers, but she was afraid he was treating her like a girl. She didn't like that, but wasn't quite sure how to deal with it yet. She ran back in and updated Sheriff Jenkins and Officer Wales.

"Shannon, are you telling me, he looks to be playing *Cops and Robbers* around the auto shop?"

"Yes Sir, so it appears, Sheriff. He is currently walking toward the back along the southern wall. I think I can take him, he's just right there?"

"No, Saleisha, we're close, and I don't think I want any of you dealing with him alone. Any word on Dillon?"

"Nothing Sir, I'm worried. He'd have called in by now if he could."

"Yeah. Me too, Officer. Wales? You hearing this?"

"Yes Sir, what is it about a full moon, huh?

"It pulls all of the water in our crazy bone to the top," Sheriff Jenkins dead-panned.

"I guess. It's a better answer than I had. I'm two minutes out, Sheriff. Siren's on?"

"No, let's see if we can keep the advantage and catch him off guard. See if you can park out of his line of sight and catch him at the back."

"Roger that!"

Officer Daniel Wales had no clue how far out the sheriff was, but he decided he wasn't going to wait. He rounded the corner of Main Street at sixty miles an hour, silent, no spinning top or headlights, with no visual on the suspect. The early dawn light didn't help matters much, fine detail was all a blur in the fighting light and the waring absence of it. He slid to a stop in the front of Danny's Auto, out of his seat belt, with transmission in park in one-fell-swoop. Out the car door and three steps running without a sound. Nothing looked off about the place, but he knew well, that a slaughter house doesn't always show blood on the outside.

Having no love for Danny or his work, this wasn't a desirable place for him, but if Danny or his pretend brother had anything to do with Dillon being missing, there would be hell to pay. First, he had a bat to catch; a moonstruck crazy with loony aspirations, possibly still hovering around back.

Wales' two hundred and fifty, stocky pounds were well handled, moving with a physical grace one wouldn't suspect from the look of the man. He had a soft look to him, but it was only the top layer. He was far harder beneath. He quick stepped, donning the departments black uniform and hat, down the left side, where Officer Shannon said the perp was mimicking the very actions Officer Wales now made; letting his pistol take lead. It didn't lower his guard that the man had no gun five minutes ago, because they had no clue what might be going on. Perhaps the young man was with a gang and if so, who knew what they might be up to?

Officer Shannon stepped out of the office and quickly locked it up (thinking if she could only teach this habit to Dillon, hoping she would have thc chance). She wanted to join the professional version of the young man's *Cops and Robbers* walk, just minutes earlier. She stepped toward the garage, scanning the area behind for sight of the young man. She didn't see him, but Whats-Her-Name, Harvored's white house spoke to her, for some reason. 'Had he gone in there? Had she let him in for some reason? Had Saleisha subconsciously picked up movement?'

More questions and no readily available answers, or as she called it, The Job. "Shannon on your left!" She called out to Wales so she didn't spook him and get shot. She trusted her fellow officer's, but thought it courteous to announce her position. She knew her duty mates well enough to know they weren't too scared to do their jobs well. They didn't shoot first and ask questions after. They didn't treat disrespect for their badges with bullets, or anger with bullying or death, as was seen so often on the news these days.

Wales appreciated the clear announcement, and kept his eye on the back of the garage, so he didn't see the bouncing red pony-tail sweeping the back of her head, as Shannon jogged toward him. "Officer," offering her a verbal nod. When Shannon was twenty feet and closing, he said, "Nice to have you at my nine, Sal" without a look at her.

"Nice to have your nine. I've got a feeling about the Harvored house, but nothing definite on this kid's whereabouts."

"Good enough, we'll check with Carie, before we work around. Should we check the garage first, though?"

"Yes, since he was the one to bring it up, and all. He was mumbling about Dillon and the garage. Dillon may be in there." Shannon thought, 'Oh, yes, Carie is her name. Never cared for her.'

"Okay. You wanna check the far corner while I check inside?"

Wales was all business, that was one of many virtues Shannon loved about him. He was a great father and husband to Holly and their three babies, that was another. "Roger that."

She'd grown up with Holly and was glad her friend had someone like Wales. She stepped past him and checked the corner, checking her left and front before scanning back toward the garage's front. Seeing no sign of the perp, she decided to run back up front and meet Wales in the middle.

She might even get to save his life; hoping the entire way, she wouldn't have to. The small front door was unlocked. The aroma of lube filled her nose, not as awful as any nail salon. She heard a faint radio and the tap of a wrench under one of three vehicles. She saw Wales as she stepped around to the open left and saw him pointing toward the ancient, green GMC pickup. Wales was closer and knelt down. Shannon waited for him to speak, but instead her fellow officer returned to his feet and waved her to the back. They scanned the rest of the fairly open shop. Shannon didn't ask, but Wales explained in a whisper toward the back, "It was just Danny, he didn't know we were on the place. Don't see any hidy-holes, you?"

Officer Shannon shook her head side to side with a gorgeous smile, "I'd say Dillon must moonlight here, because he never locks up the department, but he *is* missing and I don't want to joke about that."

Wales looked at her, almost grinned, and nodded in understanding, "You say you wanna check Carie's?" Shannon nodded in return and they stepped out to view the outside scene. "What was your reasoning, other than vicinity?"

Shannon frowned, and hesitated to speak, "I......m not sure, it just stood out to me on the way over, for some reason."

"Good enough for me. Let's look around the place first, what do you say?"

"Roger that." They could hear another car slide into place in the front of Danny's. "How 'bout we wait on the sheriff?"

"Yeah, read'n my mind."

Sheriff Edward Jenkins slid to the right of Officer Wales cruiser and made his escape less stealthily, but the difference between ages thirty-two and sixty-four was far greater than thirty-two years, it was multiplied by gravity and wear and goddamn tear. Jenkins had an irritable, yet healthy lack of respect for that fact. He also touted an immense amount of respect from his officers and the town he protected with his fair minded senses. His gray, thick hair and salt-and-peppered scruff seemed a perfect declaration that he was their elder sage, the one with a sense for what needed to be done.

Once free from the car, he made his way in the tracks of two of his best, aping their earlier approach. He was twenty-feet from the front corner of the long garage, when he saw Officers Shannon and Wales step around the far corner, guns drawn, pointed high and safe. They step towards him a few feet and waited, transmitting a sense to the sheriff that they wanted him to join them in the other direction. Fifteen-feet away, he said quietly, "Talk to me."

Shannon took the lead and explained her gut feeling on the Havored house and their plan to secure the perimeter before knocking, perhaps peeking in a window where possible. He agreed, but now with three, he told them to proceed with any questioning while he check the windows, back of the house and any outside buildings or hidy-holes. They gave the sheriff a head-start before stepping up to the front door for a knock. Sheriff Jenkins cleared the west wall and got a preliminary look of the back before he heard said knock.

Carie Havored sat on her back three steps, wishing she would've brought her coffee with her, but not enough to take the time to retrieve it. She was ten minutes into sitting here and now in a ruminating trance, eyes half focused on nothing as she stared at the blades of grass, in need of mowing, standing six-inches all over the back yard. Her red shorts were just visible in this position as the gray sweatshirt hung out over the sides of her bent lap, causing her torso to look lumpy and mismatched with her fit legs. Her knees and white legs exposed to the cool morning air. It felt nice, but mostly unnoticed by the half-awake thirty-eight-year old woman. She was almost past the concern that she let something wonderful go by without at word. She had since drifted on toward other hopes, losses and wistful beliefs - she was in a mood that was bizarrely stoic. She would have thought that she might have been spooked by another uninvited appearance, but she always thought Sheriff Jenkins was cute. And, it was almost as if she expected him. She turned passively toward him with a subtle smile, "Hey Sheriff. You just missed him." She said all of this so casually, it stunned the experienced law man. She returned to staring at nothing with no pretense about hosting her guest.

"Who?" He didn't think Tommy Havored's daughter was going to answer him. He'd met Tommy with his tour of the local fire department, before he died on duty ten years ago. "Who did I miss, Carie?"

She looked back toward him for all of a second before returning her gaze to the middle of the yard, "There was a young man that ran from the back of Danny's garage. He just ran around there all of what, eight minutes ago?"

"What makes you think I'm looking for him?"

"Oh...I...don't know, really, I just had a feeling I guess. Are you not?"

"Actually, I am. You're feelings were right. Did he do anything odd, or say anything to you?" He wanted to ask her more, questions were biting at the back of his tongue, but only because he wanted answers before any action started. Carie's demeanor was rather catchy. He felt like sitting and having a cup of Joe with her.

"No," she said simply, subtly playing with her toes on the bottom step, "Well, I was inside. I just happen to see him out my front window before he ran around the house. He did look troubled."

"Are you okay?" Sheriff Jenkins asked the young woman as he stepped closer, worried she might be hiding some injury or offense just wrought upon her.

"Yeah, just thinking." She looked into his eyes as he moved closer. She seemed to wake up completely now with a slight shake of her head, "No, I'm fine Sheriff, really. Thank you. He ran right around to the right of that old shed and disappeared. He looked as if there were much more going on than I could see, though. Please be careful if you're headed after him."

"I will Sweetheart, thank you. You mind stepping' inside and locking' up 'till we know he's out of the area?"

"Yes Sir, that's probably a really good idea."

"That's Officer Wales and Shannon at your front door. You think you could fill them in on the specifics while I look for the young man in question?"

She smiled at him for real this time and stood up, turned and entered her home. She wanted to hug the man, but didn't know him well enough for that.

Birth of The Maxx

His eye were already open, it was as if they were just finally focused for the first time. Nick was sixteen, two inches taller than the previous year and lanky as all-get-out. He didn't have any consistent nicknames in school, he was picked on randomly, mostly for his wrinkly, unwashed laundry and lack of money for anything, ever. Once for wearing girl-jeans; he didn't know, he just thought the two-toned pattern was kinda cool. He was the butt of jokes because everyone knew his Steps was Hank-The Tank-Forbus, but he was also saved from hearing those jokes, due to rumors of Officer Forbus' mythical sadism (half of which weren't true; he was mostly bark on the job, save for two severe occasions).

Nick kept his head down and though he had acquaintances from every click, he never felt safe with any of them, until Tommy. Home-life was hell, his school-life was in and out, mostly out. In between all of that was quiet moments of imagination play, and the all-too-brief stint with Skippy (Nick believed Hank knew, somehow, and ended the poor dog on purpose, relishing the awful act of erasing the boy's only friend).

There was the occasional teacher or student extending a laugh or genuine kindness and it touched Nick, but what of it. It would amount to nothing, because when school was done, Nick was gone. He would walk to the end of the earth to be as far away from the Step-Fuck as possible.

He actually found the farthest point from the man; Port-aux-Français. The French Southern and Antarctic Lands in the south Indian Ocean, the main settlement of the Kerguelen Islands. It's mild tundra climate and 45 residents in winter and 120 plus in the summer, sounded perfect. Its shallow seaport allows barges to offload supplies, it hosts scientific laboratories, technical stations, a cinema, small medical center and a small Catholic Church. The best part, no Hank Forbus. It was 18,000 kilometers from the broken down recliner, the farthest piece of land from this horrible home. The actual antipodal point was further north-east, in the middle of the ocean, so this would have to do. Oh, sweet imagination.

This particular day out of Nick's five-thousand-nine-hundred-and-thirteen-days, so far survived, involved a pivotal birth. A second fracturing broke free beneath his skin. Ten years prior, a six-year-old girl was phoenixed from his mother's abandonment. Nick was just five when he'd actually witnessed the girl in a mall. Hank took them shopping. Nick was forced to sit with Hank as he read the paper and Mom shopped for bras, whatever that was. The large man made Nick nervous, but it was a great place to watch people, on a bench, between stores. Thirty minutes in, he saw a black family, an old man, a younger woman, and even younger girl (probably his age). They stood out to the boy, because they were black, a real minority in Fairbanks, Illinois at the time. He found them richly exotic, wondering why they were so different. He watched the girl, wondering what her life was like, when the girl fell behind, drawn to a dress in one of the store windows. She stepped up to the window, while her family walked on oblivious. Nick watched silently, already having learned that life was easier when he was neither seen nor heard. He witnessed the girl turn to find her familiars gone; to see her face distort in fear, to crumple and create tears. He watched her experience the pain of being left and though his mother would never leave him, he felt half abandoned already. Her pain melded with his that day and Jay Jay was born. His empathy for her brought her alive within, to protect and play. What he didn't understand was that she was born to keep him sane in the hard years to come.

Jay Jay would be forever six and her new mate, forever sixteen. The birth of this second was as violent and tumultuous, as births can be. It was this violent first day that shaped his side, for he was merely a facet of another.

Hank bore The Maxx out of Nick like a proper, demon-midwife, hands at the ready and working hard, beating this second out of Nick's already fractured mind, without raising so much as a finger…to the boy. No doubt, Hank put the boy through his paces, day in and day out, but this was a special day, a day of surprises. This was the day that Nick's mother returned.

Nick's days routine by now: awaken, eat cereal (if there was any milk that day), walk the mile-and-a-half to school, put in his day, walk back home, explore outside or read (he'd learned a range of disciplines and psychology that way), wash dishes and prepare a meal for two, before Hank arrived (Nick always ate before, so there would be no question as to him breaking bread with the man). Nick was excited to finish a book he'd stumbled across in the school library, _Gnosis Onward: Volume III; The Ancient Atlantean Meditation_. PhD., D.D., Lewis E. Graham, taught the ancient Mystery School knowledge, found by Greek philosopher, Pythagoras. He was excited to study the practice and begin it right away. Pythagoras began his own Mystery School once he returned home, and required his students perform this meditation once a day for five years, before the first lesson. It was said that five years of this practice would give the student a clarity and focus of mind that would prepare him for what he was about to learn. Nick wanted this ancient knowledge, some mystical answer to his life of drudgery thus far.

This excitement died away as he found the driveway. There was an old Jeep parked just off the street. His first thought was hope, hidden behind a face that knew better. His second, defeat, strong, like soul strangling depression. He tried to breath through being so torn, as he jumped up on the porch. He reached his keys toward the loose lock, when the door opened. His calmed breath caught in his throat and chest; he wanted to run away, Jay Jay wanted him to run to the short, skinny woman that stood before him now. Mother Stone. He was pissed and so very happy and so very broken since he'd seen her last.

That voice was so immediately home, "Oh Nick....My Baby...." she cried as she reached for the boy, who knew not what to do. His hesitation caused her to stop, respecting his right to be pissed (it was this expectation that delay the visit for so long). Her heart was already scared and now trying not to break. "It's okay, Baby, I....I did this. I'm so sorry that I left you. I tricked myself into believing that he would chase us down and kill us both if I took you. I told myself that he would take care of you in ways that I couldn't and let us both live. I...."

Nick watched apathetically from behind Jay Jay's tears, who openly mourned within his chest. It was in this moment that The Maxx began to try and unfurl a soft, wet wing. Jay Jay was thinking this *could* be okay, maybe now everything could be good again. Nick was furious… and sad… and hurt, beyond action or words. Until the poor girl's tears won out, "Mom? How....... (tears) Why.....(a loud retching gasp)." Then a new idea came to Nick that filled him with hope and joy and movement, "Mom! We can leave now, together. We've got a couple of hours before Hank gets home." Nick was mad at her, but using her to get away would at least even the score, so they could start anew. Yes, it was perfect, to erase the baggage of the last twelve years. He could put it down and walk freely with her, the hell out of here.

Nick grabbed up the small, dark haired woman and popped her back in this physical plea for freedom. Mary's hair was longer, clothes drab (she wore yellow sweats that were too short, a thin white shirt beneath a tan knitted shawl and white Keds over short, white socks), she looked worn thin. This didn't matter, they could both do better, together. Where would they go, he considered in his racing mind. Where does she live now? "Give me five minutes, I'll grab my backpack and a few things." He was smiling, holding both of her frail arms, excited with Jay Jay's naive beliefs. "We can...."

She was shaking her head negatively and looking ashamed of herself (he didn't like this), "Nick, Baby, I...." She grabbed his hands with her own and pulled him weakly to a stop, "I'm not here to take you with me. I'm on my way to a shelter, where maybe they can help me. It's a woman's shelter and they don't allow boys...or young men," she finished taking stock of her sixteen-year-old. "I have a problem with addiction and....I need help. I can't help you. I can't be good for you, right now. I...I just wanted to..."

Nick's face glazed over for all of them, it was Jay Jay that nodded slightly, silently. The single tear condensed from the hot flush of Jay Jay's disappointment and the cold heart of old lava that crusted over completely within Nick's chest. The hardening was the freezing chrysalis that would break open to become The Maxx. The still forming trio walked in Nick's body to the sink.

He had a job to do and it would keep their hands from doing something bad. Their stomach ached as Nick picked up the first bowl and the drying sponge to the right of the sink. He started the faucet to wait for the warm water and dropped some liquid soap on the sponge. Jay Jay sniffed and The Maxx saw the crack of first light.

Mary collapsed in on herself at the door, looking in at her offspring; contemplating if she could just take him now? Could she stay clean for him, keep him safe? Could she give him something, anything to make up for all she'd left him with? She didn't feel strong enough. Would it lessen his bleeding if she just ripped off the bandage and took her leave for good? Could she just turn and walk away? No, she decided, he deserved her at her best. She would help him with the dishes, try to warm his heart and leave him long enough to get herself clean. She was in a bad way the last two years, in too many bad places, all because of the cowardice that kept her away. So, taking him was not an option, but it put her path right. She had work to do, but then she would return to take this boy where ever he wanted to start over.

This thought led her in the old house, nothing about the place looked different since the night she scurried away, a touch dingier perhaps (but her soul was too tainted to judge). She closed the door slowly, feeling of the same drapes over the small front door window that she'd put up so long ago. She dreamily made her way back, silent in her reverie and solemn in her endeavor to show her son the love, that he'd been without for ten years, was still abeat in her chest.

Nick was blurry beneath the emotional storm churning in his gut. He was oblivious to her approaching presence, her tiny footsteps, as he washed his third plate, his guts boiled up a warning. She touched him. The warmth of her hand on his back was incalculable. Soothing in a way he forgot existed. He dropped the plate and ran for the bathroom. Mary heard the door lock behind the slammed door and her son growling and gagging beyond it.

Her heart went out to him, if she could only make him believe that. She stepped up and held the old door like she had just touched him, wanting to go to him, to be his loving nurse maid, but she wouldn't break the door open to do that. He deserved whatever space he asked for.

She stepped back to the sink and continued what he'd

started, hoping to bring them both some sense of closure before leaving. She got the plate Nick dropped rinsed and on the dishrag to the left of the sink. She only hoped he'd come back out well before Hank came home. She had planned to face him, certain she could now, but just being back here made her question her own convictions. She'd become certain it was in their best interest to be gone before the man's return, when the front door behind her.

Mary closed her eyes, hoping against hope, that Nick had crept out of the bathroom and made a dash for it, wrong again. It was her husband's stunned face, quickly transformed into a grinning, dark mask of calculation. Her heart stopped, she thought, but realized that it was beating so fast it was a hum. His name was on her tongue, a stab at civility, but there was not enough breath to carry it out of her mouth.

In the bathroom, Nick wiped his mouth and pulled away from the nasty toilet to lay his folded arms onto the dirty floor and his head into his arms. His fists hit the floor as he shifted to lay in this child's pose and the solid thump reverberated into his soul and felt satisfying in an animal way. He thrummed the floor again, and again, like a tribal drummer; growling with the beating fists. The edge of both hands were already singing their defense, but the release was too pleasing. His beating grew stronger, as did his guttural mantra. He was drooling manically, wet from eyes to chin and swaying up and down on his knees, like a Shaman vanquishing a white god. The old house was barren of insulation, to the cold and to the sound shared so freely from room to room. Nick was lost to his parents last fight, however, just as they were lost to his emotional purge.

"Well, well. Mary Fuck'n Forbus. How in the fuck are you, my dear? Oh, the conversations I've had with you. Well, not with you, you understand. Considering you WEREN'T FUCKING HERE! What, nothing to say?" Hank walked his way deep inside her personal space. It wilted her like the pretty flower she was. She had no answers he was interested in, she had no space that was her own any longer. She was crack-headed enough to stroll back into his house as if he had no right for payback! She was his in Hank's play-book, and his chest and hands had a purging of their own. Mary felt the warm urine dripping from her yellow sweat-panted crotch, too frozen in fear to be embarrassed.

Hank took a cathartic breath and opened a clenched fist to rub the back of it down her cheek. He started to speak, but felt the entangling pains need to rage beyond his control. He took her tiny face his enormous hands and pulled her up nearly off her feet, lowering his head to kiss her like a one-sided love-fest. She didn't fight, but her frozen heart wouldn't allow her to fake anything so horrendous. Hank wanted to be mad that she wouldn't play along, but he actually understood. He launched her up by her head and grabbed her around the waist, pulling her into him, still the mad lover. He used her limp body long enough to realize that he no longer had enough vitality to get an erection.

He pulled her legs around his middle and held her

bottom. He pulled her face to his neck with the other hand and whispered malevolently as he rocked her from side to side like a father/daughter dance. "Look what you've done to me. I was so strong and willing for you. I know I wasn't easy, but I would've done so much for you, gone so far. And, now I'm nothing more than a bigger husk caked around a smaller heart. There is just enough spark to wish this all could've been different."

Mary couldn't move, scared to breath, heart in pain, modesty not wanting her urine rubbed into his shirt. She shook her head in double time to his waltz.

"What? I'm sorry, you wanna say something?" Hank's rage grabbed her by the scruff and pulled her now clinging body away from him so he could look her in the eye. She appeared to be feigning sleep, not wanting to deal with him. "You were always such a GODDAMN COWARD!"

He lowered her useless feet to the floor, held her there to grab the tiny pale face in the same hand and pinched her cheeks until her mouth opened. Her worn and blackened teeth exposed for the inspection of her husband's judgment. "Ahhh, had a little meth in the mouth, have we? Mary Fuck'n' Forbus! Are you a junkie now? Huh?" Hank squeezed her jaw hard enough to pull a cry from Mary, "I BET THAT'S NOT ALL YOU'VE HAD IN YOUR MOUTH IS IT? IS IT?" Hank screamed this with a fetid fury all for Mary's inhalation. His face contorted and trembled with it, his hand flowing with ten years of compounding ire for the woman squirming between his fingers.

Throughout this tirade, Hank fished his fingers in her

mouth, daring her to bite him as he dug around for her tongue...the smell of urine told him he had nothing to worry about and his anger didn't care. His anger told him that she could bite with all her might, but he would have her tongue. He clamped his thumb and two first fingers on the wet, squirming organ and pulled hard enough to pull it loose from one side of the bottom of her mouth where it was anchored into the hyoid bone. 'She couldn't even scream right,' was all Hank could think. It felt good to him, but just a the tip of a start of his welling fury.

Hank was even more pissed at her weakness, for the lack of fight in her. He didn't just want to play, he wanted her to stop him, if only she sounded stern, it might just be enough to stop him; to save herself and him from what he couldn't stop himself. So much so, that he repositioned to hold her up by the temples and attempted to squeeze her skull. Mary Anna Stone Forbus moaned cries of gibberish. He imagined it crumbling like chalk, but when it gave as easily as he'd hoped, he was as stunned as she.

Don't fight, don't make it worse; this was the mantra that kept her imprisoned with the man for so long; it was also the motto that carried her through her addiction as she failed to grow strong enough to fight her way back to the light, back to her son.

Hank was slobbering as he squished the mortal coil that clung to the woman, the life she couldn't let go of quick enough. Just as he was beginning to feel sorry for her, her pain caused her to appear to smile. He grimaced so hard it hurt his jaws and reseated his palms into the already dented skull. Hank didn't know the frontal, parietal, temporal, and sphenoid sheets of skull all met here, he just reacted; as helpless to his rage as she, her fear. All he knew was the red that snapped and bit, that prodded him on to force his feelings into this face was strong enough to win. The red was the trigger that pulled at his bullet. He was a tool to the abuse that had trained him so well.

It was where these layers of skull connected, that gave way and pierced Mary's Meningeal artery, with no skin laceration. Seeing no blood and only her eyes rolled up in her head, Hank's anger gave him one final push and he loosened his hands before slamming them together with all he had left; hammering her temples. There was a pop, that only Mary could've heard, were she not beyond hearing. Hank fumed, pulling his hands away, slowly drifting into a soft stare out the kitchen window.

The limp body fell almost silently to the floor. Mary's pain was no longer registered by her dorsal posterior insula, as it was damaged in the final injury. It ended with a pop and her vision rolled black and white like a poor television signal.

Unmeasured moments drifted by, before Hank realized he felt the beating in the floor, heard the growling from the bathroom wall. He looked down, now fascinated by the malfunctioning robot before him. Her eyes were rolled up to the point that her irises bobbed up and down like a shade pulled to full length and released. The epidural hematoma brought about by that final pop, filled Mary's skull with blood. Mary's body shut down as it struggled to function within the building pressure. This oncoming bulging brain tissue could have been corrected by a surgeon removing a piece of skull to release the blood and therefore the pressure, then repairing the lacerated meningeal artery, but Hank opted to sweep, her too, under his dirty rug. He walked her by the shoulders, over to the couch and pushed her onto it. He didn't want her dying stench in his chair. It was his only sanctuary.

It was after Nick cleaned the toilet from his sick and the floor from his raging drool, that he washed his hands, face and mouth, in that order. He wanted her to be gone when he came out. He wanted her to have changed her mind and waited for him. He angrily wished her dead, and then immediately took it back. That wasn't true, he just didn't know why it had to be so damn hard? Then, it occurred to him. He made his first real decision for himself; he would leave with her whether she was okay with it or not. She could drop him off and run off again, but he wouldn't be left behind in this shit hole ever again.

He didn't know what to expect, but it felt good making a stand for once. It was having Nick's most regrettable wish granted that broke the last of The Maxx's containment. The Maxx was sixteen but hard, virtuous in his yearning for freedom and practical in his self protection. It was The Maxx who guided Nick to a quiet, dark spot and bid him sleep while he handled the clean up that Hank lay upon the poor boy's lap, yet again. Maxx saw things in a way that brought beauty to the most vile situations. The de-sparked woman -mother- was seen as abstract lines of color in a painting; black feathers of hair, tan knit over white shoulder, curving mouth corner (twitchy), eye lid all a flutter. The newborn saw the result of dancing neurons, the flight of dust motes in the fading sunlight of the west facing window and marveled. He saw the day's light on the porch wood, worn in its white paint and inhaled for the first time. He saw the police cruiser's huge trunk lid open like the welcoming mouth of a predator, with one victim on its ledger already. He saw the darkness of this trunk accept his gift, his prize, his lost matriarch. He smelled the dog that once befriended his master and inhaled deeper. He remembered beautifully what Nick could never know and he bit his tongue ever after to keep it that way, relishing every sensation, animal-like.

Unhunted

Beyond the white house was a dilapidated shed, old white paint stood like lone feathers on gapped boards, some loose and slanted. Nick appreciated the outbuilding as he ran past it, wanting to lay down inside and gaze upon the rays of light the gaps allowed, like a hundred spotlights on the forgotten nothings; that lay about like an old man's toys abandoned by the work of their youth. The island of tall grass that held the structure aloft and apart from the surrounding cut grass, spoke of years of growth. Two saplings grew out from under the discarded structure, along the path Nick ran. He fought the urge to stop, to smell the old wood and dusty inside; the tinny tasting adrenaline at the back of his tongue driving him on. It was the taste of fear.

Behind the building was a fine cut clearing, an unused but not abandoned lot. It ran like an alley between a row of houses and a thick barrier of thorn bushes that cut off the woods beyond. Ahead, within this alley, was another lot of taller grass surrounding an abandoned house, one set of shutters missing around the window, right of the door and to its left, a window missing one shutter, with the other hanging askew and ever so slightly swaying with the breeze in a lazy, apocalyptic dance. Nick, irritable from the buzzing in his brain, ran up and kicked the door, wanting to break something.

The Maxx stopped him from entering once the door was compromised, revealing the dusty, lost home. The Maxx had Nick by the traps, like a friend, "Dude, you can't stay here. Let me carry us on, please? We'll all know when it's right, but that's not here." Nick always heard The Maxx when he spoke, but he thought it was his conscious, his Jiminy Cricket. He knew, too, that it was his wiser self. What he didn't know was that The Maxx could take over for him, take him over like a parasitic friend. He knew of missing time, but he, like the rest of us, assumed he was just lost in thought while moving in auto-pilot. Nick also didn't know this fractured part of himself, this young protector, took the name of one of Tommy's favorite animated comic-book characters. Nick would have loved it too, had the opportunity ever presented itself. Tommy kept trying to show his buddy, but Mom or Dad was always watching or the elusive chance to climb atop the roof was more appealing.

Nick looked The Maxx in the eye for all of two seconds before dropping his head in submission, grateful for the opportunity to drop the reigns, and effortlessly fall away. He was confused and scared, high on uncertainty and loss. He knew something was amiss, but he kept losing the thread of what exactly that was. Memories began pulsing throughout his body, seeming to propel him back and forth in time, to and fro in space, moment to moment, each as real as the last. Flashes of the corner of a smile, a twitchy corner; eyes rolled to the whites; convulsing hands and arms...and head. And then it was gone as Nick slept in the Fireman's carry over The Maxx's shoulder.

The Maxx carried them all, save for Jay Jay who walked beside him, holding and swinging his hand. No one else could see this, of course, it was all symbolic, but if a sugar pill can cure afflictions with the brain's belief that it will, what isn't symbolic in our lives? Jay Jay smiled and looked up to him, asking him 'why' about this and that and everything. They discussed the sky, the silly and magnificent cloud formations and every now and again, she would ask about Maxx's plan for getting them back to the tripping road (that was fun. She only ever called him Maxx). He didn't treat her like a child, but he didn't give her all of the gory details either, she was six years old. She felt the weight of Nick, just as Maxx did, but she didn't mind that. She knew in wisdom beyond her stilted years, that anything out of her control was to be accepted and dealt with. Not butted and rammed with futile attempts to change the unchangeable.

What she didn't like was the other load, the recently bared dark load, and his missions; whatever they were. He dismissed her and Maxx and Nick for their softer way, their whiny need for food and help and...whatever. He was very condescending. She would help Maxx carry them both for now, but she wondered if Maxx had a plan for losing the loser. She knew not to ask him about it though, she felt he was asleep, but they were never really alone. She thought of it like having a Siamese twin removed from your back, snip snip and gone. She hoped that was something they could do. Vexatious people made life intolerable when they were ever on your mind; worse yet inside. There might not be enough space in the world to make breathing the same air as him, tolerable, but darn sure not within the same body.

The Maxx assumed they were being followed, and if they weren't it was no biggie, his paranoia wouldn't hurt them and it just might save them. He knew Nick's car was missing and he knew who had it, or more precisely, who hid it from Nick. He'd get it back, if only for Tommy. Tommy was his friend too.

Thomas Cates drug behind by the ankle, The Maxx and the girl. He liked The Maxx. He was much cooler than Nick or the girl, but he might have to put him down, to work against him in the end. He didn't truly know if he could be put down without them all suffering the same consequences. The rules to this game dumbfounded them all. Just as Nick thought of them as figments of his imagination, their real force of taking over and laying him dormant would be a case of trial and error. Cates' saw The Maxx and Jay Jay, just as Nick did, he assumed. He didn't know Nick's own self doubt made him chalk them up to a continuation of his child's-play. This, Cates knew, was a competition, but he didn't know if there were ways to win against them; or for them to lose without him losing too.

Survival was key, but only for the mission. He lay loose as they pulled him along, watching, listening. He enjoyed the luxury of their work and their goal of protecting the whole, but the rest of the world could go to hell. Jesus Christ, most people would sell you or kill you for a goddamn candy-corn that you found in the street. The world was populated with worm fodder and sweet, innocent girls, unlike the one currently dragging him by one ankle now. She was irritating as hell and about as goody-goody as one gets. He knew her mind and it was a mix of the other two bed fellows he had to sleep with. She wanted to save the world and force the innocent to suffer through it all; to save them from the sanctuary of death, that Cates was here to offer.

Sharing their skin was too much sometimes, most times, it hurt and just didn't work, not for his mission (though he had a keen eye for opportunity and a tricky sense for how to turn their path into his own. Cates' back story was real to him and made his time stretch much further behind him than reality knew. He had work to do and they worked against it on the reg. It wasn't hard to stay ahead of them, but it was work, and to share their goddamn mind without letting them discover his intentions! Tight quarters and a mighty warmth in these rhinos! It was work not to let it all be too much.

The Maxx walked them past another gathering of four houses seemingly placed willy-nilly in a two acre space to the east before the sparse trees began to take over the landscape. Fortunately, the thorn thickets had run their course behind. He'd turned them south, leaving the houses to their back. Jay Jay loved the mood it lent the walk, a playful one by her skipping. Maxx approved because it was away from people and provided hiding places for those that might still be in pursuit. Thomas didn't give two shits, he could handle whatever was thrown at him and Nick, well, Nick slept on dreaming of road tripping with Tommy in the Duster of their remaking.

Lost Tracks

Officer Wales interrogated Ms. Havored, though Officer Shannon wanted to refute that fact. He pussy footed around a real interrogation, but she knew he knew her, could tell by their comfortable banter and was glad that Wales didn't lose his professional demeanor in spite of his obvious softness for the woman. She supposed they might have been friends in school, though she thought she might have to ask him about it sometime.

She watched the woman, the questioning and fought the urge to butt in, but she knew she was feeling petty and didn't want to be that person. She wasn't sure why this woman irritated her, there was no past for her to be upset about. So, she kept her mouth to herself and let the officer do his job. Havored was credible for what it was worth, though somewhat, lackadaisical in Shannon's opinion, as if she'd just smoked a bunch of weed, but there was no aroma or masking thereof. She decided to let it go and look around at the pictures in the woman's living room.

"So, once he ran past your shed, you didn't see him again."

"Right, he....he's just gone."

Shannon saw a small picture frame on a faux mantel on the living room wall, showing three girls, all about thirteen in Shannon's estimate. She could tell that Havored was the middle girl. She wondered where the other two were. She felt a softer spot for the woman now, as if she had a real history that was probably just as important to her as Shannon held her own. This brought the officer back to sensibility and duty. She breathed in the relief of her balance and let Wales finish what he started with no interruptions, glad she was strong enough to keep quiet.

"Alright, well, thank you for you help and you should lock your doors for a few days, if you don't already. We have reason to believe he is troubled in some way. Alright Carie?"

She looked up to the officer as she sat on the couch now, seemingly lost to something that couldn't be seen. She smiled that simple smile of some deeper understanding, one that didn't seem to make sense to her just yet, "Yes Sir, I will do that. Thank you," she added, and then with a look to Officer Shannon, "Thank you."

Shannon smiled back and nodded in affirmation. She looked to Wales who gave her a nod and they walked back out the front door together, leaving the stoic woman to her thoughts and her position on the couch.

"What do you make of that?" Shannon asked Wales.

"I'm not sure, but I have a feeling it doesn't have anything to do with the young man we're looking for. Perhaps it made her take stock of her life, in some way?"

Shannon enjoyed Wales wisdom, even if she wasn't sure that he was right, but it felt right. Perhaps Havored felt a connection with the young man, who knew and did it really matter? For some reason, right now, it did to Shannon.

Officers, Wales and Shannon stepped around to the south of the house to join their sheriff, who was just stepping back into the Havored yard on the path to the south of the shed out back. They stepped toward one another and gathered between the house and shed.

"Did you see anything, Sheriff?" Wales asked.

"What few signs there were petered out just beyond the shack, here." He gestured with a thumb toward the old storage shed. "What'd you learn?"

Shannon shook her head to the negative, but let Wales answer. He said, "She saw him run at the house and around it. She thought he was coming to get her, that he was going to hold her hostage simply because of vicinity, but he just ran on by. She seemed bothered, but I think she's just caught up in her own thing right now. I tell you that, only because it might be more than that, but I just don't think so."

Sheriff Jenkins looked down between their feet as he seemed to think this over. He rubbed a finger and thumb at the salt and pepper scruff on his chin. "I caught some of that as well, and I know well enough to know that you've got good instincts and I trust 'em. Any other feelings either one of you'd like to share?" He looked from officer to officer.

Shannon felt compelled, "Since I was the only one to actually speak with the young man, I guess I'll tell you what I picked up. I don't think he meant to be deceptive in anyway. He genuinely seemed to be seeing someone and, I think, hearing them. I'm not sure if this invisible one was speaking to him at all, but I got the feeling the other one was speaking to me, in the boys mind that is. It was the way he was looking from me to the other. Having said that, Dillon is still missing, as far as I'm aware. That is what prompted the alert for backup, he asked for Dillon. That is really all I know, but it feels to me that this boy has a foot in more worlds than this one. He may be in as much danger as anyone else."

"Noted, thank you Officer. The question now is, do we check every house due east or go back to the office and see if we can find anything out about Dillon? Let's do both, Shannon, go back to the office and keep us updated on Dillon. Wales, you check the Shelly block, you know, Webb Shelly's place?"

"Is that Mortin Shelly's mom and dad's place, back over beside Timothy Duncan's?"

"It is. Go door to door, keep your eyes out and trust your gut." Jenkins turned back toward the shed as if he were done; orders given, talking done.

"Sheriff, what are you gonna do?"

He turned back to Shannon, all business, "I'm going due east, see what I see. See how good my tracking skills are."

Tommy and The Maxx

School was never a favorite place for Nick, and still a damn sight better than home, even before Mom got the hell out of Dodge. She was always sad and somber. A subdued parent makes for a depressing childhood; speaking of half-life. After she came back and so suddenly taken out for good, The Maxx was wrenched into being. He was bright and ravenous for life. He would peek out from over Nick's shoulder, studying the world and gleaning what could be learned from Nick's experiences. A week later, too curious to stay inside, The Maxx met Tommy.

Nick had been hiding in plain sight, in Geography class, as he did in every other class, when The Maxx watched the young, dark and curly headed boy sit in front of Nick. He was fascinated by the boy's approach, audacious was the only word The Maxx had learned yet to convey such leanings. Later, perspicacious would better fit his thoughts on Tommy.

"Hey," he whispered to Nick, turning his handsome, bright eyes on them. Mr. Janson had finished his twenty-minutes of teaching and now was time to take notes from the lessons on the board and from chapter twelve for a test tomorrow. "I was thinking. Why don't we buy Old Man Duncans' old jalopy. I was looking it over yesterday, ha, there is a tree growing through the back floorboard. Isn't that funny?"

"I don't know anything about cars." The Maxx knew this was true, but he was attempting to prod more out of his benefactor. 'We could try?'

"I know some, but, we'll learn the rest together. Come on, Dude! You always turn me down. I've been trying to get you to join me forever now."

"I just...I can't just come and go as I please. I..."

"I'll get my dad to talk to your dad."

"My step-dad..." Nick corrected him, "and, that's probably not a good idea…he," rolling his eyes to the side.

"Your step-dad, sorry. Look, Dad'll make it okay, and if he can't, we will. I'll get it all set up and...It'll be fun. We can go riding around in it. We'll share it."

"Are you gay?" Nick lashed out in anger, disbelieving the young man could really just like him as a friend. It was pent up yearning to escape, and words from the very man who kept him that way.

Still, Tommy looked compassionate, "Don't be that way. I don't believe I am gay, but who knows. I don't find you sexually attractive, though, if that is what you are asking. I just think you're cool, or could be if you'd ever wake the fuck up." Okay, his face hardened on that last bit. That hurt Nick, to know he would dare strike out at such a big heart who only ever showed kindness.

Silence bit at Nick, he felt ashamed. He placed a timid hand on Tommy's shoulder, closed his eyes and said, "I'm sorry. I'm afraid my step-dad may be wearing off on me. Thank god you want to."

Tommy laughed, "Well, I don't want to rub off on you. I just want you to help me bring an old car to life. I never said anything about anyone rubbing anything." They both laughed at his slight toward Nick's homophobic tone.

The Maxx was eager and in disbelief that Nick was

going to brush this off and avoid Tommy. He would have too, if The Maxx hadn't stepped forward. Nick would never remember that lost moment, or how he and Tommy had surpassed the differences between them. "You know what," The Maxx said with a smile, "I will do it." It was the first complete smile Tommy had ever seen on the boy and he was enamored with it.

"There you go! You won't regret it, Nick, this is gonna be fun." The Maxx grinned through Nick's face. Thank the Gods for The Maxx.

Graduation Morning

The Dodge, Duster's keys felt heavy in Hank's hand. When he was done putting on a tough face for the boy, he marveled at the weight of them. It was almost as if they were a talisman of some sort, a sacred object in some magic curio shop in China Town somewhere. Sitting silently next to the box that contained Gizmo (the gremlin maker), waiting for that perfect, forever home. He reflected on the boy flashing at him when he demanded the keys. There was something, a flame that bore into him. He saw strength, but the heat of it was felt. He pretended not to know what to make of it, did his best to forget it altogether, but it led him down an alley of nightmares that night.

As usual, Hank drank himself to sleep (it was the only way to stop the PTSD of how big a fool he was for Mary…and the blood…the feeling of her skull giving in his hands), this Saturday night, watching Ultimate Fighting Championship (sometimes Nova, sometimes the History Channel). He always watched the replays, he wasn't going to pay the bastards for their precious pay-per-view live matches, not when that sixty-nine dollars would buy two weeks worth of beer. He enjoyed the sport, though, and watched the free replays as often as he could. It was match number 203, before falling asleep ten minutes in to the hour long UFC's Favorite Knock Outs. It was actually a minute long commercial for Insta-Light that Hank fell into. His brain saw the man tripping in the dark on his way to his garbage can in the commercial. His eyes witnessed the man tossing the garbage into the air before his subconscious mind created its own ending to the ridiculous commercial as he fell into sleep.

Hank found himself in the scene, actually catching the airborne bag of garbage. He thought, 'Geeez, at least make it a believable toss, dammit man.' Hank felt the weight of the bag and the need to shoot it back like a basketball, when he was distracted by the Insta-Light coming on. It was a battery powered security light, but when it came on, it proved only to expose the darkness all around. Hank lowered the bag and looked for the ground beneath him, but there was none. It was eerie, like he was surrounded by space. Hank was six-four and well over two-hundred pounds since he was sixteen, just over three-hundred since not long after the boy's mother left. He thought he liked space, because the world was always too small for him, hell, even his favorite chair was too small and mostly broken down at this point. This much space was troubling, however, very discombobulating.

As soon as he really began to question what he was standing on, the light suddenly shot upward away from him. Then, as his body began to realize it was turning with no surface to contain the gravity that pulled at him, he knew he was falling away from the light, falling from his place in the world. He felt no wind in his hair, just as he heard no whoosh of wind rushing past his ears. He began to question this vacuum, if it was the atmosphere-less space he'd heard so much about, as he slept through programs like Nova.

His mind fought to understand where he could be falling to and then trying to comprehend if he was indeed falling. It seemed as if he was flipping in place with the light rushing up away from him, but now he was simply lost to the twisting darkness, not even sure if he was twisting now without the light for visual confirmation. He felt nothing, even as he tried to feel his own middle with his hands. He couldn't feel himself, even the sense of moving his hands were lost to the nothing; as if his lost eyesight stole all other senses. He began to speculate whether his body still existed at all. Was he just his mind now, with no feeling, just thought?

Hank was lost to the confusion of size and space with no sight or sound or physical feeling. It was when the sheer vastness of that possible space began to scare him, making him feel the raised hairs on the back of his neck, making him dizzy, that he saw something. He could see a light, a pin prick in the utter lack of anything. And, yes, he was twisting ever faster, or the light was dashing around him at impossible speeds. The visible scene could have been the sun for its overpowering pull of his eye. It was simply a growing spec of light, it quickly became a shiny scalpel lunging at him out of a room.

It was only after he felt the flesh of his face open and began to drip that he realized it was Mary's hand and that she was standing in his kitchen. She grew out of the darkness like a fish-eyed-lens caricature of herself, the reflected light coming from the old tan tile of the kitchen floor (simply a fleck of background behind her thin stalk of a body that grew wider as it grew closer to him), so that the lethal blade and raging hand blocked out the scene as it slashed across his vision.

Hank jumped back into his senses, the cool beer

wetting the dome of his stomach, seeing that he was back in his dirty living room, in the old, comfortable recliner in front of an infomercial of HerSnuggle. Hank's attention was so quickly taken by the curvy, skin-toned pillow, that his fear of the nightmare was quickly overridden. It was the attractive woman snuggling up around the product that drew his eye and middle heat, or what was left of it in his mistreated body. He couldn't stop his mind from wondering about modifying the pillow to meet his particular specifications for sex before snuggling, but his bladder and laziness overrode the dusty, sexual desires and urged him to the bathroom. CLICK sounded the television, followed by the CREAK CREAK of the lopsided chair and the old wooden floor with every step to the lou. He was in his routine again, feeling nothing but the pain of being heavy and forgotten to his youth, save for the small shudder preceding the pushing away of the troubling darkness and the shudder of the warm urine leaving his body. Hank CREAKED his way to the broken down bed and found sleep again.

He slept in his rut, and that familiar, unremembered darkness until just before dawn. The growing light streaming over the details of his bedroom, through half turned, thin blinds, began to catch his almost closed eyes. They were the disturbing, open eyes of someone sleeping, looking dead and disturbing to anyone who sees them. The sparse decor in the room, were the same objects that the boy's mother had decorated with before she left him harnessed with the boy. An old dresser, centered across from the foot of the bed, matching night stands that were skinny legged and simple with a foot high, short back-shelf that was open and sat above the lower table top. An antique coat and hat rack in the corner, just out of reach of the open bedroom door. There once were two lamps that sat upon these small top shelves on either side of the bed, but Hank broke them both in two separate fits of anger after Mary left. They weren't replaced because he didn't need light to sleep.

The coat and hat rack was a golden pole upon a simple splayed foot. It terminated six-feet above with four six-inch hooks symmetrically placed with a decorative crown at the top. The crown was actually the logo for the Crowning Stand company that made the very popular racks in the twenties before going bankrupt during The Depression. Hank had not moved anything, not because he didn't want to see change, but because it never occurred to him. Everything worked where it was and he never thought about it. He didn't know how much better it would feel to move these three items, much less the items in every other room, if not replacing them altogether. He was too preoccupied with carrying his shitty life around on his tired shoulders to notice or imagine that things could be different. He had beers to drink, a chair to ride and endless, meaningless television to watch. It actually called to him, because it was his meditation. He didn't connect or even register half of what he saw, his mind was free to roam and plunder and be, like his physical body never was.

It was the growing light on the unpolished, golden surface of the hat-rack that caught his sleeping eye. He was a side-sleeper, and though it hurt his overly encased ribs to do so, he couldn't fall asleep if not folded up in this fetal position. He never questioned why, he just did, but if he could've articulated why, he would have said that the house was just too quiet. He didn't sleep with a fan because Mary hadn't bought one and he didn't buy things, he didn't shop. He used what he had and didn't question. The white noise of a fan might have given him some added peace and deeper sleep, but his was not to ask why. So, one ear lost to noise, buried up into his pillow, was just enough to cover that eerie quiet.

He slept on the edge, facing out toward the door even though he had the entirety of the old queen sized mattress to himself. With one armed folded beneath his pillow growing numb, he saw the reflected pink light of dawn on the golden rack as a crack of light that was suddenly opened. It was a streetlight shining directly into his eyes and what opened was another eye looking back at him... No, hmmm, the enormous lid of a car's trunk? His police cruiser's trunk, as he began to realize what must be happening. The crack of light was the outside world and he was tied up in his trunk, bound so he couldn't move, and the boy was standing before him, seven years old and crying. Hank could smell death or rot or something similar.

Hank was surprised to see the boy crying, assuming the tears were for him. Was he hurt, tied up and kidnapped and the boy was here to save him? The boy's tear tracked face seemed familiar, from a specific moment, but what? Now he saw the pajama top the boy was wearing, faded and thin, but Hank could make out the little white, trash-can robot, or toaster or whatever the hell it was. "Ohhhh, this is...that....Oh GOD NO!" Hank's lamented moaning was all that would come. He realized with terror that he was where that damn dog had been. Sometime after the boy's mama left them, he hit the German Shepherd, he thought. It was here, in his patrol car's trunk, where he put the broken mutt. The terror that raised his hackles was the shape the dog was in. Hank began to feel the injuries the dog had died from: a broken spine bending severely in the middle, two broken back legs with two exposed bone ends showing from one, and a bloody, dented head.

He knew he was the goddamn dog now, he was the broken mutt and the boy was here to bury him (there was one other possibility, but Hank's mind wouldn't go there, it clamped to the mere thought of who else he might be, the woman, the fuel for his sleep-limited, drunken nights, rendering comatose the rest of his brain). Hank cried realizing the moaning was his own broken voice trying to escape the now broken body.

Hank didn't remember terrorizing the boy before tripping off to bed, but he knew it was cleaned up and assumed the boy had taken care of it. He also remembered finding the bloody rag under the kitchen sink three days later. It was the rancid smell that made his stomach churn. He beat the boy for being disgusting and taught him a lesson about evidence. Hank's mind knew the scene must have gone similar to what the boy was now showing him. The boy was trying to stop crying, trying to touch him before pulling him free of the car and fighting the need to throw up the entire time.

He was speaking, mumbling as if to the animal, but Hank couldn't make it out. He figured the boy probably said some dumb-ass, touchy, feeley, bullshit, his mama would have said, about love or heart or good...please! Hank cried, now angry, and watch as the boy pulled him out of the bathroom sized trunk. He saw the edge of his house's roof and the far off neighbors junked up lot behind his own house. The boy laid Hank down carefully (as carefully as a seven-year-old weakling can) and retrieved Hank's shovel and dug and cried and dug and cried. Hank tried to look around, but couldn't change his line of sight, stuck on the scene at hand. He watched the boy and tried to scream him aware, "Boy! I know you hear me, Boy! I'm not the Goddamn Dog, DO YOU HEAR ME? HEY! DON'T BURY ME, NICK!"

Finally the boy walked back over to him and used his hands to grab at something below Hank's sight. Hank could see he was being pulled toward the boy, closer and closer until his sight appeared to show him falling into a hole, A GRAVE! "Nick, please, I'm not dead. I'M NOT DEAD, KID!" Hank's moaning only grew in Hank's mind as the small kid-sized shovelfuls fell over his sight. "AAAHHHHHHHH! MMMMMMMMMMNM!"

Hank lurched up in this last scream too quickly to realize it was the hat rack that started this nightmare. He was out of breath and drenched in sweat. The thin sheet he slept with was a dirty white and half off of him, exposing his left leg up to the same colored tighty-whiteys that were his pajamas. "Goddammit," he purged between heavy breaths before groaning to stand and walk to the hall bathroom to pee blood, as he had been most mornings for the last six months. He didn't like it, but the show must go on, right? What could a man do? He was struck by how badly he wanted to live. He couldn't understand why. Then, he realized that he was scared of what came next; what had he earned from his actions in this life?

Graduation Afternoon

Hank was disturbed. He'd never been a healthy sort, was raised with a trashy diet and held firm to that fine tradition. He ran in high school gym, but was always the last to finish because of his weight. He wanted to be a runner. Watching the young boys and girls around him run so fast, it looked so effortless, like they were flying. He wanted that, but getting picked on over and over again, "…slower than my Grandma," "Look'it his tits bounce," defeated him. Easier to hate the skinny little shits, than to be like them. So, his momentum increased with his weight. It was easier to push people around half you weight. Mary had made him happy once, or as much as he knew how to be, but she was so timid, scared of her own shadow. He couldn't get her to be herself, to be bold and open with him. Not that he was good at sharing feelings, but she had nothing to share, ever. He wondered if she had the capacity to think. He hated to believe that she was using him to give her boy a Dad, but it was hard to discount; especially after she left.

Since then, Hank hadn't slept a whole night through. The beer was self-medication. He didn't want to go to bed, but he so wanted to sleep and sleep some more. He was exhausted and there was no end in sight.

He remembered the feeling of the trunk, but not much else. The details were lost to his over-weighted, overly-pickled and overly fatigued mind. He was a man of the now. Tomorrow mattered about as much as yesterday (which was not at all), and his goal at every turn was to get to his chair, beer in hand and numb his brain with the television. It worked, it soothed him and it kept away all of those awful thoughts that ran at him when he wasn't in that spot, in that chair, in front of that TV. It was a comfortable living death. His life outside of that numb place was irritable, awful. Depression marinated in heartache and shame, with a crumb topping of fury.

He felt that every morning, without fail, it seemed. Today was plague special. He wrenched himself from that god-awful nightmare, wiped a wet hand over his face a couple of times, combed his hair straight back, where a small part fell to one side (his thick hair his best feature), and he was ready for work. Hank wasn't a breakfast eater or a water drinker, but he was unusually thirsty this morning. He drank two glasses, gazing out of the kitchen window, but he stared through the patchy lot and the abandoned, gutted house. His mind lost in trying to figure out what in the hell the dull finger poke at the back of his head was.

It was as if there was a detail, something to do today, something important, trying to dig for it. No idea what that might be. He didn't have any appointments, ever, he didn't have any chores, that he couldn't get the boy to do; hmmm, something about the boy? What could it be? No doctors appointments, who had time for that shit? He hadn't had to wait on any services to be changed or turned on since Mary was home to do it...and yet, there was a shadow at the back of his skull awaiting his acknowledgment.

Nick slept like a baby for the first time since Tommy died. He had settled every little thing on his plate. He'd gone through the anger last evening, like a tunnel and the light at the other end was freedom. He sat with his troubles late into the night. He forgave his mother for not being strong enough, wished her well wherever she was. Felt strong in his decision not to be here the next time she came to leave him behind.

He couldn't forgive Hank, but he could leave him behind. And, that is what the next evening would bring, and exit into the real world. It was scary, because Nick was certain he was so far behind, socially, but it had to be better than this. And, he too would get better, right?

The last dark tunnel left to get through on this fine morning, was his last morning with Hank, but his mind already imagined him to the other side was; where it was worth the work he must endure today. What eased his mind, like a storm cloud blowing over without a drop, was that by this time tomorrow night, he would be out of the state, for the first time in his life. It was as if he understood that every hard thing he would ever do was already done. Now, he was hoping like hell he could just remain convinced, that all he had to do was show up. It was such a relief. There was a bump of doubt that he could stay happy, a terrible belief that he would never be comfortable with joy, but The Maxx brushed it all away with his placating tones and inside temple rubbing. He would take care of the itch so Nick wouldn't have to carry the weight of its worry.

The Maxx had very practical feelings toward Mary, but a compassion for the up close frames of her in the throes. He felt for her, for Nick, as she was dispatched in a child's anger; Hank was a grown child that reacted as such. With hands large and strong enough to kill, a hurt mind, stubborn and ignorant enough to react first and not think much after. To act selfishly and not know to feel empathy. The Maxx was glad Nick didn't see it, that he wasn't in the room to do nothing about it. The Maxx didn't know if Nick would have tried to stop it, he was too submissive, his mind hesitation at every given moment, and that amplified in Hank's presence. Nick would have had to watch his mother killed, knowing all the ever after that he wasn't strong enough, or brave enough to try. Even if it wasn't his fault, he would not ever have the strength to believe that. Maxx was relieved that as it stood, Nick could resolute himself to not having a choice, if he ever found out. She was gone before Hank was home. Gone without a word.

The Maxx, wearing Nick's submissive face, stepped into the living room, trying not to show just how exhilarated and scared he felt. Wouldn't tip his hand, because if Hank stood in his way, he didn't know what he would do. He didn't feel capable or even willing, but knew if he was pushed too far, again and again, he would crack.

Today was his real Free Day, the day that freedom was granted, or up to be won, more precisely). He had finished classes two weeks ago and tonight all he had on his agenda was to go through the ceremony of graduating, and then initiation was afoot. Self initiation into the real world that he'd heard so little about.

He looked forward to it, because in that moment, he was gone. He turned his head to see Hank only in his periphery, as Nick would have done. The tall and wide, frumpy Illinois State Trooper puckered his uniform, having out grown this size as well. This would be the fifth time he had to up-size his uniform since Mother Mary left them alone with each other.

"Gonna lay about and jerk off all day? You got school, better get to it!" He finally turned his head to see the boy's usual submissive glance. Just as Hank turned away he swore Nick tilted his head up to offer a shit-eating grin. He quickly jerked his head back toward the boy and only saw the lowered head, then the boy turned toward his room and walked out of sight. Hank actually shivered. He felt too goddamn powerless this morning; he didn't care for it. He felt the need to get out of the house, besides it was time for work. His fear pissed him off. He helped the screen door slam a bit harder than usual and left the wooden door open. Fuck the dip-shit. Oblivious to the fact the boy had already finished school. And that nagging item, was tonight's graduation he heard mentioned at work. He'd convinced himself that Nick wasn't there yet.

Nick awoke three hours earlier, for a workout (which consisted of push-ups, hand-stand push-ups and squats holding bricks and blocks) and a run. This was the first day of the rest of his life. It was likely to be a long night, but what of it. A nights hard work for all the years left free from the darkness. He was running away and all he had to do tonight was turn the keys and drive like hell. With the rest of this morning and afternoon free, Nick wanted to walk around town, one last time.

The Maxx wanted to see Tommy, one last time and he knew how to lead Nick along and make him believe it was his own idea. The Maxx needed the closure of saying goodbye before they were gone forever. He couldn't imagine letting Nick come back here, ever. There was nothing but sorrow for him here, why shove your own nose into that? He wanted Nick to remember the good in this town, to perhaps see some today that he didn't know existed, but coming back was not in the cards. He wanted to see every new road there was to see, until some sacred ground somewhere called to him, by name. He wanted a home that felt like a home should feel. He wanted to make some memories that weren't shuttered, that didn't have to be blinked between dark and light to hide the hideous.

Goodbye Tommy

The run/walk to the Center Cemetery was grand. The wind was still cool on this May day and the sun was just warm enough to be a friendly hand on the shoulder, a gentle kiss on the face. The city was ready for a parade, but quiet and scenic. It might have been eerie, but The Maxx was happy to be seeing their friend after so long. They'd not been to see his grave, his headstone since the funeral. They weren't sure they believed it would do any good, or that he would hear, but The Maxx needed it to mean something today, if only a symbol of their love for him. Nick didn't know where they were going until he saw the cemetery on their way. He was just walking, following his feelings, his intuition or inner voice. It led him this way and how fortunate, he might as well make his goodbyes to his only friend.

Nick couldn't remember having come this far. Perhaps he was walking on auto-pilot. He shrugged it off and walked on, now that he could see the stone archway of the cemetery; he jogged to the rows of standing stone. Third row, fifteen in from the path. Nick and The Maxx, now hand in hand, slowed to a walk as they found the sacred earth where these ancestors were buried. Was Tommy his ancestor? It sounded odd, but Nick and The Maxx decided it was like when your Uncle is younger than you, that is how it was odd. They weren't sure these bodies ever had souls and if they did, they were uncertain if they moved on and visited or knew when their forgotten bodies were visited. Still, this ground was sacred, even if death wasn't the end. Even if it was just for the honor with which it was treated by the living, an earthly shrine left undeveloped simply for those that were loved and lost.

They could see it now, it was not wide or tall or gaudy, nor was it overtly religious, which they were glad of. It was a Celtic cross, which was obviously religious, but it seemed more Gothic than a plain cross. It was a stone they enjoyed to, they rubbed the rough edges under the circled cross arms. It was a pink hued stone and it felt cool to the pad of their right hand, both on Nick's knees to the left of the grave. They lay down now between grave sites, closed their eyes and rubbed the stone. Nick whispered what Maxx pushed forth and spoke so eloquently in Nick's roomy head.

"It wasn't so long ago you stopped me from running on, and even less time has run over us since you've been gone. You made the darkness brighter with your attention and will, and often the worst of our pain fell beneath your heel, where you ground it in to depths that could hold it some, I had no right to ask you to exist, no right to ask you to come. And though you had no idea of just exactly what you would be to me, you reflected something of the heavens, something I'd no right to see. The affected atmosphere about you smelled of what could be, songs and blooms, birds and trees, desert nights, breezes billowing."

Then they spoke aloud, in unison, "That is where we're going, Tommy. To see that desert land you spoke of. Remember? You spoke of tripping Nevada. Driving too fast in our Duster, outrunning the dust we made in it. Come with me, if there is any part of you that feels me, or hears me...come with and see it too." They laughed, until tears stole the sound and clutched at their throat. "Perhaps you're already there. Are you there waiting on me? Or just blowing about, adrift with the sands?" They suddenly felt as if there were no more words; all had been spoken and more would just be so much noise. Four eyes opened, head turned toward the stone as the hand felt up and down the edges. Then they looked about, seeing the day reflected upon the line of stones all around them. One tear from two eyes, cried by both, slid silently down the left cheek and the one mouth smiled for the two of them.

They let Nick's head roll to see only the sky, hands falling to chest. They rock in the grass, watching the clouds play Red Rover, feeling like kids who don't care what anyone else might see. Until, suddenly, it was stolen by the dark figure at the far end of the row of stones. It was the far end from where they entered. It looked like an old English suit and top hat, all details of color drowned beneath soot. Dark enough to be a silhouette, but as it limped closer, shoulders twisted oddly, there was an eerie depth to it. They could hear it's feet thumping and dragging the grass as it neared. There was a growl of sorts, a mumbled growl that was more felt than heard. They fearfully understood that it would get to them no matter how fast or far they ran. Nick closed his eyes, but The Maxx forced them opened.

"YOU." The voice was deeper than a growl, too deep to get a sense of. It was more like a man than a woman...held a finger out toward them, "RUN OR WALK,

CRAWL OR TARRY, LIVE OR DIE, FIGHT OR TRY." It wasn't screaming or yelling, the growl was fear itself, but stated simply enough, not threat as much as fact, it seemed. "THIS BE THE END OF THE LINE, FOR THEE AND ME. SEE ME OR DENY THY SIGHT, BUT IGNORE NOT THE DEEPEST DEPTHS OR HIGHEST HEIGHTS. THIS WORLD IS A RIDGE OF LIGHT, REFLECTION OF DIM DAY AND DIMMER NIGHT, BUT THERE IS A DEEPER WELL IN WHICH TO DROWN AND A HIGHER TORCH TO BURN YOU DOWN."

The creature stepped bony feet on either side of Nick's head, and bent to grab his face and leaned down like a wild animal, speaking this upon his lips, "YOU ARE THREE AND SOON BE FOUR, ITS YOUR ACHING NEED THE WORLD WILL ABHOR. BUT YOUR NEXT WON'T BE DENIED, LET HIM BURN PARADISE WIDE. DESTROY YOU OR STRENGTHEN, EITHER ONE SUITS, THE CREW YOU CARRY ARE BUT CRAPS TO SHOOT." It's rotten breath too much to take.

Nick looked back to the opened eyes that The Maxx now controlled and saw the creature's wide sunset colored eyes, tilting and leaning to look deep into his own. It pulled back, it's pointing finger becoming a wrenching fist. It had them by the V-neck of Nick's only long sleeve, gray, tee. The thin fabric stretched before bringing them back to the putrid maw of the thing. The fetid creature stood their every hair up on end. "THEE AND ME ARE ONE AND ONE OF THEE ARE ME." They watched as the thing blinked into another rotten person, a feminine looking version, one that looked like it might be....Mom. Horrified by her decay and familiarity, they gasped as it blinked back...and forth and back and forth, from one to the other, closer with every next blink until it was kissing them with its open decomposed mouth. Nick and The Maxx clamped their eyes wrinkled shut and felt the ground pound them in the back before they felt the absence of the rotted hands.

"Jesus Christ!" Jay Jay screamed at the back of them. Maxx didn't know she was watching and turned to her. Nick thought it was his own scream. He wondered now, "*One of thee are me.*' What the hell was that? What does that mean?"

Consoling her was a grand distraction and Maxx was glad for it, anything not to think, to absorb whatever message was just given. He did his best to console her, it seems she didn't see much, it was the jar of being dropped that woke her to the surface. But, damn, how much of hell did you have to see to get the picture, to feel the emitted essence? Maxx and Jay Jay convinced Nick it was time to go and he did as his intuition told him, as long as it was telling him to get the hell away from anywhere that thing might be.

Survival

Thomas was pissed completely off. These pansy asses were too scared to get him the hell back to where he could be of some use. This cocksucker, The Maxx, was taking the lead and for whatever reason, Cates couldn't over take him. He wouldn't turn away just long enough, the fucker was strong, far stronger than Cates would ever admit to any of them. Every time Cates tried to break through, typically just a step forward (that's how it worked the first time, at least), but when The Maxx was ahead it seemed there was an impenetrable glass wall. It would simply not give when The Maxx was in the lead. It was different with Jay Jay too, but not impossible. All he could do now was piss and moan, irritated at the lack of possible movement, or semblance of control. Goddammit, he was a mover and a shaker, he got shit done and needed to move, to stand and stretch and work his body. Being dragged by the heels, like a slug trailing behind….Grrrrr…irritated the shit out of the killer.

The Maxx walked with Nick and Jay Jay now, the trio breaking the same stride, pressing into the same steps. This was the first time, since the walk home from the cemetery that they all three walked together, side by side by side, sort of. It was nice, like it was that day, though there was something off that day. That thought went unfurled any further, like an umbrella's trigger fingered at, fidgeted with, but left unopened in the end (for fear of getting their hands slapped by the superstitious fearing a deceased love one).

"I could use a break, how about you two?" The Maxx asked his family. "Yes," expressed Jay Jay immediately.

"Sure, why not?" Nick added not realizing he was actually being carried along. Cates left well enough alone, knowing his black sheep position amid the bunch. He wasn't really sure if they knew about him, really. He knew they saw him earlier. He felt their eyes in the sky as he stood upon the rock and watched Nick drive by in his precious little roadster. Their eyes were upon him, the little black girl and the teen boy, but he didn't know if they knew him or how he fit in. He wondered if they could know him as he knew them? He wondered if he could overpower them in the end? It pissed him off, but it was just a challenge and Cates was good at those, very good indeed.

They were, The Maxx figured, three good miles from the center of town, roughly an hours walk (though this was a total guess). He wasn't sure what they were running from, but felt it was best to keep at it. They sat upon the low limb of a large tree, scattered amongst many, blocking their view from the path they entered on. It felt safe and fitting for a break and look out, because there was enough large trees to hide. After a few minutes, they all were on board with laying back upon the grassy ground below, the rise of the tree roots were buried beneath the soil and grass, just enough to make a fine pillow for the foursome. Cates was especially on board, he knew what might just come of it.

Survival .2

Cates smiled at his sleeping family, the smile-a-mighty-jesus (that is what one of Nick's teachers used to say about a great big smile and why we should all wear one. "This," she would say pointing to the corners of her upturned mouth, "is the smile-a-mighty-jesus and he is in your heart when you wear it." He wore it now, chuckling silently at the old memory in his skin. Not all of Nick's memories were available to Cates, but sometimes they just bubbled up on occasions like this.

Nick was exhausted from the adrenaline, the unaccounted for bang to the head, the unremembered bruised leg, a forgotten torqued knee, and running all night and day. Jay Jay's little boy metabolism was tired from the walking and The Maxx was in front for longer than he'd been in a while, it's hard to hold up three personalities (the fourth took it out of him). Cates was riding easy up to this point (just a weight for the others to drag along and he had imagined every heavy thought he could muster), and now it was his turn. He didn't mind carrying their sleeping carcasses. While they slept, he could get back to his mission. He tried to imagine a door in Nick's head, one he could lock them behind. It might just slow them down and then, it might not do a damn thing, but it wouldn't hurt to try. Thomas Cates began his/their walk back west, he would need to retrace all of their steps to get back to their Duster. Once there he could head for his place and begin again. As he walked he replayed the scene with Officer Dillon.

What Nick had missed was the square of duct tape that Cates had folded inside out, into a two inch square, to block the door catch. Cates lulled Nick into holding the door closed, so the dome light wouldn't come on. If the cop saw the door wasn't shut, his death would have to come sooner. So, Cates kept silent during the car ride back to Cate's Place, the sacred Gates of Tara. Cates just watched while Nick drove to the Sheriff's Office, pissed that the boy would have the gall to try and get him caught, the audacity to fuck with his mission, little cocksucker. He didn't seem to bat an eye when he lurched forward for the first time, his birth, and jumped out to grab the girl; but Cates had tired himself in that first mission, hiding the girl and her blood from the boy.

He could see the officer walk into the headlights, puppcting his shadow on the fantastic formation. It made their skin crawl to let the officer so close to his saved girl, but Cates knew discipline, and waited until it was clear before pushing the back door open. He also had a disciplined bladder, because this numb-nuts had yet to relieve himself of the piss that woke him, before he decided to play hero. Cates would piss for him and all over the cop he was about to relieve of consciousness.

He slid out of the car, ran soft footed, to the Gates of Tara and saw the law man's flashlight and hand at Deborah's neck. 'Ewe, this fucker!' Cates was in motion before the beam turned on him. A foot to the man's chest knocked him over Deborah and against the rear wall of the formation. He hesitated only out of shock, as the falling fucker kicked Deborah in the face as he was pushed to the wall. Cates knew he'd done that, that it was his own fault, but was pissed at the man for being the one to make such brutal contact. "You fucker!" He launched again, but the hesitation was just enough for the officer to raise his flashlight and strike out; the cop's power lessened by the breath he just lost. Cates caught the blow on the top left side of his head, hard enough to make him see a green flash of light, and bring blood. He was quick enough to continue his assault, though, and caught the officer's hand before he knew he was even going for it and forced the man to one knee (too goddamn close to Deborah's head). He landed his licks with more accuracy and evil intent, splitting the officer's skull and laying him out where he knelt, which was all over the poor girl. "Goddammit!"

Cates did his best to drag the man out of the formation and off of Deborah as carefully as he could, so as not to upset the poor girl any further, cursing the whole way (because his anal sensibilities couldn't stand every touch of the law man's dirty fucking feet on the beautiful, pure girl). He twisted his knee as he turned to exit the formation with the one-hundred-and-eighty pound man in tow, stepping into a divot he wasn't expecting. He could feel the slow and irregular pulse under the man's arms, where he carried him, knowing it meant he hit him hard enough to cause more than a concussion, possibly a hemorrhage from the weak pulse. He pulled the man a hundred-feet out of the stone temple and offered him unceremoniously to the desert night. Cates would have left it at that, but the trapped rage at every accidental kick upon Deborah's body drove him to add a second kick to the temple. Then, he wrote Nick's name across the uniformed chest and would have pissed all down Nick's leg, had it not been for having to share it.

Cates was headed to the car when he realized the flashlight he taken from the policeman was where he'd dropped it. He thought it only fair to leave Nick's fingerprints all over it for the cops to find, but considering they were his fingerprints too, caused him to reconsider his revenge. He grabbed the flashlight, cleaned it with his shirt, and tossed it out into the darkness with an overhand toss.

Walking back to the car, he tripped over his own damn feet, really more of just a knee give. It meant that he was losing control of the body, one of the others was pulling back into the front and he needed to keep this from them, if he could. He walked knock-kneed and just as he opened the driver's side door, he realized that whoever was waking up would wake up where he was. He couldn't let the boy wake up behind the wheel. He would have to improvise and fast. He stepped to the back door, reseated them into the backseat and tried to lay as if he'd been knocked out, so Nick might try to fill in the missing time.

There was no time, he felt the boy stepping forward just as he lowered his head and lost his sight. Cates could still feel his control of the body but it was slipping. He imagined randomly the radio receiver torn loose, cord dangling, blood spatter across the dashboard and damaged radio, as if the officer were attacked trying to radio for help. Why not dash a little fear in on the boy?

Cates fought the laughter at watching his loser-of-a-master survey the scene with wide panicked eyes. He relished the push, like a tattoo for the mind (all while the boy merely sat there in the back seat). He stepped even further back into the shadows to watch the boy open back door. Cates eyed him while he searched behind the stone, forcing him to miss the girl still there. Cates watched him finding the flashlight and clicking it off to save from being seen (it was just too much), this was fun.

Now, when the boy ran to the shadows, to escape the killer obviously at large, Cates imagined himself just behind the car, thinking over his last move for the moment. If he could summon the energy to will Nick into believing that he was jumping into the car, starting it and driving away, it should clear the boy from the girl and just maybe, make the boy realize how unforgivable it was to work against fate by raising another alarm. Two birds, one piss-poor stone, winner Cates! He couldn't help but laugh at the boy falling right into the scene he painted upon his fore-mind. It was working!

Later, he had a few more Jedi mind tricks to perform. This used the last of his mental reserves, which is another reason he was pulled along by the hero and the girl the rest of the day. He had to imagine the Duster invisible, unseeing the whole of the car while Nick was approaching the law office. He was exhausted by the time he had to play Danny's hick brother, hell, he'd just barely seen the sign for Danny's Auto when Nick ran into the police station. Then, the light show, the movie in the garage. He had a blast working his mind tricks, but he was tuckered out and needed his rest. Cates fell back, passing the boy without acknowledgment and lost awareness.

Back at the Office

Officer Shannon walked back to the office. The sound of the door closing as she stood just inside, very tired, seemed a remark on just how long of a day this had already been. A look at the clock, behind the counter, further remarked on how much had taken place, and all by nine 'o five. After a few mind-drifting minutes, she made a move for the coffee pot and sat at the Sheriff's desk with a hot cup of Joe, warming her hands around her favorite mug. She leaned back and put her feet up like he does, and it was nice. Her sister bought her this mug, what, six Christmas' ago now? The white mug's decor was Droopy, under the caption, 'You Know What? I Love Coffee.' Saleisha smiled at the memory (and the voice of the animated dog from childhood cartoons), and put her brain to task. 'How do I go about looking for Officer Dillon? Who might have seen him come and go?'

Ah, she knew, Barry Thompson was known to do his road kill clean up after dark, maybe he'd seen something? It was a long shot, but the only shot she could think of at the moment. Barry was fifty-three, slightly inappropriate and funny as hell. She loved the old coot, but she had to set him straight more than once, though he was always just fine with the lines she would draw, until he was feeling his oats the next time. She hadn't had to hit or arrest him yet, but she suspected he might just push it that far one day. She dialed the phone and sipped the hot Joe. On the second ring she heard,

"I don't know who the hell is calling at almost nine-thirty

in the freaking morning, but you obviously don't know me very well?"

"I guess I do, Barry Thompson! I know you well enough for you to have offered me a Coke and a smile, with copious amounts of innuendo when last we talked."

"Hmmm...that doesn't much narrow it down for me and I have yet to place your voice. Try me again."

"You old Shit, this is Officer Shannon at the Sheriff's Department, were you out and about last night?"

His voice softened immediately, "Well, the Coke and the smile still stands, Officer Shannon. Naw, I wasn't feeling my Wheaties last night, stayed in and got drunk. Why?"

"I was hoping you might have seen Officer Dillon at some point. Just trying to verify some facts for a report." She didn't want anyone thinking he was missing just yet, since they had no clue as to what exactly was going on.

"Sorry I couldn't be of any more help, Love."

"Thanks anyway. Go back to sleep, Old Man."

"Roger that, Sexy!" he responded before the line clicked. Saleisha laughed and replaced the phone in its base and slurped the last of her coffee. She didn't want to be out of the warm beverage just yet. She yawned, raising her arms and the mug in a stretch as she did so, then stood to retrieve another cup. She auto-piloted back into the coffee room amid another yawn and as she reach for the pot, she caught sight of the primer gray car parked just north of the office parking lot. She'd forgotten about it since she arrived. She couldn't help but wonder if it might have something to do with this mess. She had no other leads to follow, might as well see what's what, besides, she didn't recognize the vehicle. She decided to postpone the coffee, if this turned into anything, it would be cold before she could get back to it, anyway. She sat her Droopy mug down next to the pot and walked out.

It was a Dodge, Duster, she noted as she walked around the back to get to the driver's side (checking the trunk was not open as she passed by). She expected it to be locked and so just shielded her eyes from the reflected day on the window to see what she could. Did one of the locals run out of gas and pull in here to get off the road? Or, maybe someone having car trouble and she just might be able to tell who owned it by some of the artifacts on display and save herself some time. She didn't recognize it as local, and the Illinois State plates told her it was either newly purchased or someone traveling through.

As she ducked down to view the inside, she noted one important finding: the buckled windshield of the primer gray sedan was caused by an impact from the inside. Her breath caught as she caught sight of what looked like a set of keys hanging off a key chain from the ignition. Officer Shannon decided to be safe rather than sorry and ran back into the office to retrieve two pair of latex gloves (she was really rough handed, so she always donned two pair).

She was just as dumbfounded, back at the car, to find the door unlocked, though it then dawned on her that if it had been locked, the keys would have been locked inside. *Four points for Officer Shannon*, she thought, noting her good luck. She knelt down, gingerly at the edge of the front row seat, not wanting to interfere with the bloody scene, or contaminate the forensics investigation that would need to be done. She scanned the driver's seat for hairs, fabric or any fluids, to no avail. The dark stain on the passenger-side floorboard looked menacing, however.

This was just a preliminary look for immediate facts, to find Dillon. She still didn't know if this car belonged to the young man on the loose, though the blood spatter she saw on his face and shirt pointed to that very conclusion. Her intuition was screaming she accept it as related. It felt too coincidental.

She tilted her head and reached around the steering wheel to the small picture wedged in the cars dash, between the plexiglass and where the dash kicked back. It was the young man in question and another dark haired one, same age it seemed, friends from their smiles. 'Or lovers?' she pondered.

She decided to takc thc photograph, to see if she could scan and run an image search for him in the database. First, however, she would take a preliminary look over the inside and then check the trunk. The only visible clue Officer Shannon noted in the back seat and floorboard was a few strands of blonde hair snagged on a piece of trim at the bottom of the door which she would come back to collect when she got suited up. Shannon stepped out and shut the back door, making her way to the trunk. Her gut was trembling with discovery.

She popped the trunk with the keys and slid them into her uniformed shirt pocket, deciding to place them on the sheriff's desk in case the young man came back unnoticed with the intention of leaving town. In the trunk, she found a number of items her eyes were struggling to see one at a time instead of all at once. Okay, spare tire under a duffel bag, blankets. The duffel bag and blankets were army green with a black stencil reading **Forbus, H**. There were a few road flares strewn about, three dark stains in the dirty trunk's fabric and two dead dragon flies. Oh, and a notebook with a pencil run through the wire spiral. She grabbed the notebook and returned to the office.

She first laid the keys on the sheriff's desk, the notebook on the counter and started the work on the photo. She scanned the image and loaded it into the FBI's database. That began a run of flashing photos and a counter, logging in the number of files that had been searched thus far and it was climbing fast. The servers that handled this protocol were massive and they were capable of comparing a thousand photos and real-time video clips a minute, or so she'd been told. She'd performed this task enough to know it was a lot like a pot of water on the stove, not boiling under watchful eyes and all. She grabbed another cup of coffee and stepped out to the front lobby. She stood looking out of the glass door, slurping aloud. She was so excited about possibly getting a hit on the facial recognition service that she almost forgot about the notebook; another piece of the puzzle. She carried her warm mug around the counter to see what she could make of it.

In the top left corner of the worn aqua colored notebook cover was the name Nick Stone in a creative hand. It was empty other than that, no scribbling or doodles. She pulled the cover open as if she was handling the Dead Sea Scrolls. She handled it with as much care, finding value in someones thoughts and feelings....and evidence. The script that wrote the name on the cover was obviously the same author of the story she found inside. She read, enraptured by the unfolding crime. It was entitled *Thomas Cates: Back at the Start,* and it began*; The middle aged man sat in the fuzzy light of the used up Sun, that allowed a threatening shroud to encroach across the flat and dusty land. He crouched upon a boulder, like a bird of prey awaiting the occasional rodent.* It went on for six pages and spoke of a sacrifice of sorts, a mission to save young women by killing them. After this story, another began, entitled: *Solitary Suicide,* and the first paragraph read;

The blade in Cate's hand was sharp. It was his special, his blade for their ceremony. He always thought of it that way. He wouldn't be here if not for Tara, chosen to carry out the work he was so focused on perfecting. Forever grieving that he wasn't about to save her. He had learned from each sweet girl saved, what scared them, soothed them, saved them from fear or ache. He wanted to warm them, caress lovingly, so they might leave this world with the joy of what was to come.

Tripping To and Fro Into the Fray

Cates would have said that he could hear the man coming, but the truth was he expected him, and was disciplined enough to wait motionless. He was twenty-six-feet up in a Sweet Gum tree with four branches held at his feet to screen him. He knew trees and plants, what was edible and what would make you lose your last three meals. He could make a fire with no tools, if he had to, gut any animal and hold a three inch pattern of arrows at two-hundred-yards with a re-curve, unsighted bow. A back story as real to him as this tree.

Fortunately, the moment required only basics, because dragging these sleeping bodies with him was a burden he wasn't used to. These other personalities were getting heavier, or, and he didn't want to admit he might be getting weaker. He simply waited for the sheriff, who passed by a hundred yards south of Cates, to walk out of earshot before climbing down and walking back. Cates was relieved he was just far enough away not to see easily through the screen of leaves he'd secured before him. It was easier, one less battle in the midst of learning to carry these numb-skulls.

He didn't have the tracking skills of a native American, but Cates was stealthy on the regular, his senses sharp. He climbed back down the tree and dropped into the leaf litter below quieter than the squirrels playing around the area. He started his trek back west, toward the Duster. The only concern he had now (other than getting to the car before the police figured out it was his ascendant's ride), was the other officer he'd heard on the police radio when Nick was talking to Officer Shannon; Winn? Winston? Waverly? Whatever?

He couldn't remember the name, though he was sure it was a "W" name, maybe. Though, he realized, he wasn't sure if it was indeed the sheriff or officer that had just passed him, and didn't care, he just didn't want to run into the other one. Cates felt sure that they would probably walk through at the same pace, spread out from one another just enough to keep eyes on one another — if they were both searching this area, that is. He stopped and scanned the area, to the north for the other officer, but there was nothing there. He waited for five minutes, quiet, and still nothing, so he moved on.

Officer Wales was still working his way door to door. The first two houses knock's went unanswered, the next two were answered with no sightings of a stranger or Officer Dillon. Wales now stood before the last house in this scant neighborhood, a single-wide trailer with multiple additions. It appeared the whole east end was the latest addition, as the siding appeared newer. There was a section to the west just different enough to be newer than the trailer. After an inspection of the perimeter, Wales stepped up on the new, large deck and gave the door a rap. He heard footsteps. The wooden door's knob sounded and opened upon Will Eppard, a man Wales knew from his time at Cold Springs High School, a small town just to the west of Austin. Eppard was a few years older than Wales, he remembered.

"Hey Man, I hope you're not here to pick me up." Eppard put up his hands, "I didn't do it." He laughed harder than the joke was funny, Wales thought, which might mean nervousness. He was pretty sure that was just Will Eppard. Wales quickly took in the scene. The middle aged, moderately lean, sandy-haired man wore a Spanky Johnson tee-shirt, it was gray with the *Reservoir Dogs* trademark, silhouetted-suits on it. He wore jeans and was barefoot. The place smelled as if he were preparing his lunch, soup and grilled cheese, if Wales were a betting man. In the doorway, Wales could see some Gothic looking memorabilia (such as Bendy and the Ink Machine and Halo figurines) and four different game systems.

"Just wondering if you'd seen any strangers running about this morning?"

Eppard looked suspicious "You mean here in our neighborhood?" Wales shook his head side to side. "Naw, Man, I only got home just about an hour ago, but I haven't seen anything around here. But..."

"Yeah?"

"When I was coming in from work, out at Bob Scott Campgrounds, where I guide for visiting hikers, I saw one of your cruisers parked out some ways off the road. It seemed odd because it looked abandoned, to me, just...felt odd"

"Where exactly was this?"

"What is that, two miles east of town? Oh, you know, out in front of Hanger's Rock."

The news got Wales hackles up, "Thank you." He offered his hand and Eppard shook it, with respect. Wales leapt from the porch without another word, back toward where he thought the sheriff ought to be. Eppard watched him go for a full minute before he decided to go back inside. He wanted to know why the officer was walking off into the woods, what was it he asked him, something about spotting a stranger? The officer was well out of ear shot when Eppard stepped back to shut the door, overcome with the chills after spotting something else. He slammed the door shut in fear.

Officer Shannon was completely unfocused. She started to continue her phone calls, back to work and all...but, then she remembered that the phone calls she needed to make were to find information on Dillon's whereabouts and, well, his whereabouts were found. Which meant she was currently out of immediate duties and…'goddamnit, he was dead'. She whispered this in an inhalation of breath that felt like it offered her nothing. Her lungs were through taking oxygen. She would suffocate right here, in shock.

She sat down in the sheriff's chair. No better, she stood up and felt like letting her body fold up limp. The gears of her mind caught on Dillon's death. She put her back against the small open wall and let her body slide to the floor slowly, feeling every muscle in her legs engage. It felt good just to make them work, rather than her consciousness. Once her butt hit the floor, she caved in and cried herself out, loud and quickly.

She gave herself five minutes to scream and moan. Once she was empty, she felt the need to flip back through the notebook. She was afraid to look back through the car, knowing she'd only contaminate the evidence if she wasn't focused on the task at hand. She only knew Terry Dillon from work and a few night's shared beers at Lafferty's Pub during celebratory occasions, such as Dillon's commendation for bravery under fire with last year's Baily Family incident. He was friendly, quick to laugh; a damn good laugh at that. 'Had,' was the word that echoed in her head. There was a light in that laugh, that struck her more in this moment, than had ever registered before.

Cates saw the collection of random houses. Then, he saw the other law-man inspecting the expanded trailer before stepping up on the porch. He was coming out of the sparse brush to the north of the fucked up suburb when he spotted the man's movement. He froze in his tracks, trying not to return the favor of offering up his own location. He ducked behind a waist high bush when the officer faced away. Anyone with good peripheral vision could spot Nick's goddamn shirt, it wasn't the brightest red and gray, but it was not Cates' preferred black. He scoped out the scene in order to be prepared for whatever came next. Might the other law official walk right up behind him?

He watched a light-haired man answer the door. If the law-man entered, Cates would make a run back toward the station where Nick's car was, but what if he didn't go inside? Six feet to the north was a shorter bush, but it was wider and thicker than the one he knelt behind at the moment. It would give him more cover if the policeman decided to join the other law-man.

The home owner never looked away and this forenoon

light made hiding near impossible. Cates was quick, but it was a risk to try the dash to better camouflage. Cates was caught off guard by the officer so quickly leaping off the porch. His chest froze over as the man ran directly at him. 'Oh Shit! I've been seen. He was preparing to defend himself at the last second, if he was spotted.

There was a full second window, three seconds away he figured, when the law-man shouldn't see him in a mad dash to the thicker bushes, but the chances of the homeowner seeing him were great; he would rather dance with the homeowner, he hoped; so, he made his move.

Fortunately, for Cates, it paid off. The policeman was off at a run, before the goddamn Nosy Nellie spotted him. Cates stood up, when the man visibly jumped at the sight of him. Cates made a split second decision.

He launched into a run so quick, the man was still fumbling to lock the door, when he dove head first through the window to the man's left. Glass rained across the brown carpet beyond the flaps of ripped screen. The man was astounded, because his windows were so high. As he watched the assailant roll to a run, he felt immediately defeated at having locked himself in with this animal.

He never expected to watch his home broken into while he was locking the world away with his expensive, front door. Eppard immediately knew he would never make it to his bedroom, to lock it's door. Still frozen in half a turn, as he watched the motion of a young man (in a jersey tee and jeans), run through the still falling glass at the wall across from him. Damned if he wasn't impressed despite, believing the boy was about to run up the far wall. He felt sure he was capable.

Cates did run two full steps of the wall, to aid in his speed at changing direction. He leapt toward the frozen gawker and closed the distance in two strides. The man grabbed at Cates' hands, now wrapped into bunches of the tee's collar. Eppard reflexively adjusted his weight against the expected push, adding his own momentum to Cates', who pulled them both backwards. Cates smiled at the shocked man, as the man's body was set in motion. Just before Cates hit the glass ladened carpet, he pushed his knees into the falling man's upper abdomen and planted his feet in the V of his hips. As Cates' legs rose into the roll, he extended his arms and Eppard was launched upside down toward the back window. It was Cates' plan to launch the man and set upon him before he could react. What happened was unexpected.

The poor man's heels pushed through the top of the glass, before, his lower back dug into the bottom eight inches of stubborn shards. Cates rolled up into a fighting stance, ready to act, but realized the fight was already over. The man's head and chest convulsed, independent of one another. The sturdy new windows held the weight of the man, as his pierced kidneys and guts bled out. The man twitched and shuddered for all of ten seconds head, until his tensed body let go. His head and chest lowered enough for his eyes to fall upon Cates. Then, with a popping snap, the glass snapped free from its frame, and the weight of his long legs launched his upper body like a trebuchet, and he was gone.

Cates watched in awe, not even proud, just amazed.

He felt no need to check on the man, to assure himself of anything. He couldn't imagine him making it through that gut wound. The best thing was get them all the hell out of here. If he could have left his troubling band of tag-alongs, he would have, but that was not yet something he'd figure out how to do. '*Now*,' he thought as he unlocked the solid door, '*for the Duster. Now for the getaway*!'

Wales jogged his way to the wood line and then fell into a quick walk letting his heart settle into a resting rhythm. He calculated that a safe walking pace, a hunting pace, would put the sheriff a mile to a mile-and-a-half further south. He knew the sheriff had his radio on him, but Wales did not. The department only had three portable radios. The sheriff had one, Dillon probably had one and the other had been on the fritz for a couple of months now. He would have to catch up to the man to redirect their search and hopefully be of some help to Dillon.

The cruiser appearing abandoned didn't bode well, but perhaps this kid had Dillon on a hunt of his own, or maybe there were others involved. The variables would have to wait, either way, Wales knew he had to catch the sheriff and get them to Hanger's Rock. Wales hadn't thought much about that place since high school. He'd been once with a friend for a fire and to imbibe forbidden substances. He felt vulnerable being out-of-towners. He'd heard stories about high school Jocks starting shit with rival schools. He didn't know, but assumed that the kids still used it today for the same reasons. It made Wales wonder, if the kid was as young as Shannon thought, if that had anything to do with all of this; the local hangout where everyone went to get up to no good. Perhaps this was a kid from another town coming to party and things went awry?

It took another twenty minute jog for him to catch up to Sheriff Jenkins. He hissed at his superior from a fair distance, so as not to spook him and risk a gun pointed in his direction. Wales discontinued his speed with the hiss, hands up in clear view and was glad to see the sheriff turn and recognize him immediately.

Sheriff Jenkins was focused on hunting. His head slowly swaying from side to side to use his sight and periphery to its fullest extent. His ears were straining for sound just as his eyes were trained for movement. He actually heard a rhythmic breaking of leaves just before he heard the hiss behind him. His trained body remained fluid as his mind raced between perp alert and friendly warning. His mind was quick to decide that the perp most likely wouldn't warn him before attempting an attack. He swiveled around and saw one of his own, Officer Wales. He stopped and waited for Wales at first, but then something in the man's walk made him believe that Wales was needing him to change direction, so he met him in the middle.

Wales quickly filled him in. "Hanger's Rock, huh? Did your class hang out there back in your day? Oh, I'm sorry, you aren't from here, are you?"

Wales just nodded, "Just once. It was never a place I cared for, but I've been there." Wales admitted as the men fell into pace back toward their cars.

"Shannon has told me stories about the place, but she

didn't act as though there had been any serious trouble out there before. You ever heard of any out there?"

"No, no more than Officers running kids off or giving them rides home."

"Hmmm, I don't like that he hasn't checked in. Let's get to him." That was the end of their verbiage as they made the long walk back to Danny's Auto. The worst of worse-case-scenarios was running through both of their minds. What might have troubled them both was how very different the scenes were from one head to another, that they could be so far off on the same case.

Wales was going to ask, but before he could raise the question, Sheriff Jenkins answered it, "Ride with me, Officer, I don't want us separated on this one." This surprised Wales, the sheriff didn't typically express his feelings or answer questions like, "Why". Wales looked at the sheriff over the top of the car as he was about to get in the passenger's side, trying to read what brought this unnerving statement on. It was unnerving because it meant the sheriff expected trouble, all Wales got was a stern look from the man in charge. Wales was a good officer, in Sheriff Jenkins' opinion, because the look was answer enough. Jenkins tabbed the lights and siren before flicking the ignition and bringing the engine to life. He was out of the gravel parking lot in a twist and forced the cruiser lower to the ground as he quickly increased the speed with a foot upon the throat of the gas pedal.

They were at Hanger's Rock in a minute and a half. They both spotted Dillon's cruiser, hoping like hell he was scouting for clues to something. No such luck. Without a word, they both understood that something was wrong, and the only hope left was that Officer Dillon was held hostage without mortal injury; or unconscious, or unable to walk. The sheriff slid to a halt twenty feet behind the Hanger's Rock, in case there was anyone using it for an ambush. The scene answered their most immediate questions. Their brother-in-arms lay upon the ground with a bloody head. Before either had time to touch a door handle, Sheriff Jenkins had a play, another reason his officers loved his charge, "Wales, I know we both want to get to Dillon first, but let's both work our way into the rock and make sure this isn't a trap. If we get shot up, we can't help him." Wales heart rate increased a notch, the sheriff was nervous and this meant, it was smart to be so.

Sheriff Jenkins parked the car facing the formation, so neither of them would be in excessive open range exiting the car if someone jumped free of the stone formation and opened fire. Officer Dillon was some fifteen feet to the right and rear of the car. Officer Wales fought the desire to look back at him as he exited in sync with his chief. Nine millimeters drawn on the first step out of the car, shoulder high with both hands, weapons pointed toward possible danger. As they stepped closer, eyes trained for motion ahead, Wales took the lead and the sheriff two steps behind. As Officer Wales made it to the short stone hallway, Sheriff Jenkins tapped him on the shoulder with a quick modification. Wales understood the circle the sheriff made his left index finger meant he wanted to circle around the huge stone and the quick jab up meant he was going to step up onto the front ledge so he could see down into the inner room. Wales was good with having someone above the scene he was about to step into. He nodded and waited for his chief to get in place. Wales noticed he would be able to see the sheriff when he stepped up into place and looked in over the wall. If anyone was waiting for someone to step in, they would likely be pointing any weapon they had at the doorway, not up over the open walls. Not that it wouldn't still be dangerous, but it was a sight better than just stepping into the house of stone.

He saw Sheriff Jenkins appear and train his gun into the hole, moving it with his view as he scanned from wall to wall. There was something immediate in the sheriff's eyes. The sheriff nodded to him and raised his gun before disappearing. Wales breathed a silent relief at the all clear, but lost it at the sight of the young girl, she was beautiful in the ray of sun that beamed straight down onto her body, even in her obvious death. Both men would dream of this image again and again; it was tragically cinematic. The white, orange and blue uniform was bright within the enclosure and smudged in places, muddy scuffs as well as bloody fingerprints. Her obviously tanned skin had paled in places and there were hematoma along the back one arm down at her side.

The footprints on her cheer uniform felt like blasphemy, on top of the assault and killing. He saw the drops of blood on the ground beyond and in the young blonde's splayed hair. There were a couple of drops on her legs, also scuffed in two places. The sheriff made his way back to Wales, after checking on his downed officer. "What do you see?"

"I think the drops of blood in here are from Officer

Dillon, it doesn't read right to be hers." Wales looked at the sheriff, 'How's Dillon?' almost fell out of his mouth and it seemed too much some how, as if he expected too much, he settled for, "Dillon?"

The sheriff looked down and shook his head, "I'll call it in. See all you can, I'll pull a kit from the car for processing." As Wales replaced his gun and shook his head at the incomprehension, his overwhelmed heart burst forth in his mouth. He stifled the cry and wiped the hot tears away.

Officer Shannon read on, she got caught up in the story, but was no closer to finding Officer Dillon. They all seemed to be based around this Thomas Cates character. She stared at the now closed notebook and then out of the window in the door, lost in thought. She'd flipped through the pages, but there was nothing else to find. Her unfocused stare was snapped into focus by the abrupt, voice of static from the office radio. She hopped to answer and found Sheriff Jenkins on the other end. "Officer Shannon, over,"

"Saleisha,"

"Sheriff Jenkins, are you okay?" He'd never called her by her first name. It was kind of a thing around the office, they all called each other by their last names only.

"Are you alone?"

"Yes Sir, the office is empty." *You are scaring me*, is what she wanted to follow that up with, but she was now of the habit to contain her emotions in this man's world.

"Saleisha, Officer Wales and I found Dillon." She wanted to shout the questions that now sped through her head, but merely breathed deep with what felt like relief. She realized that it was resolution, not relief, to know they were upon the answers, good or bad. "It appears that he was hit over the head, we're thinking with his own flashlight, because we haven't found it." Saleisha was about to ask, not able to fight it anymore, but the sheriff answered her awful question, "He's dead, Shannon."

After Graduation

Nick was nervous about so many things. He couldn't wait to leave this hell behind, but it was all he knew. Life before Hank was two or three tiny visual memories, but the feelings they might have once held were ultimately gone. What was he supposed to do with his mother's sweet smile of love and feeling of adoration, now that she'd left him behind, thrown to the wolves…well, the wolf?

What would life be anywhere else? He knew he was never happy here, but there was a comfort in having a room in a house, a best friend. It wouldn't stop him from leaving, but it was still an unanswered question that left him feeling a bit unstrung. What if he couldn't stand being anywhere else? What if he just wasn't happy, anywhere? What if he fell into trouble, strangers running out newcomers? Was it possible he might get homesick? The thought made him shudder, this was no home, whatever else it might have been.

He also had jitters, Nick was proud of the achievement of graduating high school, but crowds and having a part to play in front of said crowd brought its own tension. There was a mournfulness fighting to escape from his chest, a wish that his Mom might just show up and a not knowing if he wanted that, not knowing how he might react to her presence (The Maxx knew she would not be in attendance). There was a sour-sweet coating over all of this and Nick felt sick to his stomach. He had a feeling that he would be states away before he broke out of his own auto pilot and allowed himself to realize just where he was and what he was doing. He would go, though, if it killed him.

The Maxx had plans to help Nick in this endeavor as he was going to let Nick rest his eyes just after the ceremony and take care of just one more thing. Besides, Nick had a lot of driving to do, they had a road trip to begin! Jay Jay was deep in slumber, now. She'd been driven to remind Nick to play, to remain playful, but his nerves wouldn't settle for it. As for Cates, well, he would not awaken fully until he saw a blonde on the road three days later. He wasn't even so many lead strokes on a page, as of yet, not yet a sketch in prose who was just suppose to be a story. What Maxx didn't know is that his work tonight would be the catalyst to the killer's awakening. He would be born in the wake of Hank's ending and lay silent, gaining his footing until Deborah Marsallis was sighted upon the distant horizon. A taste of blood for the rogue lion inside.

Of course, Mary Stone was not in the audience to watch her only son graduate, nor did Hank Forbus. Nick would have never believed that his step-father actually denied the boy's age, in his own numb way of holding on to the boy. Had he known, his limp sense of father's pride, would've looked too soft. He thought Nick knew how proud he must be, but he didn't want it to go to the boy's head. They still had to live together, maybe for the rest of their lives, and he didn't want to lose his hand over the boy. They were bonded by the woman's leaving, stronger in her abandonment and tied in her murder. They shared a secret and an unspoken ligature that would forever orbit the boy around his sway, or so Hank believed. Perhaps, they could be friends when the boy grew up enough? Unlike Hank and his father, he still felt shadowed by the large, hard-handed man.

Nick was proud, but uneasy sitting in the crowd of fellow seniors surrounded by their parents, grandparents and the school's faculty. He was a good student, but not so good that he had to worry about a speech or anything. He merely had to walk upon stage and shake two hands while carrying the weight of his diploma. He was so afraid to be himself, of crowds, every public moment was a chance to embarrass himself. His heart pounded as he stood and stepped closer to each student standing before him, as they made their walk toward the stage, one at a time. He made his walk though, unsure in his stride and unsettled by the trip ahead; back to his seat (where he would have to face the crowd behind) and beyond.

There was an unexpected fructifying excitement within Nick as the ceremony closed and the class, as a unit, stood to throw their hats and scream in merriment. He got caught up in the moment and felt a bond with these kids he'd spent so much time with, for the first time in all of the days they sat together, walked together and ate together. He was fortunate their wasn't enough room for cliques in their lunch room, so he always had conversation going on around him, and they didn't exclude him as much as they just didn't force him to include himself. If they ever did, he felt put on the spot and would simply lower his reddened face. He realized he knew them, as he'd spent all of this time listening, but they didn't know anything about him. The only person that would have known anything about him was Tommy, and he wasn't here. Some thought Hank was his father, he didn't correct anyone, but he always listened to whatever they had to say about Hank. Apparently, Hank wasn't exactly loved in town; imagine that. He was thought to be a low-life, dirty cop. Nick didn't know what exactly they meant by dirty and didn't want to know. He knew he was thought less of because of Hank, but it wasn't as if he wanted to be thought more of. He just didn't want to be thought of along side Hank at all, but he understood that he was seen as a product of the man.

Nick, rapt in this first real sense of belonging, tried to get in on some photographs with his class, but realized only too late that he was not welcome. He'd taken too long to warm up to them, it was all over. Just one look is all it took, Stacey Hastings looked more confused than hateful, but his smile was erased by it. He backed slowly out of thc group, only to realize that he was a in a room full of smaller groups, none of which were his team.

He watched each group in turn, all focused on their friends and parents, expressing thanks and sentiments to the faculty that waltzed in and out of the groups like agents of concern. None of them felt compelled to express anything with him and as glad as he was of that, he too, was rather quickly incensed. He decided he didn't need these fuckers anyway. He took a deep breath, ground his jaws and made ten hard steps before he heard his name.

It was Tommy's dad, Sam. "Nick," he called again, afraid Nick hadn't heard him. Nick turned to him, the ire gone with his recognition of the voice, "I was afraid you'd left already, I couldn't find you." He stepped up and squared off, as if to read Nick's temperament, somehow asking permission for a hug without a word. Nick was just coming to this realization when the man took the chance and engulfed him in a genuine loving embrace. Nick immediately felt as though he looked awkward, he finally made his hands close on the man's back and allowed himself to settle into the warm security, the true love the man felt for him. The knowledge that some of this love was for Tommy, but Nick didn't mind, he would gladly share it. He didn't realize he had closed his eyes and leaned into the man's arms too much, until the man pulled away. "Thank you, Nick. For being my Tommy's best friend. Please know always, that what I told you will always hold true. You always have a place with us and if you need anything, come to us. Okay?" He once again stood with his hands on Nick's shoulders. "I'm serious, anything." He smiled tearfully at Nick and placed a hand at the back of the graduate's neck, gave a squeeze and walked to the door with his head down, seemingly overcome with tears. Nick watched him leave and then, with one more look around, and a touch of renewed appreciation for this place and people in general, he left too.

Nick walked back to Hank's house. His plan was to wait for the man to drink himself to sleep and then hunt for the Duster's keys. The Maxx kept his own plan to himself. Nick would leave tonight, he just had to play his part until he was gone. He drifted into a restful inner interlude on Baker Street; The Maxx came to life. To anyone watching, he would have looked like a new person blinked into the place of the slumping, slower teen, as his large, upright steps launched out of nowhere. He picked up Nick's steps with a vigor for work at hand, a task to earn the superb Road Trip. It would be a dirty task, a reddening of clean hands with effort and blood, but he would let Mary's dried blood be his fuel for the work.

The Maxx knew how it all worked. It made sense to him, that they all shared each others memories (though he was good at masking his own memories in a blinking, soothing rhythm. He knew, though, that Nick thought these memories that weren't his own, were imagination, random visions. A writer's imagination of things yet seen, yet born into being.

It was seven-thirty-five in the post meridian. He knew that Hank would be into his fourth beer by now and feeling numb, but not yet sleepy. He imagined how easy it would be to take care of all of this while the step-dad slept and wondered if he shouldn't wait for a few hours as Nick wanted to, but his hands yearned for the wheel and his foot for the pedal, just as his heart begged for departure. He also wanted to prove himself in the fight. Either way, it would play out as it should. Fighting for control of other people, who were fighting to control you, was simply unnecessary when you could just wait them out. Too many variables were best to juggle with hands wrapped in plasticity, a mind set in adaptability. People in need to control others were limited by rigid beliefs.

The Maxx didn't want to wait, a crutch that Nick relied on all too often. It even crossed The Maxx's mind to sneak the keys and let the man be, but Nick was scared of the man using his web of blue lines to drag him back. The Maxx couldn't let the law find Nick along the road and force him back, not to this. He deserved better, the man needed to be finished.

"Well, well." Hank said garishly. He didn't get up or have more to offer, because he could tell the boy was in one of those moods. The mood he recognized was The Maxx, though he didn't know it wore a different name. He'd seen the boy's eyes take on a hard, strengthened sheen ever since...hmmm, well hell, since he left that last big mess for him to clean up. Hank didn't like to put a description to the incident, it was a sticky image in his mind, a dark-flying thing and it didn't need a name and it didn't get talked about, not even silently in his mind.

The Maxx heard the step-dad announce his presence and was sure he would have said more if he hadn't stared the man in the eye, like Nick never did. The Steps didn't care for it and The Maxx enjoyed that. He enjoyed the fact that for the first time, he stared the man down and Hank quickly turned back to his beer and idiot box. The Maxx thought, 'Turn about, you Fuck,' as he stepped into the back bedroom. He just wanted to look at it, to remember it for Nick. Nick already had an old duffel bag, filled with the two pairs of jeans, six pairs of socks, six pairs of underwear, four shirts, and one blanket (not including the black jeans and white dress shirt he now wore), in the trunk of the Duster (beside the five gallon plastic jugs of coins and atop the red and black Indian blanket that covered the spare tire). Nick had packed and stowed these items just before having his keys taken away.

He had a Tackitt's Grocery brown paper bag filled with the rest of his belongings there too, so as not to be seen by anyone that might peer into the windows upon the front or back seats, say, on his walk from his cruiser to the house. That bag was not exactly filled, but it held two pictures of Tommy, a small school picture of him in the ninth grade and another of the two of them working on the Duster that Tommy's dad took. This one was in a four by five frame with a wrench on the bottom right hand corner. It also held a five inch figurine, the only real souvenir he had from his mother. It was a man in some kind of odd desert uniform, a very steam-punk slanted, pewter thing with boots, gun belts and head gear. Nick had no idea where it came from, what program or comic or series of toys it might belong to, but it could make Nick feel like he wanted to be strong enough to handle his own problems.

There was also a chlorine jug that The Maxx had added when he gave Nick a rest this afternoon. A jug filled with a homemade concoction of bleach and acetone that he'd purchased for just this occasion. He didn't have a stash of weapons to protect himself and would probably never need this chloroform he'd made, but he wanted to cover his bases in a world full of people he didn't know to trust. He'd wondered now, if it wasn't a prudent idea to try it out on Hank.

Nick had a second set of keys, Tommy's set, but they were all on the same keyring, so he would have to either sneak the keys or take them by force. He was thinking now, that when he got them back, he would put one set in a magnetic box to keep under the wheel well, in case he ever locked himself out or had his keys or car taken. He didn't believe Hank would allow him to leave, that he would have him arrested or at least brought in; knowing good and goddamn well, he would then get rid of the car for good. At least, if he waited until the bastard fell unconscious, it would allow him time to break away, or so he'd hoped.

The Maxx knew that dealing with someone who doesn't compromise or make deals, took a stonier heart. Besides, he wasn't going to leave this battle unfought. He was going to take what belonged to him, well, to Nick, fight this good fight and make their leave. The villain of unfought battles tended to show up when you least expected it and that wasn't going to happen here. This would be done before the tripping began, The Maxx was dead set on that. Let it be done.

The Maxx stepped out into the open kitchen and living room. He breathed in the scent of the old wood, dirtied from the use of one growing boy and an overweight, alcoholic, smoking alpha-dog, who growled and bit and barked. The darkened wood showing through the nicotine-stained chipping-paint and the scuffs of wear and tear. There was a genuineness, a silent sentiment about the place, but a darkness that just sullied it like mud from your shoe. It was a place worth letting go, but still a place that held him for a little while, and that was worth remembering. Even cold, ugly hands that hold you through your childhood were beautiful in your heart. He looked to the horizontal man, feet up toward the television, head back in a beer. How should he do this? A blow to the head? Strangulation? Or, could he make the man do himself in? He liked the thought of that and he thought he could run him through the paces, at least. Why not? Might be fun. Even if Nick only picked up snippets and chose to think of them as imagination, it might leave him with a satisfaction of revenge and closure. Okay, now, to piss him off.

Hank was watching some flick on Lifetime, smoking and drinking his beer like a good drunk, he heard the boy step out of his room. Nothing odd about that, except the small footsteps grew quiet, as if the boy were just watching him. Hank didn't want to turn and engage the boy, not after the look he flashed on his way in. He'd missed something, something that kept the boy out late. What was it? Should he have known about whatever it was?

He didn't think about the car he took away the night before being a catalyst, but then, he didn't much think in terms of the boys feelings. He would get hard if he had to, but it took so much energy and last night's sleepless run had him feeling aged. He hoped to avoid an altercation tonight, but damned if he wasn't feeling the boy standing behind him with a knife or something. He couldn't hear him, but felt him standing close. He tried to act nonchalant and smoke his butt as if nothing bothered him. A list of mean spirited accusations came to Hank's mind, maybe one of them would shut the boy down before he thought he was strong enough to take him on.

The smoke rising to further age the yellowing walls and ceiling of the old home. Hank couldn't fight it any more and snapped his head up just in time to see the boy's hands bludgeon the recliner on each side of Hank's head. He put his weight into pulling the broken down chair over backward. Hank felt the attacked head cushion push his head forward as the boy pulled him past the tipping point. The momentum was too much for the man to stop. His uncontrolled weight forced the chair into three pieces against the floor. The boy laughed and with a brashness that immediately infuriated Hank.

"Hahahahahaha, oh, you fat bastard!"

Hank finally slowed his roll, literally, enough to work his way up to his knees. He felt blood and fat and beer rush to his head so quick, he thought he might vomit. He looked up, attempting to find his feet, "You little, evil bastard!" Hank was pissed, but he was unsettled by the show of force. The boy had never so much as held eye contact, he'd never even looked as though he'd contemplated fighting back. Hank was going to have to get his bluff in quick. He didn't know just how strong the boy was now. Hank lunged at the boy, reaching for his neck, in order to clamp it and toss the boy head first into the wall. One quick, hard shot to put this shit to an end. The boy was too fast though and swayed back like a UFC fighter at the last second and Hank's directed weight got the best of him, over the boy's suddenly outstretched leg. He stumbled head first into the wall. This was a hard knock, as his three-hundred-plus-pounds pushed against his head and neck. He fell to his ass and studied the boy once his vision settled. He was feeling a lack of feeling in his body. 'He broke my neck.' What the fuck was he going to do now? Show his ass, "You Mother-Fucker!" He had to overemphasize the anger and downplay the dismay and end this before it got worse, he was about to lose everything.

He decided to corner him before launching himself again; the boy was quick. Perhaps he could walk in quick enough to get a handful of hair. The boy was still smirking, little shit, standing between the two open rooms. Like Billy Cochran used to do when he taunted little Hank Forbus in third grade. Hank hadn't thought about that bully in years, it pissed him off that the boy was able to drag that up at all. There was a bar to the boy's left behind the half wall of kitchen that separated it from the living room. Hank wanted to push him toward the sink and just get his hands on him. He didn't need him any particular place, just his hands on him to squeeze and hurt and stop this shit, now! He stepped up, knowing the boy would back away, wrong again.

Just under the reaching, mad hands, the boy pulled to the side and added his own weight to the hulk's spilling momentum. Pushing him past his slow feet, into the oven door handle's prominent corner with his left temple. Didn't sound too menacing, but the blood it leaked down his face told another tale. A torn flap of skin hung grotesquely, like an earring. Hank fell like a child, with a look that spoke to just how injured he was feeling.

He lay spent of breath, spent of fight. A heart attack right here in the floor, was believable. Ah, then he realized, he would just have to wait for the boy to sleep. Tonight, once he got his hands on the boy, he could make a believer out of him. He would just lay here and breathe and play defeated, see what the boy made of it. He never got to play that card, though.

The Maxx was enjoying the loss of hateful power in the man, but he felt sorry for the bastard, all the same. He placed his right shoe on the fallen man's raised hip and kicked him flatter to the floor. Either the man was truly beaten or he was playing a longer game, The Maxx figured it was the latter. No matter, he started this game to finish it. He planted a hard toe into The Step's crotch. This brought a clinched gasp and extended moan as he crumpled further into the soft flesh. The man was spent and hurt...and done.

"Goddammit! Stoppit! Stop it," Hank spat trying to catch an elusive breath.

Maxx merely took a step toward the counter, unplugged the microwave and pulled the large radiation box onto the man's lower back, it looked like a kidney shot to Maxx. Another groan and hitch of garbled vocals. Maxx was suddenly certain the man was crying. He heard the rotating glass plate inside the microwave break and thought about how easy it would be to pull a shard out and cut his throat. No, he wanted this to look like a stupid accident, and a sliced throat clearly wasn't the way to go.

He noticed it was getting dark outside as he gazed through the kitchen window, watching the fat man out of his periphery and contemplating the right way to do this. What did Hank do that might kill him, accidentally? It was too warm to rig a heater. The man did smoke, so that was always a way to go, but why not double down on the possible ways to read this. A kitchen fire would do just that, no?

Say, the *Steps* was cooking himself up a fried bologna

sandwich, which is all the fucker would eat. Everyone would think Nick left, since it was graduation night (a great night to runaway), or even just out partying (you know, with all of his many, wonderful friends), and the overeater finally had to cook his own meal. Hell, he was already in the kitchen. It could read like a stove-top fire that got away from the fat man, a heart attack, The Maxx didn't care. A burnt house wouldn't hold any clues as to him even being there and they had no nosy neighbors to see a damn thing.

The Maxx pulled the smaller skillet out from the drawer under the oven and set it on a burner, and then turned the burner on high. It began smoking almost immediately, from old grease and dust. He pulled the ingredients out of the fridge and left it open, just for shits and giggles. He never would have thought the downed man would be anal, an asshole, yes, but compulsive about anything other than abuse, no. Hank half begged the boy to shut the door. The Maxx was humored. The Maxx pulled the hot skillet off the burner and clapped Hank on a raised knee, "No!" He sounded like a mother scolding her little imp and it made him chuckle.

The old iron skillet was already getting hot, but luckily not hot enough to scald Nick's hand. The Maxx didn't want to leave his primary any injuries, he was broken enough, poor kid. He put the pan back on the burner and dropped the whole package of shitty-meat-product into it and then, the roll of paper towels. Then, inspired, pulled the sugar container from the first upper cabinet. It was a tall, rectangular plastic container. He pulled the pink lid loose and poured the whole of three or four pounds across the pan and stove top, with the last few cups onto Hank, who was watching him now with a look of confused disgust.

The Maxx would have thought the man was merely mad that he was beaten, but he knew now that the man was horrified by the mess. This dirty, gommy excuse for a broken man had a thing about misplaced items, other than his dirty uniforms, obviously. How bizarre.

The Maxx went through a couple more cabinets and set up the tea container and tea bags as if he were making some. The Maxx planted his left foot just out of Hank's reach and raised his right, the muscles pulling like a spring, and shot it down into the side of Hank's raised knee, forcing the joint open to the floor. Hank barely moaned, but it was a sustained grimace that sounded awful. The sugar bubbled and flamed up, catching the plastic meat packaging to flaming and dripping. The scattered granules didn't domino the flames down the counter, as he'd hoped. So, he grabbed a ratty oven mitt and spilled some grease from the searing bologna. As the flames grew larger along the trail of grease and igniting the various piles of sugar, smoke began collecting at the ceiling. The Maxx bent down to Hank and slapped him across the face, sort of jovially, and said, "You ignorant bastard, you could have made this more, something I could've learned from. And, at that, I guess Nick did learn from all you offered, or I wouldn't be here, would I?" The man didn't flinch or groan or even flutter his eyes. He just looked at the boy, probably wondering who the hell he was. The Maxx was off to seek brighter rooms, bigger outdoors and grander days...leaving this man to his own reaping.

Job done, results in progress, time to get the Hell out!

Just one more thing, he thought, stopping on his walk out of the flaming kitchen. He stepped back over Hank and grabbed an unopened bag of flour. One that he'd looked at most everyday since his Mom left. Flour was not a product needed for sandwiches and cereal. The Maxx stooped away from the hovering smoke with a cough as he stepped back over the man and out of the kitchen. He popped the old adhesive on the thick papered bag, pulling the entire top free and tossed it toward the back wall of the kitchen beyond the man and the fire. It was a cleansing act to destroy the old bag that had been a daily reminder that his Mom was gone, but he also knew that flour dust ignited in open flame and could cause an explosion. He ran to the door, ducked out without a look back at the Sodom and Gomorrah that might turn him to stone.

The Maxx walked casually to their car and initiated the growling engine. This relaxed his guard just enough to allow Nick to see through his numb gaze. He breathed, settled into the cassette blaring "Holy Diver" from *Dio* (one of Tommy's favorites from his dad) and just took in the scene, breathed it in one last time. Nick began by recognizing that he'd made it back from the graduation. He was in the car and it was time to go. Then he saw more.

The Maxx was able to feel Nick watching and stepped forward enough to cause Nick's vision to be broken into tiny clips that could easily be associated with a movie or dream. There was a flash-bang from the dusting of flour first, then the smoke found escape through cracks in the facade. The light inside the dark home began to dance, to whirl and gambol. The darkening day allowed the body shaped flame to dance with dazzling effect. It looked lighter than Hank, in inspired movement, birthing new flames as it bounced from wall to wall, surface to surface. The Maxx could only imagine the burning human oil that must coat the walls with each impact, leaving enough to hold a smaller flame and burn long enough to catch. Toppling end tables and waltzing ablaze.

Even with this limited view, shuttering with The Maxx's help, Nick and The Maxx both were lost to the sight, enraptured by all that it meant, in the way that tragic events could be beautifully significant and with a merit and gravity of the unseen. The Maxx knew that Nick could and would always deny the truth of what he was seeing, but that deep down he would feel the achievement; just as he felt the loss of his mother without the detail of truth that swayed like a flag above his head.

The Maxx pushed forward a bit more and took the first patrol out of town until it was safe to allow Nick forward again, to drive and enjoy the first tastes of freedom. Nick drove until Cates would see the blonde in practice and in real time, search her out on Tommy's old phone. The Maxx watched the scenes fly by from time to time as he stepped up and back. They all did though, Jay Jay joined them, relishing the wind that crept in as Nick rolled the glass down and Nick, though unaware of them fully, was finally free enough to allow them to roam about the cabin, so to speak.

Out of Dodge?

Officer Shannon had given herself twenty-minutes to grieve (which was about fifteen minutes longer than she'd planned to allow), she wept in the tiny bathroom (just big enough for a good cry, she thought) and cleaned herself up with a superbly cold splash of water in the face. "Pull it together, Girl." She'd put the call into the team now that she thought she could do it without breaking down. They would all gather at Lafferty's tonight and toast the man, honoring his time on the force, his perseverance to righting the wrongs presented him and the loss of who he was. Typically, they would all be called in to help man the scene, but with no leads on the mysterious young man and little to do but protect the coroner while he made the call on Terry Dillon and Deborah Marsallis, the sheriff put Wales on the prowl around the area the suspect was last seen.

With the calls made, Saleisha wanted to delve back into the writing. It read like a novel, but it gave her the chills, now that she knew the parts about Deborah were real. How long had he been watching her? And, could it really be that poor, young kid? This was a journal written in third person, if it were written by the boy. Or, she realized, perhaps he was recording the actions of another; making him an accomplice. All she could do was wait for the evidence to be found. She started to put the thing away, many times and just couldn't stop thumbing page after page. She would go through ten blank pages and close the book, bored and horrified. Then she would succumb to the curiosity that was yet sated and try to pick up where she left off. It was a horrible loop that would last most of the day for the shocked young officer.

Cates still carried the lot, but he was strong enough for that. He was born on the trip here, after all, and had a rejuvenating rest after his Jedi mind trickery. His birth was marked by the blonde in white, orange and blue, a Mustang in young, tanned skin and toned muscle. Nick had inklings of the killer, dashes of imagination and possibilities that he thought were great story fodder, but the spark of Cates' reality were blown upon the air at the sight of her falling through the air. Glistening, form exposed, graceful. He found her school page, her name, and his own need. Cates was born as she walked away on her own. His back story forged to give reason, and her sweet life cut short in the walking air of a young, invincible feeling woman.

He now crept up to the Sheriff's Office window with care and saw Officer Shannon, his old buddy, old pal, flipping through Nick's notebook. He knew it was his story she was reading and he felt nothing about her having it. Though, it might be best that they left that behind. It could only serve to make Nick's awareness of his presence more likely and he liked that they were all fairly disconnected, disjointed (what better to control them with than chaos?). He was also proud of himself. He was a precision instrument, disciplined in many arts with a body like a steel trap, ready to fire at the whisper of a touch. He was so good, that even if he were caught, he wouldn't be found. Nick would be found; naive, simple, foolish Nick. Even if they dissected the young man, they would never find

Thomas Cates. He left no markings, no evidence of where he'd been or what he'd done. He was an invisible, floating ghost with evil on tap.

He forced himself to stop watching Officer Shannon at the counter and stepped around to the car. She had the notebook, he noted, so she might have the keys, but he would check before he just let her in on his whereabouts for no reason. She couldn't pull herself away from the words, he couldn't help but find a sense of pride in the fact that she found his story so compelling. He would try not to kill her, if indeed she had the keys, as she seemed an innocent too. Sometimes though, lesser innocence fell victim to the greater good and this just might be one of those times. He found no sign of keys.

Well, she knew what Nick looked like, so pretending to be here for any other reason was not going to help him. Unless... He decided very quickly not to think this out, to just react, be spontaneous and to be quick. He didn't feel he had much time before the entire calvary showed up. He stepped around the car and ran for the door. He slammed himself inside and up to the counter for as much surprise as possible. The more off guard she was, the better.

"Officer Shannon, I didn't know when I was in here before, but I know what happen to Officer Dillon. Please, you have to protect me!"

She was alarmed at his rush, and scared standing here. Cates stepped up toward the space between her and the offices and spied the tangle of four keys on the desk in the first room. He pretended to breathe heavy and look alarmed to keep up what little facade he came in with. He was as close to the keys as she was and he hid his intentions better than her. Her eyes told the whole story, as they bobbed from him to the office across from her, where the radio was. Where her gun might be. He would have to take her now. He liked to let his prey run to him whenever possible, however, and so let her fear guide her straight into the trap of his arms.

She was good, though, he watched her catch her breath and swallow her fear down. She must have realized she was showing her hand, she must have felt herself becoming the rabbit in a staring contest with the fox and fought the situation with all she could. Good on her. It was as though she were being possessed by another person as her demeanor changed before his eyes. Her shaking ceased, she stood taller and broader and spoke with a confidence seemingly just inhaled, "I need you to tell me what happen to Officer Dillon?" She said this with a knowing that made Cates' proud.

Cates knew she was trying to settle him into conversation mode, a tactic change, but he didn't need to distract her any longer, he needed to get the hell out of Dodge! He was watching her wrists in his periphery as he held her eyes with what looked like his focus. He snapped like a steel trap and ensnared her right wrist, then her left when she attempted to punch at him with it. Now he had both arms controlled and her pushed back to the wall. Before she could even think to knee him in the crotch, he gave her a Glasgow Kiss, right to the center of the forehead, then a kiss on the mouth, as she slowly reeled from the stud she caught in the impact with the wall. He could feel the fight drain away as the tension in her arms dissipated. He let her slide gently to the floor behind the counter and leaped into the office, grabbed the keys and was off in one fluid motion. He wanted so to lay beside her, rub her cheek and talk to her now that she would listen without interruption, but he had a new mission now, his priority escape.

He departed the building, climbed into the Duster, pulled the door closed with his left hand while he twisted the ignition with his right. The engine growled to life. He wasn't exactly hiding, but he didn't need any extra attention, so, he pulled the stick into R and fought the need to speed all the way out of town; all three blocks. He reached the border of Austin with a WHOOP of celebration. He sorta kept to speed limits on his way to Cold Springs, Fallon and Reno. He thought Reno would make a nice second stop for another mission, but the mission's presented themselves as they would. He didn't decide, he merely answered the call and so it would be whatever it was. For now though, he was free, they were free, thanks to him and he would enjoy this road tripping for as long as they allowed him to do so.

Another key to when the next mission would begin, he wasn't the only one invested in this body and would have to take a number, until he increased his power to take charge.

Just how far down do you wanna go
We can talk it out over a cup of Joe
And you can look deep in my eyes

Like I was a super-model   uh huh!
It's just you and me baby
No one else we can trust
We'll say nothing' to no one
No how or we'll bust
Never crack a smile or flinch or cry
For nobody   uh huh!
So give your ID card to the border guard
Your alias says you're Captain John Luke Picard
of the United Federation of Planets
'Cause they don't speak English any ways
Everybody knows that the world is full of stupid people
So meet me at the mission at midnight
We'll divvy up there
Everybody knows that the world is full of stupid people
So I got the pistol
So I get the pesos   That seems fair!

Banditos / The Refreshments

Tripping Nevada; After the Math

Nick wondered how exactly he came to be back in the Duster and wondered if he might have dreamed about the girl and the cops. Ha, probably because of that story he was working on, huh. Made sense, the blonde was a touch too ironic after having written about a dead, blonde cheerleader. He was coming up to a sign for Historic Middlegate Station and felt he needed to stop. He was starving and he was tripping, after all. You could stop when you wanted while you were road tripping. His stomach overrode his mind for a minute, but he found his way back to the thought-train he'd been on. He just couldn't place the time, the dark time as he thought of it, missing and black. Had it all been a dream. Must've been, but then he noticed the blur over the right of the windshield and front seat was still there. There were blurry spots on his shirt, which hurt his eyes as they tried to focus. He brushed at them but his hands were a ghost through a wall. He wanted to know what the hell that was all about, but was more immediately concerned about where Tommy's picture was. That was all he had of his time with his only friend...well, he knew better. *This mighty machine is quite a souvenir, no doubt!*

Nick wondered if he would ever know as he happily raced away from it all. He was free and tripping again, just the way he liked it. He pondered while he sauntered up to the Middlegate Station, stretching like a cat the whole way, if he shouldn't go back to Austin. See if it looked like it had in his dreams. See if anyone had seen him come through. He felt pushed away from the idea, but he didn't know why.

He would not go, but the thought did intrigue him. He tried to imagine waking up on the rock this morning and packing up to drive through the town of Austin, but there was no connection to the thought.

After a fine meal and another few hours of driving, The Maxx slept, unneeded for now and relieved to be away from the trouble that might have been; not aware of how they escape either. He slumbered upright, in Nick's holding until the next time.

Cates slept deep in the satisfaction of a mission complete, as well as a side project safely hidden from his inti-mates. He didn't want his roomies to know of the power he'd discovered. He didn't want it used against him, he was the user. He knew he was the black sheep of the bunch, but the less they knew of his comings and goings, the better. Life between three innocent spies was tricky when you needed to be unseen, but it could be done with enough discipline, and he was just the man for the job.

Jay Jay hung from the window, gasping in the ninety-mile-per-hour wind the Duster produced with a steady old-school growl. Clung tight in her right arm, safely inside the car, was her tattered brown bunny, Mr. Raindrops. He was her only ever birthday present, a yard-sale prize. The quarter that bought that gift for her by her Daddy was the only thing ever given to her...that she could be happy about anyway. Her Daddy was always sweet to her, he was just hardly ever there. He was definitely absent when she needed him to protect her from her mother, her cousins and her aunt. Jay Jay was scarred so very deep, that she never thought she could feel such happiness as she did right now.

The evening was coming to a close once again and she was so very happy. She wasn't sure what all had happened, but they took care of her again and she was relishing their freedom. She didn't need details, nor the urge to be apart of everything. She was six and, now, happier than she'd ever been. Something more was complete, though she wasn't clear on what. The bright shine of every sunny day was in her face, a kiss upon her cheek and the darkness that was her home was far, far away. She caught troubling glimpses from time to time, heard weird beeps and buzzes, smelled clean chemicals, but they were just scary movies for her, a chill inducing episode that could be turned off and left behind.

What should have bothered her, she thought, was the tar-smeared burnt man in the back. He stunk and worse than that, his bright yellow eyes burned and beamed out of the black lidless face, watching her every move. He would moan at her from time to time, but he seemed indifferent to her avoidance. No need to ask him what he said if she couldn't understand him. She didn't like him, he scared her, but he was a part of all of this now. Sometimes, life gave you lemons, and you simply stayed out of the kitchen until you could squeeze the life out of them. Besides, they wouldn't let him get her. She had happiness to feel and feel it she would. Her hair was pushed back from her giggling face as the car sped passed the brambles scattered at the road's edge. "Zooooooom!" She saw the blur of red fur, a fox maybe. "Zoooooooooooooooooooooom!"

The End
4/15/2015 to 11/13/2018

This Ones for You, Sam! Miss Ya Buddy!

Joey Thomas is an Arkansas Native, ever evolving seeker of Truth and JOY! He is a better man because of people like this good looking gentleman to his right and indebted to his entire family for their Love and Support. He is the author of The Slater Family Sagas, TWISTED, TURNED, & BENT and HELL BENT, available at www.amazon.com and www.barnesandnoble.com. Seek the JOY, trust Your gut, and Love Yourself so You can Love everyone else. Oh, and BE Yourself, no one else knows how.

Author's Note

I wrote this book because of my curiosity in psychological afflictions. I've always believed that psychology is akin to autism, in the fact that there is a spectrum. We all have intricacies of character that might fit into Obsessive Compulsive Disorder, or Dissociative Disorder (once termed multiple personality). My research into Tourette Syndrome was an eye opener; those afflicted often describe it the way I always thought of OCD. That the tics and outburst are to keep the world from blowing up, figuratively and sometimes, literally, from their perspective. I'd always assumed they were neurological in nature, since they are physical tics. I've seen two documented cases of Tourette's being "cured" and one male seemed pleased with the outcome, while a female, who's family felt as if they got their daughter back, was herself not pleased, because it led her to other psychological malfunction. Her coping mechanism was removed, essentially, and it felt as disturbing if not more disturbing to her mental stability. Interesting.

I remember well, an interview with a gentleman who was diagnosed with Asperger's Syndrome. During research of one possible aid, he was shown a video of two people interacting. He didn't catch the emotion and described the interaction in a clinical fashion. Then, after his brain was exposed to a laser treatment, he comprehended the emotions of the same interaction, for the first time in his life. He expressed in a later interview that it ruined his life. He told of sitting in his car immediately after the treatment and crying listening to classical music. Then he began to remember moments in is life, to reflect on interactions as far back as grade school and began to feel the emotion that he missed in the moment; kids laughing at him, making fun of him. He was devastated at the understanding.

I have recently told my BFF (Bert), about something I've always done and never thought too much about. I find myself, while watching TV, imagining making patterns around the carpet, or around patterns in the carpet, or even around tables, with my feet. Little triangles, typically. I don't have to finish this before I can do anything else, and if I stop, nothing bad will happen, but why would my mind repeat this imagination play? Is it an unseen connection with the sacred geometry that exists around us? Is it a meditative reset for me? Does it allow my brain to clean while awake, because I have trouble sleeping? I don't know. But, it does interest me. I bet we all have little things like that, and some of us more prominent patterns with more at stake if we don't perform the rituals that our brains dictate we make, when they need to be made.

What drives us through our days and interactions with people? Why is one kind and the other hateful; because they are triggered? Sure. And, some of those triggers are easily explained and lessened with self-analysis. But, what about psychopaths and those with Charles Bonnet Syndrome (involving hallucinations of little people, disembodied faces, music and geometric shapes, and what might be described as ghosts)? What about Alien-Limb Syndrome?

Charles Bonnet Syndrome is actually thought to be an eye disorder, how fascinating is that? So, when the retina is damaged, it is believed that other parts of the brain try to fill in the details and cause hallucinations. Parkinson's causes paranoid hallucinations? How crazy is that? So, not only do those afflicted lose control of their body, but also touch with reality.

If we all have habits or thoughts that don't quite work with the social construct we have been handed, it begs the question, does our strict outline of acceptable behavior needs some renovation. This, I believe, is the reason we have so many comedians and triggered individuals (that is a joke, but any comedian will tell you there is truth in it). Because our social construct raises parents who have one or two acceptable futures for their children and fight to keep them in line with that narrow path, via pride and disappointment. In other words, Control, so our children don't embarrass us or live embarrassing lives that bring them hardship. We all have been children, and in my experience, we all want to walk our own way. We all have to learn our own lessons. So, we fight those fighting us and rebel, in varying degrees. But, then, we tend to try to control our kids when we become parents, because they rebel and become like our parents; a broken non-nonsensical loop. Control is not the answer.

I am no expert, but I did raise one. My daughter, Crystal, is a psychologist and I do love picking her brain and letting her make me laugh. She could be a comedian; which makes me question what I did to trigger her. Right? I do ask myself these questions, because what makes me right? What will I ever be an expert at? Our top experts, at least in my opinion, are basing their expertise on the findings of other experts, all of which only ever saw 0.0035% of this world we live in. I do believe that we can experience more than that, I'm beginning to understand that mystics have and are doing just that (with ancient plant medicines and meditative practices, energy work), but how much of the reality around us should we base our religions and scientific findings on? I feel like it should be more than 1%. Again, just my opinion.

Dissociative Disorder always fascinated me. How a person can split off into personalities, tools to get through whatever needs to be survived; like a Swiss-Army-Man: protectors, intellects, hard-asses... There is research that speaks to personalities taking on different physical traits, eye color, size, etc. I think these are slight, not like Bruce Banner and his Hulk, but still. How amazing, that our minds can change the physical. Look at accounts of psychic surgery.

There is a man who speaks of adding bone into a broken bone, with meditative imagery, beginning two weeks prior to surgery. He didn't want to be cut open. So, he imagined filling in the divot in his hip bone with a piping or pastry bag. The surgeon wanted another X-ray the day before surgery was scheduled, and they found the missing bone filled in with what looked like concrete. That is magic in my book. So much more than we've been taught life can be. My Sweet Grandma Thomas always told me I could be anything I put my mind to, and I knew she meant it, but I'm still surpassing the limits of what I think she meant. Life is so beautiful when you see it like your child-self experienced it. More than just being playful, I think it is a lessening of our time restraints, uninvolving ourselves with the latest celebrity blitz or political shit storm. Getting outside, into nature, outside of our comfort zone, trying scary shit; like hiking or traveling into this big-bad world.

I don't mean to say that your afflictions, disorders, or syndromes are all in your head. I don't think anyone makes up such suffering, as well, I don't believe everyone considers such symptoms as a curse or feel as though they are tragically stricken. What I do mean to say, is that I believe our brains, in conjunction with our best physical selves (which unfortunately entails our best diet, one based on nutrition and real, not sick, foods), are capable of rewiring, rebuilding, and becoming whatever we put our minds to. If not, then there is something in our way, a trigger point that needs to be sought out and forgiven or loved as we all should learn to love ourselves. I met my five-year-old self in meditation years ago and picked him up, hugged him close, and apologized for all that I put him through; for all that I've blamed him for, in my erratic teens and twenties.

I grew up to be reckless with love, I was naive and manipulated and my loyalty and innocence abused. It left me with PTSD, I realized this just recently, in 2022. Once I realized what it was, it subsided in a major way, but I still found myself laying awaking, attempting to fake it until I make it, to sleep. That actually stopped with my first Ayahuasca retreat. I can't explain in enough detail the JOY and RELEASE it gave me. From my own pressure upon myself, my time-line for projects, work, improvement. I have slept like a beautiful baby ever since. The lovely, amazing souls we bonded with in those three days are lifelong family now. I recommend Ayahuasca to everyone.

From the studies and shared experiences of all psychedelics, I believe they can all help us get beyond ourselves to our best self.

Perhaps, then, we could all LIVE AND LET LIVE without ostracizing groups or individuals that look, act, or feel different. Abnormal is not something to be eradicated. Mutants don't need to be controlled, just loved like the rest of us. We should all try to grow up and treat those around us the way our youngest children would, with compassion and kindness. Dig that, and I was born in Grubbs, Arkansas! Eat your heart out Glenn Campbell! A Great Arkansan, may he rest in peace!

I also, adopted the mindset long ago, that every failed relationship, I walked myself into. I was the one ignoring red flags and letting things go, rather than calling out bad behavior. I was attracted to triggered people who I wanted to show how magic life can really be. I did this without knowing what I was doing or learning the tools to help them get past their blindfolds of trauma to really see what was around them. To all of them, I apologize for not being more helpful. I also forgive myself for being foolish, submissive, and walked on. I am better for it all and I don't let anyone walk on me (save for my grand-daughter, Lawson, who sometimes gets away with it), but the right mindset has to be found. I am grateful for my failed marriages, especially for the babies they spawned. The world is better, brighter, and bodacious-er because of them. I also am grateful for the lessons I chose to learn in the process; more importantly, for the courage and instinct to make that choice.

I write to teach without teaching. I write to council

myself, and if it helps you, I am so grateful for the ability to reach you. I write to discover and learn and hike about this mountain of imagination that I believe exists in the ether about us all. The unconscious link between us all, where all ideas, great and small, come from. I could be wrong, about so many things, so gut instinct has to count for something.

I question everything, again and again, until I can eliminate everything possible, except one simple truth. I do think the most important thing to be, is open to being wrong. Open to someone else's perspective, until you prove it wrong for yourself. We don't all have to end up on the same page, but it would be nice if we could stop killing, persecuting, and judging each other for the page we are on. Which, again, comes with improved psychology. Love You Dear Reader and THANK YOU for grabbing me up and spending some time with my words. It means ever so much to Me.

And, remember, Everything is Already Alright, Always. The struggles you find yourself wading through are already over. And, even though there are struggles still awaiting you, they too, are already overcome by the Peace and Joy you seek. Time is not linear, we just perceive it that way. You are sublime, perspicacious, and Joy personified! 3/15/2023

P.S.

The Maxx was a beautiful animated series, that my brother turned me on to, based on Sam Kieth's American Comic Book, created in 1993. It was originally published monthly by Image Comics until 1998. They published 35 issues, before being collected in trade paperback by DC Comics' Wildstorm imprint.

The first appearance of the character was in *Darker Image* #1 by Image Comics in March 1993. The comic book, starring an eponymous purple-skinned hero, spawned a 13-episode animated series on MTV that originally aired April–June 1995. Starting in November 2013 and ending in September 2016, the original series has been republished by IDW as *The Maxx: Maxximized* with new colors and improved scans of the original artwork by Sam Kieth and Jim Sinclair. In 2018, the Maxx featured in a five-issue crossover series with Batman, published by IDW.

The series follows the adventures of the titular hero in two worlds: The real world and an alternate reality referred to as the Outback (presumably named metaphorically after the real Australian outback). In the real world, Maxx is a vagrant, a "homeless man living in a box", while in the Outback, he is the powerful protector of the Jungle-Queen, who exists in the real world as Julie Winters, a freelance social worker who often bails Maxx out of jail. While Maxx is aware of the Outback, Julie is not, though it is integral to both of their stories.

The comic book series was adapted into an animated series as part of the MTV program *Oddities*. The show covered *Darker Image* #1, *The Maxx* #1/2, and issues #1–11 of the regular series and depicted the introduction of Julie, the original Maxx, Mr. Gone, and, later on in the series, Sarah. Therefore, the TV show did not go into the same depth (e.g. revealing the origins of all the characters) as the comic series.

In 1996, the complete series was released on VHS with a runtime of approximately 2 hours. In 2009, it became available to stream on MTV.com, though only to U.S. audiences. On December 17, 2009, *The Maxx* became available on DVD exclusively through Amazon's CreateSpace "Manufacture-on-Demand" program; it contains every episode of the TV show and also includes audio commentary on each episode, plus interviews with creator Sam Kieth and director Gregg Vanzo.

All of this according to www.Wikipedia.org. The Maxx - Wikipedia

I'd like to thank these bands for these songs and the energy they inspire. The poetry. And, the way they make the muses dance!

The song, ***Banditos*** by The Refreshments was released in 1996 with the album *Fizzy Fuzzy Big & Buzzy*. A great song to rock out to!

The Winger album Better Days Comin' was released in 2014, every song is amazing, ***So Long China***, being just one of them. A favorite band of mine!

Hour 1, a jamming song from the Scorpions in 2007

with the album *Humanity: Hour 1*. Great band!

Thanks for the memories, Scoob! ***Scooby-Doo*** is an American media franchise based on an animated television series launched in 1969 and continued through several derivative media. Writers Joe Ruby and Ken Spears created the original series, *Scooby-Doo, Where Are You!*, for Hanna-Barbera Productions. This Saturday-morning cartoon series featured teenagers Fred Jones, Daphne Blake, Velma Dinkley, and Shaggy Rogers, and their talking Great Dane named Scooby-Doo, who solve mysteries involving supposedly supernatural creatures through a series of antics and missteps.

Scooby-Doo was originally broadcast on CBS from 1969 to 1976, when it moved to ABC. ABC aired various versions of *Scooby-Doo* until canceling it in 1985, and presented a spin-off featuring the characters as children called *A Pup Named Scooby-Doo* from 1988 until 1991. Two *Scooby-Doo* reboots aired as part of Kids' WB on The WB and its successor The CW from 2002 until 2008. Further reboots were produced for Cartoon Network beginning in 2010 and continuing through 2018. Repeats of the various *Scooby-Doo* series are frequently broadcast on Cartoon Network's sister channel Boomerang in the United States and other countries. The most recent *Scooby-Doo* series, *Scooby-Doo and Guess Who?*, premiered on June 27, 2019, as an original series on Boomerang's streaming service and later HBO Max.

In 2013, *TV Guide* ranked *Scooby-Doo* the fifth-greatest TV cartoon of all time. Scooby-Doo - Wikipedia

Amazon.com: GNOSIS Onward - The Story of How We Begin To Remember eBook : Graham Ph.D. D.D., Lewis, Hensley D.C., Mary Helen, Stucker, Thomas: Kindle Store

Droopy is an animated character from the golden age of American animation. He is an anthropomorphic white Basset Hound with a droopy face; hence his name. He was created in 1943 by Tex Avery for theatrical cartoon shorts produced by the Metro-Goldwyn-Mayer cartoon studio. Essentially the polar opposite of Avery's other MGM character, the loud and wacky Screwy Squirrel, Droopy moves slowly and lethargically, speaks in a jowly monotone voice, and—though hardly an imposing character—is shrewd enough to outwit his enemies. When finally roused to anger, often by a bad guy laughing heartily at him, Droopy is capable of beating adversaries many times his size with a comical thrashing. Droopy - Wikipedia Nostalgic to my four-year-old self.

CSI: Miami (***Crime Scene Investigation: Miami***) is an American police procedural drama television series that ran from September 23, 2002 until April 8, 2012 on CBS. Featuring David Caruso as Lieutenant Horatio Caine, Emily Procter as Detective Calleigh Duquesne, and Adam Rodriguez as Detective Eric Delko, the series is the first direct spin-off of *CSI: Crime Scene*

Investigation "transplanting the same template and trickery —gory crimes, procedural plot and dazzling graphics—into [a new city] while retaining the essence of the original idea" *CSI: Miami* was executive produced by Carol Mendelsohn, Anthony E. Zuiker, and Ann Donahue, with the latter acting as show-runner. The series ended on April 8, 2012, after 10 seasons and 232 episodes. Following the series finale, Nina Tassler credited *CSI: Miami* as a "key player in CBS's rise to the top", stating that the series "leaves an amazing television legacy—a signature look and style [and] global popularity". In 2006, BBC News published an article stating that *CSI: Miami* was the world's most popular television series, featuring in more countries' top ten rankings for 2005 than any other series.
THANK YOU for the entertainment, I believe I watched them all!

The Bovine Cul-de-sac
Chapter One
by Joey Thomas

He thought nothing of the darkness he stepped into, shutting the light away as he pulled the garage side door closed. It was a mundane chore that became something more as his eyes hesitated to adjust to the black night. Jose Alvarez hefted the garbage bag into his right hand to give his left shoulder a break. He thought loudly to himself, 'I'm not scared of the dark. I've done this a hundred times, there is nothing out here that can hurt me.' There was just enough white noise from the wind to feed his ears all sorts of imagination fodder; someone just behind him, a horror flick monster running from across the street, a sniper sliding a bolt action into position lining up two sights between his eyes, a hungry wolf circling its prey. He scanned the darkness and heard something, a thump that couldn't have been the wind, but then, what was it? He squinted at ten directions of similar darkness before he felt more frustrated than fearful. 'If you're not scared quit acting like it.'

He was at the large green plastic garbage receptacle now and he unconsciously asked for a time out from all of the lurking dangers of his imagination as he pulled the top open to place the bag in its designated area. It was like going to the bathroom in dangerous conditions or running yourself out of breath. Being attacked in a vulnerable position like that was against the rules. Time out was only courteous and proper, everybody knew that. It was the pirate's parley request for, 'hold on a minute, I have words that might stop you from killing me'.

The THUD sounded again, but his eyes found nothing in the limited light that could claim to be the culprit. He shook his head at just how silly he was being as the sound thumped again. His hand was frozen just over the green plastic suburban feature, his head turned severely to his right still scanning for danger, when the bag was hammered out of his hand from the left. He quickly turned to the left and saw a large black-and-white, ever growing pattern collide with his face. Knocked off of his feet, Jose landed flat on his back with a HEEEEWWWW, leaving his chest empty. He produced a couple of shallow groans before his body finally relaxed enough to inhale.

Jose breathed deep twice in a defeated pile on the ground before raising his head to witness the cow tearing into the white garbage bag ravenously. He was quite confounded by the sight. He'd just been attacked for his garbage. He watched in disbelief as the cow pulled the half-eaten cherry toaster pastry so masterfully from the torn plastic bag on her first try. He remembered Gil having thrown it away two mornings prior, saying it was just too sweet to finish.

A paper towel and several spent tea bags fell out of the hole as the bovine threw back her head and provided gravity the chance to help slide the yummy, cherry sugar-crack into the recesses of her large mouth. Jose was helpless to move, stunned by what he was seeing. He was also relieved that it wasn't a werewolf; until he saw the Holstein glower back at him as it backed away into the darkness like some hideous creature in a horror movie (except with the side to side waddle of a cow). Jose had visions of Gary Oldman in Bram Stoker's Dracula, but with the three stooges directing (like some fan fiction of a Scooby-Doo episode). Jose would have sworn the cow rolled her eyes with a slight head shake as she disappeared, as if judging his ineptitude; or warning him not to seek retribution. He shook his head in frustration, before giving in to his laughter. He laid his head back to find a sky full of stars and an appreciation for the forced moment to see it all. His hands behind his head now, he breathed through the laughter and realized tomorrow was Monday.

Garbage day was big in the cul-de-sac and he couldn't leave his Maddie with a ripped bag lying in the yard. He saw a dramatic and fiery shooting star cross his line of sight and gazed at the constellations that dotted the sky before him. He picked one out in particular and thought about how odd the world could be and was pretty sure he loved its peculiar ways. He lived with a pretty unique collection of people and he couldn't imagine wanting to be anywhere else. He grunted, thinking of how old he sounded as he turned over to his knees, to getup and retrieve another bag from the garage.

So Long Dear Reader

Joey Thomas

www.ingramcontent.com/pod-product-compliance
Lightning Source LLC
LaVergne TN
LVHW091253150826
845673LV00006B/1407
* 9 7 9 8 9 8 6 1 4 8 1 4 4 *